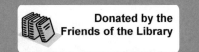

ROSIE LOVES JACK

To my brother, Guy, who made me the person I am.

—M. D.

Ω

Published by

PEACHTREE PUBLISHING COMPANY INC.

1700 Chattahoochee Avenue

Atlanta, Georgia 30318-2112

www.peachtree-online.com

Text © 2018 by Mel Darbon

Cover image © 2021 by Zoë Williams

Interior illustrations by Nancy Leschnikoff

Design and composition by Lily Steele

Cover design by Adela Pons

First published in the UK in 2018 by Usborne Publishing Ltd.,

Usborne House, 83-85 Saffron Hill, London EC1N 8RT, England

www.usborne.com

First United States version published in 2021 by Peachtree Publishing Company Inc.

Printed in January 2021 in the United States of America by Lake Book Manufacturing in Melrose Park, Illinois

10 9 8 7 6 5 4 3 2 1

First Edition

ISBN: 978-1-68263-289-5

Cataloging-in-Publication Data is available from the Library of Congress.

Content Advisory:

Please be aware that this narrative contains depictions of alcohol and drug use, verbal and physical abuse, sex trafficking, and mentions of suicide.

ROSIE LOVES JACK

Mel Darbon

PEACHTREE
ATLANTA

TEEN WITH DOWN SYNDROME MISSING

Fears are growing for a sixteen-year-old girl with Down syndrome who has not been seen since leaving home five days ago.

Rose Tremayne set off for her Pathways course at Henley College just before 9 AM on Friday, December 12, but never arrived.

Police want to speak to a caller who rang the college in Oxfordshire to say Rose was unwell and would not be going in that day. Chief Inspector Tim Jones, who is leading the search, said it was possible that the teenager, of Rupert's Lane, Henley-on-Thames, was making her way to Brighton, where her boyfriend is currently staying. "The recent heavy snow- falls and resulting prob- lems on the trains mean her journey won't have been straightforward," he said. "I would urge any member of the public who thinks they may have seen Rose to contact the police immediately."

He added that Rose's parents were desperately worried and anxious for news.

Rose is described as 4' 11", with a pale com- plexion, green eyes, and shoulder-length red-gold hair.

She was last seen wear- ing a black duffel coat, black jeans, a cream cable- knit sweater, distinctive purple Dr. Martens boots with a rose design, and carrying a purple fake fur bag covered in badges.

one
december 2nd

I put my phone down and clean a circle on the glass
to look for Jack. I can't see him anywhere. Jack always gets
here at three. It's three and a quarter now.

It's Christmas outside. I like the lights on the tree in the
square. They go blue...then green...then red...then white. I
like blue best. It looks like the moon shining. And hundreds
of stars. And everyone's breath is coming out of their mouths
in clouds.

I try writing Jack's name in the window mist.

It's noisy in the cafe today. There are lots of students from
my college here. They've taken all the sofas up. The girls
have tinsel on their heads and they're joining in with all the
Christmas songs, but real Christmas is three weeks and two
days away.

Jim is laughing at something one of the girls said. I like

Jim 'cause he's always happy. He wears a green stripy apron with a pocket at the front, for his phone and some mints for fresh breath con-fi-dence.

It's going to be three and a half 'round the clock soon.

My friend Jess walks by and waves to me. She comes into the cafe. Jess helps me with literacy at college on Tuesdays. She's cool. I want to get a silver nose stud like her.

"Hi, Rose, good to see you. I love your new Doc Martens, they're sick! Oh—that doesn't mean they're—"

"YeahIknow. Ben told Mum her meatballs were sick, and Mum said it was a revolting expresshun."

"True, haha! Can I join you?"

"Course."

"I'll miss seeing you when I'm away."

"I don't want you to go. I like you coming to help us read and do writing on Tuesdays."

"Six months will fly by. I can't believe I started planning this gap year seven months ago and now I'm off next week, it's crazy."

"Will you come back to help after?"

"I hope so, but I don't know for sure. I'm probably going to have to find a proper job to pay for me going to university, so I might not have Tuesdays free to help you and Lou any more."

"I wish I could go away with Jack."

Jess takes my hand. "Perhaps you will one day."

"Only if Mum and Dad are with us, or someone."

"I thought you did quite a lot on your own together?"

"In Henley-on-Thames. And once in Reading with Jack."

"Where is Jack?" Jess drops my hand and peers out the window.

"Don'tknow. I'm worried."

"Nothing to worry about. He'll be in the art room and have forgotten the time. I was like that with my photography A level."

"It's ICT today. Jack hates computers. P'raps he doesn't want to see me anymore."

"Don't be silly! Have you checked your phone?"

"Lots of times."

"Give him a call and I'll get us a drink. Your usual?"

"Yesplease. My healthy option, please."

I kiss my Jack on my phone screen before pressing the button to ring him. His voicemail picks up.

"Hey, it's Jack. I can't talk 'cause I'm busy. Leave me a message. Ta."

"Hello, it's Rosie. I'm sitting at our table and your hot choclet's gone cold. All the squirty cream has gone invisible. So hurry up. Love you."

Then I ring him again, just so I can hear his voice. I wish it was his real voice.

"Here's your green tea, Rose, be careful, it's very hot."

"I know, thankyou."

"Hey, sweetie, your tongue is out again. Remember what we said? It can make people stare."

5

"I didn't see it sticking out."

"No probs. Did you get hold of Jack?"

I shake my head. "I think he's with Emma Golding. He told her he loved her in Drama."

"We've talked about this, Rose. Jack does NOT love Emma, they were just acting in a play."

"He said, 'I love you' to her."

"It was just pretend, not real, okay?"

"Okay... But he said he loved Emma two times."

"Jack loves you, he doesn't want to be with anyone else."

"Then where is he?"

Jess looks at her watch. "He's late, even for Jack, so let's hope he hasn't done anything dopey."

"Whatd'youmean?"

"Well, Jack has been a bit arse-y recently."

I don't want to look at Jess for a bit. She's all wrong about Jack.

"I didn't mean to upset you, Rose. Jack's great, I like him a lot, we all do, but he can...overreact."

I turn my face away from Jess.

"Rose, look at me, I'm not being mean. When you first met Jack he was much more chilled—"

"That's 'cause of me."

"Yeah, I get that, lovely, he's been coping with his anger so much better since he met you, but since his gran died he's been getting worse again."

"Jack cried and cried when his gran died. He loved his gran best of all after his mum."

"I'm sure she loved Jack very much too, which is why he's been finding it so hard. But lots of people don't understand why Jack is so angry. You and your friends might in your part of the college, but not everyone in the main part of the college does. All they know is that he shouts and swears and hits out at them."

"Jack's brain got hurt when he was being born."

"I know, Rose, and that's very sad, but people can't see that his brain is hurt inside his head, all they see is the nice-looking Jack on the outside, so they don't get his fighting. He's frightened a few of the students. Nadia Johnson's mother complained about him."

"Henevergetsangrywithme." I shove my chair back. "I'm going to check for him outside."

Jess sighs. "I'll watch your stuff for you."

It's nighttime on the street already, 'cause it's winter. Jack always meets me just before the dark comes.

The cold air nettle-stings my face. I pull my sweater up over my nose to stop it, but then my middle freezes. I put it back and wrap my arms around me. Whichever way I look, I can't see Jack. I don't feel right inside me. I check the time. It's gone past an hour. Jack is never that much late without telling me.

Toby Varley knocks on the window of the bus as it goes

7

past. He's waving his arms about and pointing up the hill. I don't know what he's doing, but he's always silly. He's in Pathways with me at the college, but Toby needs LOTS of help. I'm very in-de-pend-dent.

I go back into the warm and get my coat. "I'm going to find Jack. Something's wrong."

"He'll be fine. I bet you meet him on your way up the hill. Aren't you going to finish your tea? If the cafe were on *fire* you'd usually finish it."

"OhnoIforgot! Jack filled up my head." I drink my tea to the bottom of the cup. "All gone. ByeJess."

"See you soon, Rose, take care."

I pick up my bag and head to college. I look over my shoulder at the bright lights spilling out of the cafe window. Jess is laughing into her phone.

My feet keep slipping on the snow 'cause I can't walk fast enough to get to Jack.

All the students are going in a different direction to me. Jack's face isn't coming down the hill with them. He's vanished.

I can see the college at the top. It's the same size as my hand. I push my legs harder up the hill. They hurt by the time college is bigger than me.

As I run through the parking lot I see a police car. The light is spinning in a circle on the top, making the snow blue.

Inside the building the corridors are empty. My boots squeak on the floor. I tiptoe along to make them hush. The swing doors at the end burst open and make me jump. A police lady runs through the gap. She stops to find her breath and asks, "Did you see a young man in a gray hoodie go past this way?"

I shake my head. She turns and goes back through the doors. My heart has a race in my chest. Jack has a gray hoodie.

My legs can't decide which way to walk, so I make them go to the art room. It's Jack's best place. When he was little, his mum told him to paint all the angry monsters fighting in his head. To get them out. He painted all the time after that. He's the best artist ever. Everyone says so.

I'm worried as I go up the stairs. Please be there.

I open the art room door, smiling my special smile for Jack. It's empty.

I so wanted him to be here. I try not to get upset. My head is too muddled to sort it all out.

I check my phone again. Still nothing. Maybe Jack went home instead of meeting me? I don't want to think that. Or about the police lady.

Street light from outside shines into the room. It makes shadow shapes across the wall. I shiver. Something taps on the window, which makes me drop my phone. It clatters across the floor. I stand very still and listen for anyone coming. I hear something breathing in the darkness. All the hairs on my arm stand to attention. I watch as the paint cupboard door opens by itself. My mouth un-shuts but no sound comes out. In the gap,

9

I see an eye looking right at me. I scream. A body leaps out of the cupboard and grabs me. A hand stops my mouth.

"Don't scream, Rosie," a voice shout-whispers in my ear. "It's me, Jack."

He takes his hand off my mouth, and I push him away. "Whatareyoudoing? Youscaredme!"

"Shush!" Jack puts his finger on my lips. "We can't make a noise."

Jack's face is white and full of fear, but a bubble of angry pops out of me. "Why are you hiding in there? I waited and waited but you didn't come. I got upset."

Jack grabs my hand and pulls me into the cupboard and shuts the door. It smells of damp paint. I can't see Jack very well, but I can feel his body shivering against mine.

"Whatisit?" I whisper into the dusty air.

"I fucked up big time, Rosie."

"Don't say that word! What's happened?"

The dark starts to go away and my eyes see Jack's looking into mine. Then he groans and lets his head fall into his hands. "I've ruined everything."

"Stop being a drama person. You're scaring me. Jess said you've been scaring lots of people at college. And one of the mums com-plained about you."

Jack holds my face and says, "I couldn't help it. I lost it in ICT. That prick, Davidson, wound me up and wound me up. Bastard!"

"Stop it! I don't like mean words. Whatdidyoudo?"

Jack won't look at me now, so I pull his face round. "Tell me."

"I smashed a computer. I couldn't control myself, Rosie. Then...then, shit!"

"What?"

"I threw a chair at the window."

"Jack that's badbadbad."

"A bit of glass flew into Mrs. Foster's eye. Oh God, Rosie, there was blood everywhere. I never meant to hurt her. I'd never hurt anybody, you know that, don't you?"

"Yes... But you did."

Jack looks at the ground. "The police came and it was horrible. They were asking hundreds of questions. Mr. Dean shouted at me, then Mrs. Foster grabbed him as she went by on the stretcher and told him that I didn't hurt her on purpose and that she won't press charges or anything, but—" Jack takes a big shuddery breath...

"What does that mean?"

"Press charges?"

I nod.

"They won't send me to prison—"

"Nonono! Not prison!"

"No, it's okay, not prison. But, Rosie, remember when I kicked the art table and it fell down?"

"I do. You broke Sam's work."

"And they said I might have to go away to some place and deal with my anger? What if they send me away now?"

11

I start crying. "They can't send you away. What will we do? We need us. I stop your angry, Jack. And you make me strong. You make me Rosie."

"And you make me a good Jack. When you're with me, Rosie, all the darkness vanishes and my brain calms down— even more than when I paint. You take away the black inside my head and turn it into colors."

I touch him gently where he showed me his brain had got hurt. He puts his hand over mine and kisses my wrist. He looks at me with eyes full of frightened.

"I'm so stupid! We can't be apart, that's why I ran away from the police so they can't take me. I need you, Rosie. I have to find a place to hide, so we can be together."

Jack folds his arms around me. I bury my face in his chest and smell his Jack smell. Lynx and sweat and lemon shampoo. He strokes my hair and whispers, "Rosie, Rosie, Rosie," over and over again.

I don't want to leave the cupboard. They can't take my Jack away. I kiss his eyes and his lips and the soft bit at the bottom of his ear. He trembles when I touch him.

"I love you, Rosie Tremayne," Jack says softly.

I'm about to answer him when the door flies open and a flashlight shines in our faces. All I can see is white in my eyes. I scream and Jack pulls me to the back of the cupboard with him. I bury my face in Jack's chest and wrap my arms around him, so I can't let go.

"Come on, you two," a prickly voice says. "We've been looking everywhere for you, Jack. You're not helping yourself by running off like that."

A police man with a big frown on his face looks into the cupboard. A police lady next to him shakes her head from side to side. She comes in and takes my arm.

"Leave us alone! Take your hands off my girlfriend!"

"Come on now, let go of him, love." The police lady tries to tug my arms away from Jack. He knocks her hat off, sending it flying out the door.

"Jack, don't! Calm down." I try and stop Jack doing anything else but the police lady pulls me out of the cupboard.

"Let go of him now, it's for the best."

The main art room doors swing open and Mr. Dean, the principal, comes in. He's all out of his breath.

"Have you...found him? W...what are you doing here... Rosie?"

"They're taking my Jack. Stop them taking my Jack, Mr. Dean."

"They have to...Rosie. Where is he, off...officer?"

The police lady nods at the art cupboard. The police man drags Jack out into the art room. He's trying to sit on the floor but the police man won't let him.

"Control yourself, Jack," Mr. Dean bellows at him. "You're making things ten times worse."

The police man stands Jack on his feet. "Let's get you to the car. Your mother is waiting for you at home."

Jack struggles to reach me, but the police man holds him tightly by one arm.

"Rosie! I'll come back and get you. Wait for me at our special place!" He swings his fist out at the police man, who grabs it and yanks Jack's arm behind his back.

"Enough! Or I'll handcuff you if I have to."

Jack stops fighting and goes sad all over. The police man leads him out of the room. He looks round at me and whispers, "I'm sorry."

I twist myself free, then run after Jack. Mr. Dean shouts my name. I catch Jack and hold on to him as hard as I can. The police man marches Jack along, making me run with him. "Don'ttakehimaway! Pleasedon'ttakehimaway."

I stumble and let go of Jack. The police lady catches me as I fall.

"JACK! JAAAAACK!"

The doors slam.

He's gone.

two

"I don't feel like talking, Mum."

She strokes her finger over my forehead. "All right, darling, but it might make you feel better if you do."

I turn my face to the wall. "I haven't heard from Jack in eight days."

Mum sighs. "He has a lot to deal with, Rose."

"He could text or call. Hedoesn'tlovemeanymore."

"Maybe it's best you forget about Jack and let him sort himself out."

"I'll never forget Jack. Jack took away my lonely." I pull my duvet up to cover my face. When I peep back over the edge, Mum has gone. Mum's upset. I always talk to her, but I can't now 'cause she doesn't understand about Jack. No one does.

Jack. Where are you? Why haven't you called me? What did I do bad?

I take my phone out from under my pillow and send Jack another text.

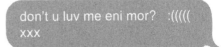

don't u luv me eni mor?   :(((((
xxx

That's eighty and two texts I've sent him. No texts back. I went to bed early at seven and ten bits 'round the clock.

So I could think about what to do. It's not working. I throw my covers off and go and look out the window. A piece-of-orange moon plays hide-and-seek with the clouds. I hold it between my fingers. I wonder if Jack can see it too.

I can't shake off my gloomy head. I'm falling deeper and deeper into sad. I shut my eyes and make my head think about a happy time with Jack. All I can see is his face full of frightened as the police man takes him away through the college doors.

I pick up the photo on my bedside table of me and Jack dancing. He didn't stop smiling at me for the whole dance. I sit on the floor with my back to the radiator and rest our picture on my lap. Behind me in the photo I can see my best friend, Lou. In her new motor-wheelchair. With red wheels with silver stars on. We've been best friends since we joined college. She can't talk by herself or walk by herself. Except her arms and legs move all on their own sometimes. Once she hit Toby Varley on the nose by mistake and made it bleed. I look after her and she looks after me. She's very clever.

I trace my finger around photo-Jack and it helps me back to that memory. When Jack kissed me for the first time. That was seven months, one week, and three days ago. I was at the Monday Night Club, which is a disco just for people who are special. At the youth center.

I watch as Jack Darcy shoots across the parking lot. He does a hardflip around Mrs. Dean's car on his skateboard. Then he does a spinny thing in time to the disco music spilling out the door. He's such a show-off. He stops by Jamie and Sandra who are kissing under the Horse Conker tree. Jack high-fives Jamie and kisses Sandra on the cheek. I don't like him kissing her...but I don't know why.

"What you lookin' at, Rose?" Elaine, our supervisor, presses her nose against the glass and peers outside. "You watch out for that one, my girl. He'll break your heart. Tsk! How did those two sneak out there? I can't turn my back for a minute. You lot know you're not allowed outside." She walks off grumbling.

Jack spins 'round on his board and catches me watching him. He blows me a kiss as he races past the window and heads for the doors. I push back from the window and nearly fall over Lou in her wheelchair. Her iPad voice shouts at me, "WATCH IT!"

As I stand up straight the door flies open and Jack Darcy races around the edge of the dance floor before he does an ollie in the middle of the room.

"SWANKER," Lou says on loud.

Angus Jones whistles loudly with his fingers and everyone claps and cheers. Jack holds his board up in the air and bows. Toby Varley tries to whistle with his fingers like Angus, but it sounds like

17

a fart. Everyone starts to laugh. Jack winks at me, but I turn my back and help Lou with her drink.

"YOU'VE GONE BRIGHT RED," Lou voices. I glare at her but she sticks her tongue out at me and pushes her finger down on the keyboard. "YOU'RE INTO JACK."

"Are you?" a voice says behind me.

I turn 'round and Jack is standing looking at me with his sky-blue eyes. His dark brown hair keeps falling over one of them. I feel all wobbly and my words won't speak.

"Dance with me?" He smiles and it makes me go all pleased shivery. Then he takes my hand. And I never want him to let it go.

"GO, ROSE!" Lou cheers and waves her arms around her head. Jack laughs and takes me onto the dance floor.

After a while, a slow song comes on and Jack pulls me in close to his chest. I look up at him and he bends his head down to kiss me—

"Why can't you leave me ALONE?"

Ben's shout reaches into my happy thought and snatches it away. He slams his door, and I can feel the shake through my feet. I was just about to kiss Jack. I try and get the picture back in my head. It's no good. My brother has spoiled it up. Little brothers can be a pain. 'Cept he's not little; he's very big for fifteen years old.

I go to the bathroom to get some water. Downstairs, Mum and Dad are talking in whisper-shouts. I lean over the stair rail to listen. It's me-talk.

"It's not fair, Mike. You can't do this to her. What harm would it do to let her have the postcards Jack wrote?"

Cards? Cards Jack wrote? I don't know what Mum's saying.

"Keep your voice down, Sarah. What harm? I'd have thought that was obvious. She needs Jack out of her life now. You give her the cards and she'll think she's going to see him again."

"She's heartbroken, you could at least stop her thinking that he doesn't love her anymore."

"Good, I hope she does think that, then she'll get over him sooner rather than later. It's no good looking at me like that, Sarah. What if Jack hurt her?"

I want to shout to them that Jack would never hurt me. Ever. I hear Mum tap her fingernails on the table. She does that when she's upset.

"I'm not stupid, I can see the risk and I *obviously* think it's best they forget about each other, but he's not all bad, Mike. Rose has been with him for seven months, so if you thought he was that much of a liability, why didn't you say something before?"

Mum's words make knots in my head. There are too many to make sense of them all. But I get that my mum wants me to forget Jack. I fold my arms around me where her words kicked me.

Dad's voice is getting shoutier. I try and catch up with what they are saying.

"...nobody would listen, as usual. Whose side are you on anyway?"

19

"No one's, everyone's—oh I don't know, it's not about sides. I just think we should give her the postcards."

"Over my dead body!"

"Shush! Stop shouting."

I can't hear anymore 'cause someone shuts the kitchen door and Ben has put Li-turgy on very loud in his bedroom.

My feet are glued down on the carpet. My back slides down the wall where I am, so my bottom sits on the floor. I go over what they said. Jack sent me cards. Why would Jack send cards? Why didn't he phone? Or text? Cards... Dad has cards from Jack. *My* cards.

Jack still loves me.

Mum doesn't want me to love Jack anymore.

Dad hates Jack.

I think Dad took my cards from Jack.

Dad *stole* my cards from Jack.

I must find them.

I go back to my bedroom and wait. I curl up in a ball on my bed. I feel tears run down my cheek. I have a waterfall on my face. I'm too unhappy to wipe the wet away, even though it tickles me. I climb under my duvet to make my crying quiet.

My clock says it's halfway 'round the clock past twelve. That's the time I put my alarm on for. I squashed it under my pillow so it only woke me up. Mum and Dad are in bed 'cause I can hear Dad snoring. I can go and look in his office room now.

It's very dark, so I have to find my way by walking my hand along the wall. I touch something spidery and nearly scream. I bite my dressing gown to stop me.

The floorboards are creaking. I try not to step on them too hard. I'm sure I'll wake somebody up before I get downstairs. My heart is wave-crashing in my chest.

It's taking me forever to get to Dad's office. That's where my Jack cards will be hidden. I know, 'cause we're not allowed in there. Not many more steps and I'll be there. I know I'm half down the stairs 'cause my foot gets caught where our dog, Winniebago, chewed the carpet. I reach the bottom and creep past the kitchen so she doesn't scratch at the door. Then I run to the office on the tops of my toes.

The office door is shut. I twist the handle and nothing moves. I try again and give a little push with my shoulder. It swings open, and I fall through the gap. I stay in my fallen-over place on the rug. Not daring to move. After lots of bits, I pull myself up. I mouse-quiet shut the door and switch the light on. And wait until no one comes.

The room is a mess. Dad's papers are piled all over the place. His laptop snoozes on the table... I'll never find my Jack in here. I don't know where to look. I pick a file up and look under a magazine. They could be anywhere. I start to get gloomy but tell myself off. I've got to put my shoulders back and be strong.

I open drawers. I pull one out too fast, tipping it up. Lots and lots of pens and paper clips fall everywhere. I'm sure Mum will wake up now. She can hear a dropping pin.

A door opens and footsteps walk along the ceiling. They stop. I hold my breath until my lungs are about to pop. The toilet flushes. The footsteps walk away and vanish.

I must hurry up. I push things out of the way and turn things upside down. Dad smiles out from a holiday in France photo, on the top of his desk. I turn it flat, so I can't see his face.

On the floor, Dad has built up some boxes in a tower. I rip the lids off and throw out anything in my way. I don't care. Then I remember I don't want him to know I've been here. I put everything back.

It's all taking too long.

In a middle box, I find a card with my name on it. And then more cards, all with "Luv Jack" and lots of his draw-ings on the front and back. I've found them. I hug them to me.

I sit down on the rug and spread the cards in front of me. One, two, three, four, five, six. Six cards. Jack has written nearly all the days. I snatch up each card. First, I look at his drawings on the front. He's drawn the cards specially for me. So I can read the pictures. To help the

writing. He always does that to help me with hard homework and stuff.

I can see his picture head with monsters jumping out of it.
Jack paints the monsters in his head to throw his angry out.
There's a little fly on one card buzzing 'round the edge. I don't
know why he's there. And then I see a picture of Jack crying.
That makes me more sad than I am.

I read the words after the pictures. I'm not fast at reading
but every card tells me how much Jack loves me.

I need v Rosie. I luv v 4ever.

That makes the sun shine in my head. Then I see why he
didn't text me or call me. A picture of his phone explodes on
one card.

Im sori Rosie. I throo my mobile
at a wall and broke it. I was cracy
about going away from v. I stood
owtside my howse in the sno and
swor at Mum. I woodnt get in the
car. Mum showtid at me. I sat in
the bak of the car and lisend to
our song over and over agen al the
way to Bryten. Ther waznt enny
luv in the air tho. I didnt say good
bi to Mum. I woz to sad. Then I
felt even sader.

Rosie Tremayne

61 Cromwell Aven

Henley-on-Thames

Oxfordshire RG16

I picture Jack in the snow. His hurt is my hurt. All inside me. I wipe my eyes with a tissue. Then I read how lonely he is.

> Ware r u? Why dont u rite? I cant bare anuther day wivout u.

Then I find the bit that breaks my heart into pieces.

> Dont u luv me enny more?

I cry for Jack and I cry for me. I hide my face inside my dressing gown, so no one can hear me. Then I cry it out, so I can find my strong.

I wipe my nose on my sleeve and put the cards in order. One, two times Jack has written where he lives in Brighton.

> Manor House Farm, Woods Lane, Hassocks, Brighton, BN6 7QL.
>
> I kopid that from a leeflet on the hall tabul at the howse. Its the 1 paynted wite with see-green shuters like ur eyes :)

I pick up all the cards and hide them in my pajama pocket.

I'm angry-hurt with Dad. He tried to rub me and Jack out. I'm sad-cross with everyone.

I make a plan in my head. I'm going to find Jack.

I can do it.

I am Rose.

three
december 11th & 12th

It's halfway past the evening six. My purple bag is packed and ready to go. Clothes. Pants and socks. Make up. Money. My Jack cards are in the secret pocket inside, all zipped up. I like Jack being safe. Best of all, my little blue butterfly brooch is pinned on my coat. I don't wear it to college 'cause I don't want to lose it. Jack gave it to me after we saw a blue-sky butterfly in the Butterfly House at Chester Zoo. It landed on my hand then flew onto Jack's nose. My grandma laughed and said it was watching over us.

We liked that.

I push the bag under the bed. I don't want anyone to see it.

I hear the door slam. Mum's home from work. She looks after young girls who aren't very happy and need help. I usually sit in the kitchen at ten past the six o'clock to hug her when she gets in. 'Cause her job can make her sad sometimes. I don't want to hug her tonight. And I didn't want to kiss her goodbye when she got out this morning either. I was tired and cross-patch, and my tummy hurt from being sad-sack at her and Dad... And I have to lie to her. It's bad to lie.

"Rose? Are you there? I've got takeout hot chicken from Marks and Sparks."

I take a deep breath and shout down, "OkayMum, coming!" I know I have to try to be normal Rose. 'Cause I don't want Mum or Dad or Ben to guess I'm up to something. I worked that out all by myself.

"Tell Ben to come now too please and make sure he's washed his hands."

"Yeahsure."

I check again that my purple bag is tucked under the bed before I go downstairs. I knock on Ben's door but he doesn't answer. He's probably got his ear pods in. I just go in. He's squashed up against his wall mirror looking at his nose.

"What part of 'knock before you come in' don't you get?" Ben grumps at me. His nose looks very red.

"I did knock."

"Knock louder then."

Mum bellows up the stairs, "Are you two coming?"

Ben looks at me and grins, before rushing toward the door. He stops when he sees I'm not following him. "What's wrong with you? Come on, I'm starving! Go!"

We race downstairs, pushing and shoving each other.

It makes Mum cross.

"For goodness' sake, you two, are you ever going to grow

out of that stupid game?" Mum sighs as we get stuck in the doorway trying to get through first. "What took you so long?"

"Ben was squeezing a spot."

"Shut it, Rose."

"But you were."

"Lay the table, please, Rose, and Ben, you do the drinks. Dad will be home any minute now—talk of the devil, here he is now."

"You're right, Mum. Dad *is* a devil. With big red horns!"

Mum looks surprised at me as I'm never grumpy like Ben. Dad bursts through the back door and swings Mum around. Mum gets all giggly and tells him to stop. I want him to stop too. I want him to go back to work. My unhappy makes me not like him.

Ben shakes his head at me and pushes his eyebrows up. Dad goes over and messes his hair, which makes Ben very cross. He spends ages making it flop over one eye. Like Jack's. Jack's does it all by itself.

Dad tries to kiss me on the top of my head. "No cuddle for your old dad tonight?" He tries to wrap his arms around me but I pull away. He claps his hands together and makes a smile that doesn't look happy. "What's for dinner then, Sarah?"

My phone shivers in my pocket and I snatch it out, hoping it will be Jack.

How r u? Has Jack text u?

28

Lou. I swallow a lump in my throat. She cried when I first told her Jack had gone. And everyone at college gave me a group hug. Mr. Dean said we had to stop as we were blocking the corridor. Lou said she had my hurting inside her too. And she wanted to make me happy again. Only Jack being back can do that really. Yesterday, Lou sent me an email at five on the clock, with lots of photos of us all together. She put a talk bubble coming out her mouth on a picture of me and her hugging. It said, *I LOVE YOU. You're the best friend EVER.*

I want to answer her text but I'm too un-happy at the moment.

"Put that phone away, Ben," Mum says, pointing her finger at Ben.

"Rose is on her phone. Why pick on me?"

"Don't mouth your mum," Dad says to Ben.

"Christ, Dad! Why can't everyone get off my back?"

I look at Ben and sigh. "There isn't anyone on your back."

Mum and Dad start giggling and even Ben starts to laugh. I make an even bigger sigh.

"Let's eat before it all goes cold." Mum uses her no-nonsense voice. She waves her hand around the table. "Eat, eat!"

I push some peas around my plate. One falls off and rolls across the table. Ben goes to flick it, but Mum gives him her eyebrow look. You don't argue with Mum's eyebrow. Dad's talking about work now. He makes ad-verts for the TV and the radio. And in magazines. He gets overexcited when he

29

has a new idea and flings his arms around. He nearly knocks his wine over. Mum has gone all pink and chatty. I watch them. I can't talk. I can't eat. My insides turn over and over. I have to miss work tomorrow. I have to find Jack and be with him. I don't know if I can do it. I don't know if I can leave my house. My Henley-on-Thames. Can I get to Brighton by myself? Mum and Dad say I can do whatever I want. I can be in-de-pen-dent, but even that stupid word is too hard to say.

Inside me I have a big talk with myself. *You walk to Waitrose on a Saturday on your own, Rose. To go to work. You pack all the people's shopping bags all by yourself. And stack the shelves with food. Toby has to have a super-visor from Henley College. You go on the number three bus to Henley College when Mum can't take you. You go to Jim's cafe on your own every day. Nearly every day. You go to the river park with your friends when it's sunny. And you go for lots of walks with Jack; and you go to the cinema with Jack all by yourself... That's all in Henley-on-Thames but once you went to Reading with Jack too. That wasn't very nice. But, remember, Jack's mum took you and Jack to Brighton. And she left you both for lots of bits of time. AND Grandma told you that you can do most things on your own.*

She should know 'cause you see her lots. Remember she took you to London and let you look in Topshop without her... You see, Rose, you are very in-de-pen-dent.

"Earth calling Rose! Hello? You were miles away. Where have you been?"

"I'm sitting at the table eating my dinner."

Mum looks at me with a smile that isn't in her eyes. Her eyes are down in the dumps.

"You've barely touched your food. It's one of your favorites."

"I hope your chin isn't going to actually rest on that plate!" Dad teases Ben.

"Why? Are you the chin police?" Ben pushes his plate away. Dad is about to speak, but Mum puts her hand on his arm and shakes her head. "Could we have one meal that doesn't end in an argument with you and Ben? Thank you... Rose, darling, are you feeling okay?" She rests the soft bit of her hand on my forehead. "You haven't got a temperature but you're as white as a sheet."

"I'm going to bed, Mum. I'm not hungry."

"Oh, Rose." She rubs my back. "You go on up and I'll bring you some hot chocolate in a bit."

"Nothankyou. I want to be with just me."

As I go out the door Dad says, "Give it another couple of weeks and she'll have forgotten all about Jack."

I march back into the room. "I won't. I'll never forget about Jack."

I run upstairs making my feet stomp on the stairs. Winniebago tries to follow me. I send her back to the kitchen. Her tail hides between her legs. I need to be with just me. I need a Jack plan.

31

I text Lou. She will help me. Best friends help each other all the time.

> How do I get to Bryten on the trane?

Y?

> Im going to c Jack

When?

> Don't know soon

U got another card from him then?

> No ☹

Good ☺

> Y good? I want anuther Jack card

Ur dad would c the other cards had gone if u had, cuz u said he gets to the post 1st as he's up early

> Yes I did I 4got that

How come u r going to c Jack then?

Just am

Tell me when u do X

Ok XXX

I put three kisses 'cause I feel wrong that I'm not telling her the truth.

Cool. Give me time to work out the journey to Brighton and then I'll email it to u.

☺ XXX

I can't tell her I'm going tomorrow. I don't want to get her in trouble.

I sit on my big cushion and try and see Jack in Brighton. It won't come. I go to one of our happy places with just us. By his garden pond.

The night has come out. All the birds have gone to sleep. The moon shines in a white ball on the water. Jack and me sit on the bench by the pond. We watch a frog puffing its chest in and out in the moonlight. It makes us laugh. We kiss for a long time, not wanting to let each other go. I snuggle up to Jack to stop the wind making goose bumps on my arms. The trees moan and rustle and tap their branches on each other. A lady fox shrieks in the distance. I shiver.

"What was that?" Jack says jumping up from the bench, making me startle.

"What?" I scared-whisper into the air.

"That." He points at a tiny black shape swooping over the pond. Then another and another. "OMG! They're bats! Rosie, look at the bats. They're so cool—they're catching the flies."

He takes my hand and we crouch down low and watch the bats dancing over the moonlit water lilies. I rest my head on Jack's shoulder and close my eyes and listen to his sing-song breathing in the dark...

I kept waking up last night. I had to check my purple bag. I did it three times—to make sure I hadn't forgotten anything. Clothes. Money. Jack cards. Tube train map that Grandma got for me when I went to the biggest Topshop ever, in London. Snacks.

I'm more tired than when I went to bed. I want to climb back under my covers and wake up again. With Jack next to me. That would be the best.

Daydreaming is no good. It won't find Jack.

I go over my journey. Lou worked it out for me. I still didn't tell her I was going today. I have to go up high to London to get back down low to Brighton. I don't get why you can't go in a straight line.

Lou wrote my journey out for me last night. She always does the difficult stuff for me. I help Lou with everything else. Eating. Getting her books. Dancing in her wheelchair at discos...and getting her to all the places she needs to be. Especially in college.

She made my journey to Brighton on her laptop and sent it in my email box. I printed it out on my new printer on my desk which I got for my college work. Ben was jealous, as he has to share Mum and Dad's. He'll get his own when he goes to Henley College.

I look very hard at Lou's email. I'm not great at reading, but it helps keep a memory in my head. I put the paper flat on my desk. I tick as I read. I'm using a green-leaf pen.

1.) Henley-on-Thames to Paddington Station. (Get a train before morning 10 on the clock or you'll have to change at Twyford.)

2.) At Paddington get the under-the-ground train to Victoria Station. District and Circle line. Yellow line. Seven stops. Going west.

3.) At Victoria Station get the Brighton train.
On top of the ground. 1 hour and 1 minute
to Brighton.

4.) Find Jack. Look at his address on card
number 5. I think you said number 5.

I pull my bag out again to check the cards. It is number five. Tick. My sweaty hand smudges the number, so I go over it with my pen.

I can hear Mum going downstairs for breakfast. A bit of sick comes up in my mouth. I picture Jack in my head. He smiles at me and sticks his thumb up. I finish my list ticks and go down to the kitchen.

"How are you feeling, love?" Mum peers at me closely. "You look wiped out. Why don't you give college a miss today? I can work from home if you like—I've got a huge amount of paperwork. We could have a duvet afternoon and watch a film?"

"NO!"

Mum steps back, frowning. "Don't be like that, I'm only trying to help."

That makes me feel wrong inside, but I can't stay at home. If I do, I don't think I'll ever go and find Jack. It has to be now-go. When I have talked myself into going to Brighton.

"SorryMum. I'mokaythankyou, Mum. I want to go to college."

"You're right, best to keep busy." Her finger gently strokes my face. Her nice makes me not so brave. "Have some toast, darling, you can't go to college on an empty stomach, especially since you didn't eat anything last night."

The radio talks quietly on the shelf. Mum turns it up to hear the news. I'm thinking so hard about what I'm going to do I only hear bits of the radio man.

"...*taken on her journey to school...found in river...dead for several days.*"

I go all cold and goose bumpy. I don't understand everything the radio man said, but I know a girl got taken away and killed dead. That's badbadbad... I'm going on a journey to Jack. All by myself...but she was only twelve years old, and I'm sixteen and ten months. I can look after myself.

"I can't bear to listen to it," Mum says switching the radio off. "That poor girl and her poor, poor family, having to go through it all." Mum's voice sounds broken up.

Ben charges into the room and grabs a bit of my toast. "I'm late, have to meet Angus." He rubs me on the head as he goes past.

"Gently, Ben, and goodbye to you too." Mum half laughs. "At least he spoke this morning." She smooths down my hair where Ben ruffled it up. "I don't know." Mum checks her watch. "Right, ten past eight, we need to get going or we'll both be late. Are you *sure* you want to go in today?"

I'm not. But I have to. Jack needs me. "Let'sgoMum."

We go out to the car. Winniebago wants to come with me. She follows me out the door and tugs at my coat. I wish she could come with me. Like Toto in *The Wizard of Oz*. 'Cept Winniebago is too big to go in my bag.

"For goodness' sake, what's the matter with Winnie today? I don't need this. Here are the keys—go and sit in the car, Rose, while I put this wretched dog in the kitchen. What on earth have you got in that bag of yours? It looks like it's going to burst."

I slide into the seat. I put my bag under my feet so Mum can't see it. I clip my seat belt on. You must always wear a seat belt. In my pocket I have a Jack card. A little picture-fly buzzes all over it. I read it to help me have brave.

Im siting on my windo sil. Its 3 in the morning and I carnt sleep. A fli is buzing rownd my room. I didnt think u got flis in the winter. It feels like its inside my hed. Im going nuts wivout u. I need u. I need ur kisses. And ur smile. To stop me being me. Im bloing smoke rings up to the moon. Can u see them? The wind is ici cold. I wish u wer here to warm me. Im sinking into blak. Wats the point of me wivout u? Iv got to get ovt of here. Pleeze rite. Hope u stil luv me. I luv u the size of the sky. Jack XX

Seb thinks my art is the dogs boloks. ☺

Rosie Tremayne

61 Cromwell Ave

Henley-on-Tham

Oxfordshire RG

Jack isn't Jack without me.

Mum slams the front door. I put my card away and hold my hand over my pocket. I keep Jack safe and warm.

Mum jumps in the car. "I had to give Winnie some bacon bits to calm her down. I don't know what's got into her. Oh no, is that the time? It's eight twenty-five already, we need to get a move on."

Mum chatters all the way to college. I'm glad 'cause I don't want to speak. Mum would know something was up with me. Like Winniebago.

She drops me off at the corner of Dean Street with easy parking. She leans over to hug me. "Oh, you're wearing your butterfly brooch. I thought you didn't like wearing it to college?"

"It makes me think of Jack."

"Yes, of course." Mum does a big sigh. "Bye, Rose, I love you, my darling."

I hug her tight. I don't want to let her go. Then I think of Jack. "Bye, Mum. I love you too." I get out and stand on the pavement and watch her drive down the road. A semi truck comes 'round the corner and blocks her out. I go and hide myself down the side bit of the youth club hut. Near to the college building. No one can see me. It's freezing cold, but I'm sweating all over me. I get my phone and ring Jess. I have to ring Jess 'cause she's like a grown up. My heart is hitting my chest so hard I think it will explode out.

"Hi, Rose. You okay?"

"Yesthankyou. I mean no. Idon'tfeelwell. Ineedyoutotell college."

"I'm not in college this morning, Rose. I'm all packed and ready to go to the airport. I'm off on my gap year, remember? I don't have much time. Why can't your mum ring them?"

"No! No, Jess. Mum can't. She's at work already. College will be cross if no one rings."

"Well, okay then... I guess I can ring them. I'll do it as soon as we get off the phone, but make sure your mum lets them know too, as soon as she can."

"I will." I'm about to say *I promise.* I can't. That would make it a worse lie.

"Keep warm. I'll see you when I'm back. Love you. Woohoo!"

"Bye, Jess. Thankyou. Love you too."

I see my face in the window of the youth club hut. I don't want to look at me. Over the road I hear the college bell go for starting the day. I pull my hood up and walk up the high street to get to the station. My breath steam-train puffs in and out. I dig my hands down to the bottom of my pockets to stop the cold biting them. My fingers find my lucky sixpence coin that my granddad gave me when he was on top of the ground. I hold it tight.

My bag bumps against my leg all the way up the road to Henley-on-Thames train station.

40

The ticket man is on his mobile phone. I get my list out to check what I need to do. My hands are being clumsy, and I drop it. It floats down to the floor and flies away from me. I try and stop it with my boot.

"D'you need a hand, miss?" the ticket man shouts through the speaking hole.

"NothankyouI'mokay."

I'm not. I'm hot and bothered up. I have a talking to myself and pick my list up off the floor. I go over it but it doesn't look easy any more. I need a ticket to London Paddington... Do I get a different ticket for the Victoria bit? And Brighton? I tap on the glass to get the ticket man to help me.

"I'll call you back in a minute. Now, what can I do for you, young lady?"

I hold my list up to show the ticket man. "Ineedlotsoftickets andIdon'tknowhowtodoit."

"Whoa, slow down, love, let me have a look at this—pass it through that gap there." He takes my list and holds the bit of paper out in front of him. Like my dad does. A hundred miles away from his face. He smiles at me. "No problem, we can sort all this out here."

I smile my nicest Rose smile at him.

"For a start, there's an easier route I can show you—"

"Nonono. I have to do my journey. I know it in my head. Lou told it to me."

The ticket man shakes his head. "It's up to you, missy, but

you're making it difficult for yourself. Now, do you want a single or return ticket?"

"Return, please. I'm bringing Jack home."

"So, return today?"

I look at him and I realize that I don't know. "I think so. Will I need a ticket for Jack?"

"He can get a ticket at the other end. Are you sure you're going to be all right, love? Don't you have anyone to travel with you?"

I make myself as tall as I can. "I'm fine thankyouverymuch. I'm in-de-pen-dent."

He frowns at me as he pushes the tickets through the gap. "As long as you're sure... That's thirty-five pounds and fifty pence, please."

"That's *all* my birthday money. But Jack is the best present ever."

"I've put your tickets in the order you'll need them, but you can always ask the ticket collector at the other end to help you."

"Okaythankyou."

I put my change with my Waitrose work money. I hold tight to my tickets and walk to the far end of the station. So I don't have to talk to people. 'Cause I'm always friendly and chatty. I pull my hood right over my face to keep it hiding.

Through the trees I can see the playground on the other side. My grandma took me there when I was little. I can hear the children shout. When I close my eyes I'm on the swings. My grandma pushes me higher and higher, until my feet touch the sky. The wind blows over my face, tickling my skin. I point my toes out to tap the clouds. I like that picture in my head.

I keep my eyes closed and go over everything I've done all by myself. I'm pleased with me. I sorted my tickets and I'm going to be on the train very soon. I think about Jack and his smile when he sees me later. My stomach flutters.

"Hi...R...Rose. What are y...y...you d...doing here?"

I come back to the ground with a bump. It's Danny Parker. He's in my Pathways classes at college.

"R...R...Rose?"

"How did you know it was me?" I whisper to him.

" P...p...p...purple...b..." He points twice.

My purple boots. My purple bag. I'm stupidstupidstupid. Everyone can see I'm Rose. I get up and stand behind one of the station pillars. Danny Parker follows me.

"Go away, Danny!"

He looks sad at me but carries on standing next to me. "What are you d...d...doing?"

"Nothing."

"Why have you g...got all those t...t...tickets?"

I shove them in my pocket. "I haven't."

Danny scratches his head. "You're b...bonkers. I saw them."

I look around to make sure no one can hear us. "I'm going to find Jack. But it's a *secret*. Promise not to tell anyone?"

"I like s...secrets."

"Promise?"

"C...c...cross...m...m...m—"

"Okaythankyou. I believe you."

"H...here comes your t...train. It's a diesel multiple unit with a top speed of a hundred and forty-five miles per hour." He gets out a notebook and writes in it, before he walks up to the very end of the platform.

The train whistles 'round the corner and slowly stops. Lots of students get off. I don't know any of them to talk to. That makes me feel better. I'm about to get on the train when I see Mrs. Roper getting off it. If she sees me, she'll take me back to college. I have her for speech therapy today. I run back behind the pillar and hide me as much as I can. I see Danny running up the platform toward me. I make the word "NO" with my mouth and shake my head from side to side but he keeps coming. I make a cross face.

He runs straight past and shouts, "Mrs. R...Roper! Can I w...walk up to c...college with you?"

I'm shaky all over as I jump onto the train. I peek back over my shoulder and see Danny holding onto Mrs. Roper's arm. He looks 'round and grins at me. I give him a big wave. I find a corner seat and rest my face against the window glass. It cools down my hot cheek. I smile at myself. A lady in the next seat smiles back at me. Mum says I always make people happy.

The train starts to move.

I'm on my way to Jack.

Nothing can go wrong now.

four

Paddington Station makes me invisible. People rush
past. I like being invisible Rose.

When I look up, I see a soldier standing on the wall. I
don't know why he's here. He's not real. My granddad was a
soldier. This soldier looks very young. He's wearing a helmet
and a knitted scarf like my grandma made for me. And a big
heavy coat. It must have been very cold where he was fighting.
I bet he was scared. Granddad said the bombs were loud and
made the men scream. This soldier is reading a letter. I think
it's a letter from his girlfriend. I bet his dad wouldn't take it
away from him.

I need to stop wasting my time up and find the tube train.
So I can get to Jack. I pat my bag where I've put my postcards
from him.

I hope that soldier over there went home. I hope I get Jack home.

I need to find the tube train sign. I remember it looks
like a planet. My granddad used to look at stars and planets

through his telescope. I have to get the District and Circle line to Victoria. Yellow line. Seven stops. Going west.

My bag is heavy so I rest it on the ground. A little boy runs up to me. He has a red balloon on a string. He stops in front of me and peeps 'round his balloon.

I shout, "Boo!"

The little boy squeals.

A lady grabs his arm. "Come here, George!"

"George playing with girl, Mummy."

"Not now, George."

She frowns at me and drags him away. The little boy keeps looking back over his shoulder. I watch him until he disappears behind people's legs. All I can see is the red balloon, bobbing up and down.

I must get a move on. District and Circle line to Victoria. Yellow line. Seven stops. Going west.

I don't know where to go. Everything is so big and busy. I make my eyes move around the station. People get in the way. Then I see a lady with a big hat standing under the planet sign. I keep my eyes on the sign so I don't lose it in the people.

"Watch where you're going, love!"

"Sorrythankyou. I have to watch the planet."

The man looks at the ground and walks away.

The lady with the hat is hugging another lady now. I follow people down the steps to where the trains are. People don't care if they push you.

I don't like under-the-ground trains. When I came to London with Grandma we went on lots of them. She said she didn't like them either. They're dirty and smelly and they scream at you.

At the bottom of the stairs a loud voice talks into the air. "LADIES AND GENTLEMEN, DUE TO AN INCIDENT AT BAYSWATER, THE DISTRICT AND CIRCLE LINE IS SUSPENDED UNTIL FURTHER NOTICE. PAS-SENGERS ARE ADVISED TO SEEK ALTERNATIVE ROUTES."

District and Circle line. Is that mine? District and Circle line. Yellow line. Seven stops. Going west. My stomach turns upside down.

I sit on a bench. I need to get to the big map on the wall, but lots and lots of people are covering it up. I get my little pocket map of London out of my coat. You can go on different trains. So I can work it out.

The colored lines tangle up in my eyes. I tell myself off in my head. Don't be silly, Rose. Take a deep breath and trace the lines with your finger.

I get a pen from my bag. A fat, fat, FAT boy sits next to me. He's squashing me out the way. Drops of water run down his head. He uses the end of his scarf to wipe them away.

His chin shakes. "What are you gawping at?"

I look down at my map. I make believe I can find a new train. It's a mess now. I'm going wrong already. A tear falls

48

from my eye and splashes on the paper, spreading over the red line on to the yellow.

The fat boy nudges my leg. "You okay?"

I can't speak. My words would fall over each other. I shake my head.

He sticks his big face into mine. "Where are you going?" He gives me a tissue. It's not a nose tissue 'cause it smells of tomato sauce and has writing on it.

"District. C...Circle line."

"That's it?"

"Yellow l...line. Vic...toria Station."

"Right, so you need to find another way. Here, let's look at your map. By the way, I'm Lawrence."

"Okayyes. I'm Rose Tremayne."

"Nice to meet you, Rose Tremayne."

He holds out his hand. It's hot and sticky. I wipe my hand on my coat. Lawrence copies me.

"Sorry I was such a grouch just now, but I hate coming down to London. I can't stand crowds."

I nod 'cause I know what he means. "They swallow you up."

He laughs. "Yeah—that's just what they do." He pretends to gobble people up. His chins jelly wobble as he opens and shuts his mouth. I laugh at them. "They'd have a problem swallowing me up though, wouldn't they?"

"Yes. They'd need a very big mouth." I look at him all over.

49

Lawrence's face smiles but his eyes look wrong. He clears his throat.

"You have a couple of options here to get to Victoria, Rose Tremayne. One means a few changes onto different lines, the other is simpler but will take longer...simpler but longer, d'you think?"

"Okaythankyou."

"Right you are. Anyway, I'm going to King's Cross, so we can go together if you like? We have to take the Hammersmith and City line, that's pink and all you do from there is take the light blue Victoria line straight down to Victoria Station. It's a few more stops but better than lots of changes."

He smiles at me. A real smile. His cheeks make his eyes go away. "Ready? I'll write it down for you when we get to King's Cross."

"Yesplease."

He makes a lot of noise getting up. "Pink line first... Hammersmith...and City. Phew! Can I take your bag for you?"

"No!" I clutch my bag tight. "It has all my Jack in it."

"That's a bit scary. You're not some axe-wielding maniac who carries round bits of their victims in their bag, are you?" He laughs, making his belly jiggle up and down.

"Did you make a joke?"

"Well, no, just ignore me. You ready?"

"Yesthankyou."

I follow Lawrence back out into the light. He looks older than me and a bit older than Jess who is eighteen and a half.

He doesn't walk fast. He rolls from side to side. People move out of his way. They don't do that for me. When we get to our tube entrance, he has to stop. His breath wheezes in and out.

"Areyouokay?"

He nods and stands up properly. "Got your ticket?" He holds a bit of black plastic over a big yellow button. He squeezes through the gate.

I look at my ticket and put it on the button. Nothing happens. "I'mstuck."

"Put it in the ticket slot. Take it back...and walk through. Mine's an Oyster card."

"My mum likes oysters, but Dad says they're yucky."

"I wouldn't know, but I wouldn't want to munch on something that was still alive, gross. Right, we're going down there. Where are you going from Victoria then?"

"Brighton."

"Nice, I haven't been there for years. You can get the best cotton candy by the entrance to the pier and the biggest portion of fish and chips under the arches. Careful, mind your bag doesn't get caught on the escalator—it's quite hairy, isn't it? A bit like a sheepdog. Cool badges though."

There are pictures of a boy jumping high in the air in every picture on the wall going down. I wonder who he is. And why all the pictures are the same.

51

The tube platform is very hot. It smells oily and dusty. There are a lot of people, and it's hard to move. I don't like it down here.

A group of school boys are laughing and pointing at us. I want them to stop.

"Oi! Shrek! What you doing away from your swamp?"

"Come on," Lawrence says. "Let's move further up the platform."

I look up at him. His face is full of hurt. "Don't worry, I'm used to it, Rose."

But his eyes are watery. He looks away. And I understand. I pull on his sleeve.

"Mum says to ignore people. They don't understand. They haven't been brought up pro-perly."

"It's hard to ignore me and they're right, I'm Shrek."

"You're not a Shrek, you're a Lawrence."

"Thank you."

He trumpet-blows his nose into a hanky.

A warm wind blows on my face. I can hear a rumble. It gets louder and louder. Then a train shrieks out of the tunnel. The wheels spark lightning onto the walls. I'm not so scared with Lawrence next to me. He pulls me forward when the train stops and I follow him. Someone shouts, "MIND THE GAP!" as he helps me toward the doors.

"THIS IS PADDINGTON. THIS IS A HAMMERSMITH AND CITY LINE TRAIN TO BARKING. CHANGE HERE FOR THE BAKERLOO AND DISTRICT AND CIRCLE LINES."

"Quick, the disabled seat is free—you can sit there, Rose."

52

I sit on the seat next to it. "Why don't you sit there, Lawrence?"

He looks at his feet. "I'm fine standing."

Nobody speaks. We're all squashed together. The clackety-clack, clackety-clack fills my ears. No one else notices. They just keep reading. Or yawning. Or looking at their phones.

"THE NEXT STATION IS EDGWARE ROAD."

Lawrence sways backward and forward with all the standing people. "Four more stops until King's Cross."

"THIS STATION IS EDGWARE ROAD. THIS TRAIN TERMINATES AT BARKING."

Lawrence rubs his eyes. I get a Jack card out of my bag.

Rosie, this is tuf. I cant liv wivout u. I hate being in this place. Ware r u? I cant draw you enny more. My pencil wont work. I cant paynt ennything good. I cant rite stuf ither. I can say the wurds out lowd but my hand cant put them on the paper in the rite way. Im rubish. Im hiting my hed now to tri and push sum klever into it. R u over me? Im not Jack without u. Im sori, Rosie, Ive left u on ur oan, and Ive never felt so loneli. Why havnt u writen? I hav to get home to u. Wait for me. PLEEZE.
Luv u. Jack ☹

Rosie Tremayne
61 Cromwell A
Henley-on-Than
Oxfordshire R(

Went for a run on the beech today with Seb. I wantd it to be u. Remembr wen we walkd along the sand and jumpd ovr the waves? I mis u the size of the sea.

The words mix up. Then I can't see them at all 'cause my eyes are full of sad.

"What's up, Rose?"

I don't want to share Jack here.

The train starts screeching. Lawrence stumbles forward. We all fall sideway as the train pulls us with it. My heart clackety-clacks with the train as it screams to a stop. It goes dark.

The lights start winking on and off. The next-door lady says, "Not again!"

People moan and sigh.

Lawrence's face appears and disappears. "You all right?"

"Whyhavewestopped?"

"Don't know. Take a deep breath, that's better, we've probably stopped to let another train get out the way."

The lights keep winking. Then they come to stay.

Lawrence's eyes are full of worried. "You're very white, Rose."

"I don't like tube trains. They're too deep in the ground. What if we stay here forever and I never get to Victoria Station?"

"We won't be here forever; we'll be off soon and at Victoria in no time."

"Howdoyouknow?"

"This happens all the time."

"SORRY FOR THE DELAY. WE ARE CURRENTLY BEING HELD AT A RED SIGNAL. WE SHOULD BE MOVING AGAIN SHORTLY."

"There you are, we've stopped at a signal, that's like a red traffic light."

"Iknowthankyou."

The woman next door to me unwraps the scarf from her neck and puts her hat on her lap. "It'll start getting very hot in here soon." She smiles at me. Her eyes are green. Just like mine. "Why don't you take *your* hat off? You'll feel the benefit more when you get outside."

"That's grandma talk."

"I'm not a grandma quite yet, thank you very much. My son has left home and is on the dreaded gap year, but my daughter is still at university."

"Jess who comes in to help us at college is going on a gap year today. My dad says it's just a holiday so you don't have to work."

The lady laughs out loud and nods her head. "I don't think my son would like that explanation."

The lights flicker on and off again. I want the train to get a move on. Bird wings are flapping in my tummy.

Lawrence's fringe has gone dark and is stuck to his forehead. He undoes the toggles on his jacket. It looks just like our picnic blanket.

A baby cries. Some people are talking in words I can't understand. They talk very fast. Lawrence pulls a packet of cookies out of his bag and holds it out to me.

"Custard cream?"

"They have lots of sugar. You should snack on fruit," I tell him.

He looks at the floor. "Won't make any difference."

"Yesitwill! I have to watch my weight *all* the time."

Two girls with big round earrings and ponies' tails on top of their heads keep staring at me and Lawrence. And pointing. It's not nice. Lots of thoughts mix up in my head.

Lawrence opens his mouth to bite his cookie and then puts it in his pocket. "So, tell me why you're going to Brighton, Rose."

"To see my boyfriend, Jack."

One of the girls with the hoop earrings snorts her fizzy drink out of her nose. It sprays over Lawrence.

"Christ! Can't you watch what you're doing?"

The blonde girl copies his words in a silly voice. The lady next-door to me frowns at them. Everyone else looks at the floor.

Lawrence stands in front of me, so I can't see the girls any more. When he speaks his voice is quieter. "That's nice you're seeing your boyfriend, Rose. How long have you been going out with him?"

"Seven months, one week, and five days."

Lawrence whistles. "Nice one, the longest I've ever been out with anyone was a month, give or take a couple of days."

"Jack and I are going to get married and have babies."

I hear the two girls shriek. "You gotta be kidding? That's insane."

Lawrence clenches his hands in fists. He takes a deep,

deep breath. "How many are you going to have?"

"Two. A boy and a girl."

"I think you'll make a great mum, Rose."

"My dad doesn't think so."

"He doesn't want you to grow up; my mum's the same about me. I'll probably be looking after her until I die...or she does."

"Dad lets my brother Ben go to parties, go to Reading, and do lots of things on his own with his girlfriend and he's only fifteen and two months. I wasn't allowed to do that when I was fifteen. That's not fair."

The lady next door pats my arm. "It's because you're a girl, parents always worry about their daughters more."

"No. It's 'cause I'm different. Mum calls it being special. I hate being special. So does Jamie. He goes to my Henley College. Jamie has Down syndrome too. Jamie wants to be one of the lads and go to the pub by himself and get married. I told him we can get married. Paula Knight's mum has Down syndrome. We're all different, just like you. They said that at Henley College. Some of us can be in-de-pen-dent and some of us can't. Emma Wilson won't ever be. She's very muddled up in her head. She has to go to Bishopswood School in Sonning Common, not my mixed-up college."

Lawrence scratches his cheek, which is all shiny. "I get what you're saying but my dad, when he was alive, was much stricter with my sister."

"I hate that my dad makes me different to Ben. 'Cause Mum says I have way more sense than him. And do you know my dad left me in Tesco once? All by myself. Jack and I would never leave our little girl by herself in a shop. We'd make the best mum and dad. I know we would. And we wouldn't hurt our baby. Not like the real man on the television who burned his children in a fire. I saw his picture in the newspaper. We'd never do that. We'd love our baby and keep her safe and teach her to play Doctor Who."

I fold my arms and look at Lawrence in his eyes.

"That was some speech, Rose. You go for it." Lawrence high-fives me.

The lady next door pats my arm. "I hope you get your Jack, I really do."

Lawrence beams at me. "I love *Doctor Who*, it's my favorite program. Who d'you want to play?"

"The Doctor of course. 'Cause she's brave and cool."

"I'd like to be a Dalek...exterminate, exterminate."

"Daleks aren't real. You can't be a Dalek."

Lawrence doesn't hear me 'cause the train groans, stumbles forward and starts to move. Someone cheers.

Lawrence yawns such a big yawn I can see all the silver in his teeth. "Thank God, we're moving again."

"THE NEXT STOP IS BAKER STREET. CHANGE HERE FOR THE METROPOLITAN AND BAKERLOO LINES."

The lady next door to me stands up and puts her hat back onto her head.

The train squeals to a stop.

"THIS IS BAKER STREET. STAND CLEAR OF THE DOORS, PLEASE."

As the lady gets off the train, the two girls who were staring at me and Lawrence push past her. She says something to them, but they just laugh and one girl says a very rude word.

I feel cross and unhappy at the same time. I put Jack in my head to make the feelings go away. All he brings is a sad memory. When Jack and me went shopping together. At The Oracle in Reading. You can shop, eat, and go to the cinema there.

Two girls and two boys followed us 'round the shops. They tried to trip Jack up and pull my hair. They shouted rude words at us. We went to McDonald's by the river and got a cheeseburger and Filet-O-Fish for me. 'Cause I don't like beef. The mean boys and girls sat at the table behind us and threw their chips at our heads. With BBQ sauce on. They got stuck in my hair. No one stopped them. Jack got angry, but I wouldn't let him be. I just wanted to go home. I cried. They laughed and laughed and made cry noises like me. We had to leave our food behind. And I always clear my plate up.

We went back to Henley-on-Thames early. Mum was surprised to see us. She got angry when we told her what happened. Then she got sad. She told us to ignore them. 'Cause then they'd get bored. It's hard to ignore people when they hurt your feelings. And it makes you scared. I cried myself to sleep.

Lawrence pats my arm. "Only three stops now."

King's Cross Station is beautiful.

I'm standing in a floating spider's web. It changes from pink to purple to blue. In the middle is a Christmas tree, standing on a white box. It nearly touches the ceiling. It's covered in lights, like hundreds of raindrops. When I go closer, I see the tree is made of green Lego bricks. I just stare and stare.

"Are you coming?" Lawrence calls over to me from his place by the wall. "You need to get a move on and so do I."

I'm too busy staring. The roof is a bubble. It's snowing all over it. Snow is like magic. It makes the world go quiet. It covers all the dirt and makes it clean and white. When the sun shines it makes a million diamonds twinkle on the ground. Then you can walk over stars.

Lawrence drags me over to the wall. There's half a luggage cart sticking out of the bricks with half a suitcase and half a cage on it. On the wall it says "Platform 9" with a number three over a number four next to it.

I squeak at Lawrence, "It's Harry Potter's platform! I love *Harry Potter* the same as *Doctor Who*. Look!"

Lawrence takes my arm. He has a stern dad-face on. "You need to get a move on, Rose, and start focusing on your journey as the weather's getting worse. Have you got a pen? Because I need to write down your route to Victoria."

**********1414
Number of item(s):   1

Barcode:31738010794772
Title:Rosie loves Jack
Due Date:10/28/2021

10/7/2021   1:39 PM

I nod.

"Rose! Pen?"

"Okaythankyou."

Lawrence frowns at me. "Are you going to be all right getting to Victoria?"

"Yeahsure. Circle line to Victoria. Yellow line. Seven stops. Going west."

"No, that's what you were going to do, remember? You have to concentrate, Rose, and stop looking at the tree. Stop looking at the Harry Potter trolley and just stop doing anything except pay attention to me. Right, that's better, you have to get the Victoria line, which is the light blue one, then it's five stops to Victoria Station, SOUTHbound. Okay?"

I get a pen from my bag and hand it to Lawrence. He's right. I have to be grown up. I have to get to Jack now.

He writes down my route and gives me back the piece of paper. I make him say the words three times so I can keep them in my head.

Lawrence is frowning and pulling at a fluffy bit on his chin. "I'm worried about you, Rose. Who's meeting you at Victoria?"

I stand up as tall as I can. "Thankyou for helping me, Lawrence. I have to get my train now."

"You might get lost. It takes ages to get to know the underground system. I really think—"

I put my hands on my hips. "Lawrence, I can get a train all by myself. No problem."

61

Lawrence smiles. "I'm not saying you can't, but it's chaos because of the weather. Anyone could get stranded in all the confusion and cancellations."

"Nothankyou, Lawrence."

"Why don't I come with you to Victoria?" He looks at his watch. "It's ten fifty-three now...I'm sure I can move my appointment half an hour."

I shake my head. "No thank you, Lawrence."

He holds his hand out to me. It's soft and warm. "Okay then, if you're sure."

I tippy-toe up and kiss him on the cheek. I can see the lights from the Christmas tree in his eyes.

"Thank you, Rose."

As I walk to the underground sign, I keep turning back. Lawrence hasn't moved. He waves. I take one last look as I go down into the dark. He's still there. He looks small.

I go down a long snake-tunnel. It goes on forever. I put my shoulders back. I'm brave. Jack is at the end of all my journeys. People ant-march in a line. I can't stop to put my bag in my other hand. If I do, they'll march right over me. My arm is burning in my shoulder.

In front of me I can hear music. Someone is singing. But I don't know what the song is. Or why it's in this place. Jack would know the song. He knows lots and more than me. It gets louder as I walk.

'Round the corner a man sits on the floor with his guitar

on his lap. He shouldn't sit on the ground. He'll get very dirty. He has a hat with a feather on his head. And a black hat on the floor with money in it. I know these people. We have them in Henley-on-Thames. On holiday days. I feel sad for him 'cause no one stops to listen. I stand next to him by the wall, as I like his singing. I tuck my bag behind my feet. I can wake my arm up now, as it's gone to sleep. I listen to his song.

The music is happy and sad. And full of magic. A lady smiles at the man and throws a gold coin into his hat as she rushes past. The gold ones are the best.

On the other side of the tunnel there is a big, big picture in a circle of butterflies and bees. And lots of insects. It's beautiful. I don't know what the writing means. Butterflies flutter all over the circle. The colors paint rainbows in me.

I close my eyes and let the man sing in my head.

Dream Jack holds my hand and twirls me around. He shapes the words with his mouth, "I love you." He smiles and lets me go. And watches me dance. I'm the ballet lady in my grandma's music-making box, spinning on my toes. I'm a wind-blown tree. I'm a dandelion clock floating wishes up to the sky. I drift on clouds and pop the sun with my finger tops.

I peep through my eyes and the picture butterflies float off the flowers. They flitter in and out of my arms. Jack catches a tiny blue one in his hand. Its wings beat the patterns of the song. It glows in the shadows. He lifts his hand up to his lips and blows

63

the butterfly to me. He laughs with happy. I am me dancing. I am free. I am Rose. I wave to Jack and laugh with him...

The laugh turns into a wrong laugh. I open my eyes. My happy crashes to the floor. Two teenager boys nudge each other with their elbows.

"Look at the dancing monkey!" one says with a nasty smile. "Her tongue's hanging out. Yuck!"

"Leave her alone!" a voice shouts next to me. A lady with a baby in a bag on her front frowns at the boys. "You should be ashamed of yourselves."

"Yeah," someone echoes behind me.

The blond boy grabs the dark-haired boy's arm and sticks his middle finger at the lady. They run. They shove a man with a suitcase on wheels. They criss and cross away. Their laughing vanishes with them 'round the corner.

The kind lady gives me a worry look. "Are you okay?"

"Yesthankyouverymuch. Thankyou for helping Rose."

"Don't take any notice of them. They're just silly boys."

"My brother Ben can be silly. But he's not nasty."

The singing man has stopped. He smiles up at me. "What's your favorite song, little lady?"

"'Love is in the Air.' It's mine and Jack's song. It was my mum and dad's song, but we borrowed it from them. 'Cause it happy-sings what we feel."

"Yeah, I can do that one." He shuts his eyes and does a

little hum first. Then he starts to sing about love whispering in the trees. And thundering in the sea. And he doesn't know if he's dreaming.

The lady takes my hand and we dance together. She holds her baby bag with the other hand. People stop rushing past and join in. Some clap to the music. Everyone is smiling at me. The sun comes up in the tunnel. It shines on the walls. It shines on me. It lights up all the people. We dance and dance.

When the singing stops, everyone claps and whistles and stamps their feet. Silver and gold coins shower into the black hat on the floor. I feel my cheeks pink-flush with happy. The kind lady kisses the top of her baby's head. I peek into the baby bag.

"This is my Amelie." She kneels down to let me see her. The baby coos at me. She looks just like me.

"Isn't she beautiful?" the lady says.

I nod and stroke the baby's soft hair.

The kind lady smiles a big smile with all her teeth. She puts her head on the side ways. "Who are you with, sweetie? You're not traveling on your own, are you?"

"Yes." I stand up tall. "I'm going to be with my Jack. I can look after me."

"All the trains are topsy-turvy because of the snow." She looks at her watch. "It's eleven fifteen now. I could easily take you to your next stop, if you like?"

65

I get my tickets out my bag and my list from Lawrence. I show them to her. "See? I can manage, thankyouverymuch."

"You can...? I mean...of course you can." Her voice wobbles. But her eyes shine into mine.

"I'm in-de-pen-dent. I work at Waitrose on a Saturday and sometimes at Jim's cafe when he's run off his feet."

The kind lady laughs. "That's wonderful, really wonderful." She looks at her watch. "I have to go, now." She wraps me in a hug. The baby wriggles against me. "Bye bye." She waves at me before walking out of sight.

The singing man starts another song. People carry on their journeys. I pick up my bag and get my purse. I put some money in the singing hat. The man winks at me. His song follows me as I go. Walking in time with all the people. A warm wind blows the hair off my face. I hear the clack and whistle of the tube train. Victoria line. Light blue. Five stops going south. I hug myself inside. I'm taking me to Jack.

Not long now.

It's easy.

five

Victoria Station has even more people than Paddington.
I don't know how to get through them. I keep saying, "Excuse-
meplease." But no one hears me.

I have to find my train. I can see the train-time board, but
not what it says. I wish I was taller.

A lady with an orange bobble hat takes it off and shakes it.
Drops of water splash my face. "Sorry, love." She hands me a
tissue. "Here you go, dry your face with that."

It smells of peppermint.

The man next to her stamps snow off his boots. "My toes
are going to drop off, Pam, let's get a cup of tea to warm us
up while we wait."

I look at the man's boots as they walk away and hope his
toes don't fall off. The train-time board keeps changing the
light-up letters. It says the same word under a lot of the trains.
People look cross. My neck hurts from straining up to see.
I split the word up in my head, can...can-kelled. I don't see
what that means. I can't see the lady with the orange bobble

hat to ask her. I try again. I break the word up into pieces. They trick me by jumping about.

A man talking on his phone throws his bag on the floor. "Typical! Canceled. First sign of snow and they can't cope. That's the second time this week they've canceled my bloody train."

I understand what the word on the board means now. Can-*selled*. My train has been taken away. I wonder where it's gone. A voice speaks into the air, but I can't catch it all. I'm inside my head bubble, and the world is hushed up.

I hope my train comes back soon.

Every time the train board changes my heart spins round.

But it still says the same word.

CANCELED.

My feet have gone icy, and I can't move them. A hand on my shoulder makes me jump.

The lady with the orange bobble hat puts her face in mine. "You still here, love? You look frozen."

"I have to wait for my train to come back."

"It could be ages yet, if at all, but they'll announce it when there's a change. Do you understand everything on the board?"

"I listen to the train-board voice telling me 'cause reading is more difficult. My teacher says I have knots in my brain. They need untangling, so I can think straight. I don't think some of the knots will ever go away."

"Dear, dear, that's a shame. Are you here by yourself, love?"

"Yes. I'm all by myself. I can do lots of stuff all by myself. I cook dinner on Wednesday night with Ben. Though I do most of it. And I have a Saturday job. And—"

"That's nice, but you don't want to get stuck at Victoria on your own in this weather. Have you got someone you can ring to come and get you?"

I nod. "Lots of people."

The man with her, whose toes might fall off, tugs her arm.

"Are your toes okay? Did they drop off?" I can't see through his boots.

He throws his head back and laughs. "No, they were all there last time I checked." He has furry earmuffs on now that make him look like a teddy bear. "Come on, Pam."

She shakes his hand off. "You ring someone then, but why don't you go and get a hot drink in one of the cafes while you wait? It will warm you up from the inside."

"We'll try and get a bus, I think that's our best bet." The man checks his watch. He smiles at me and leads her away through the crowds.

I'm shaky. I think the cold has crept inside me and frozen everything up. I only had a bit of toast at breakfast. I can see a coffee shop by the sign for platform seven. That's my lucky number, so I decide to go there.

Through the station entrance I can see snow falling in a white curtain. Everything has lost its shape. The sky has tricked the street lights into coming on. But it's only halfway 'round the clock past twelve. There's a line of people at the bus stop, curling 'round the corner. Everyone's stamping their feet. The cafe is full up, and it's warm and steamy. People's shoes are dripping puddles on the floor. I join a line that stops and starts toward the counter. "What can I get you?"

"Hotchocletplease."

"Y'what?"

"Hot choclet, please."

"Anythin' else?"

"A flapjack, please. I like them 'cause they've got Jack's name in. And they taste nice."

The cafe lady smiles. "That's sweet. Four pound twenty-five, please."

I have to put my bag down and find my purse.

"Hurry up." The man behind me sighs. "I have a meeting to get to and I don't want to be late. Isn't someone with you?"

The cafe lady glares at him. I put my purse on the counter. She helps me count out the money.

She drops some coins back in my purse, smiles again, and looks 'round me to the man. "What can I get you?"

I stand to the side to wait for my drink. I look 'round for a table to sit at. I can't see one.

"Here you are. Careful, it's very full."

The lady puts my hot chocolate onto the tray. My bag is heavy, and it's hard holding onto everything. The busy man knocks past me, spilling my drink.

A bit of me wants to go home.

I see a girl with pink and green hair sitting by the window. She has a hat like mine. Made from black felt. With a greeny-brown feather tucked into the hat band. There are two seats at her table with big rucksacks on them. The boy next to her is resting his head on his arms. As I walk over, she sees me and pokes the boy with her phone and says something. He leans over and pushes one of the bags onto the floor.

"Thankyou."

He grunts at me like Ben and puts his head down again.

I tuck my bag on my lap and put my hands 'round my mug of hot chocolate. My fingers tingle. I can feel the heat buzzing inside them. My nose feels like it's blushing.

Through the window I see the man who doesn't want to be late. He's waving his fist at a train man.

The train speaker voice starts to talk and everyone sits up and listens. The trains haven't come back yet. I'm scared I'm never going to get to Brighton. I try and guess what Jack would do. I make a Jack picture in my head, but I can't get his mouth to talk to me.

"I don't know what to do."

"What don't you know what to do?" the girl with painted hair asks me.

I didn't know I'd talked out loud. I feel silly. The boy next to her is rolling smoking bits up in a square of paper, like students at my college do. He scrapes his chair back and goes out the door.

71

"No, I don't want one, thanks," the girl shouts after him. She looks at me and shrugs. "Guys! Your purple boots are so cool. I LOVE the roses painted on them. I saw them when you came in. Look at mine."

She swings her leg up onto the table knocking the salt flying. "Shit! What d'you think? I painted the daisies myself."

"You shouldn't put dirty boots on the table."

She grabs the salt shaker rolling across the floor and hiccups. "The table's dirtier than my boots."

Her pink tights are full of holes. She puts her finger through one of them and rips it some more.

"Your legs must be very chilly."

She throws her head back and laughs. When she's stopped, she leans across the table and taps my hand. "Hang on, didn't you ask something? Oh I know! What is it you don't know what to do?"

I pull my hand away. Her makeup is smudged under her eyes, and her breath smells like my dad's when he drinks some Scottish whisky. She keeps staring at me, so I answer. "Idon'tknowhowtogettoBrightonorwhattodoifnotrainscomeback."

"Ha, ha! You sound more pissed than me. I didn't get any of that except for 'Brighton.' What's your name? I'm Paris. After the city. Thank GOD I wasn't called Baghdad or Dusseldorf. Ha ha ha! Sorry, I talk too much. It drives Leo mad. Leo's my boyfriend. The one having a smoke."

"My boyfriend is Jack. He's in Brighton. I'm going to find him."

"What d'you mean *find* him? Has he got lost? You could

72

always go to Lost Property." She laughs again making herself choke on her breath.

When she's finished coughing I say, "I don't know what you said."

"Just ignore me. Leo doesn't get me or my jokes either. Can't you just ring him, you know, ring your boyfriend?"

"His phone got broken up."

"Okay, I like, still don't get how he's lost, he could easily use another phone. He must have mates."

"Jack was taken away. My dad won't let me be with him. He hid all the cards Jack sent to me. I thought Jack didn't love me anymore."

Paris looks at me with her mouth open before banging her hand on the table. It makes me jump. And the people behind her.

"That's outrageous! I'd tell my dad to eff off if he tried to stop me seeing Leo...that's if I had a dad." She takes a sugar lump out of the bowl on the table, bites a bit off and drops it in her Coca-Cola. It fizzes up out of the bottle. She catches it with her mouth and does a big burp. She clamps her hand over her mouth. "Oops, pardon me."

"Is your dad dead?"

"Nah, I just don't see him."

"Why not?"

"I hate him."

She frowns and takes another big mouthful of her drink. "I've always hated him."

I feel sad. I can't work out hating my dad. Dad lets Ben chill with his girlfriend in his room but makes a fuss about Jack and me being in my bedroom. That makes me unhappy. And he lets Ben stay out until eleven on the clock at the weekend. I have to be home by ten. That makes me cross. Now I'm more angry with my dad than forever before 'cause he won't let me see Jack... But inside me, my heart tells me I love him.

"Why d'you hate your dad, Paris?"

"Why do I hate my dad? He's an arsehole, that's why."

"You shouldn't swear."

"Why not?"

"It'srude."

"I quite like swearing, it says what you feel. Shit, bollocks, bastard...don't look like that, I'm teasing you. You can take your hands off your ears, I won't swear again—promise! I'm talking bollocks, oops, sooorry. God, I'm pissed. Sorry again."

I open one eye. Paris drinks some more Coca-Cola. It spills down her front, but she doesn't wipe it off. She stretches her arms above her head then points her finger at me.

"Where were we with *your* dad? I know! Why won't he let you see your boyfriend?"

"They think he's going to hurt me."

"That's ridiculous; everyone gets hurt when they're in love. I sometimes wonder why we bother with any of it as most of the time you're miserable. Is it like that with your boyfriend?"

"Jack makes the sun shine in my head."

74

"Oh my God, that's so lovely." Her voice trembles. She presses her face into her napkin leaving black and green on it. "Wish I felt like that with Leo."

Leo comes back in, reaches under the table and drags his bag over my feet.

"Paris! Get your stuff, Gaz has a party on and we can crash at his tonight."

"What about our train?"

"What train? They're all fucked, so let's go."

Leo shakes his head and snowflakes spin down to the floor. Paris puts her hand out to catch one. "I want to go to Paris, the city of love and romance, where my mum conceived me."

"Yeah sure, we'll go tomorrow, now come on. Jeez! How much have you drunk?"

He tries to tug her through the door but Paris pulls his hand off her arm.

"We can't leave Rose."

"Who the fuck's Rose?"

Paris points at me. I won't look at him. His face is full of ugly and he said a very bad word again.

"Christ, Paris, she was on her own before. What is it with you? You're always picking up bloody weirdos."

I turn my face to him. "I'mnotabloodyweirdo. I'm Rose." He talks under his breath making Paris glare at him.

"Shut up, Leo, there's an announcement."

We all listen.

75

"WE ARE SORRY TO ANNOUNCE THAT ALL SOUTHERN RAIL SERVICES HAVE BEEN CANCELED DUE TO THE SEVERE WEATHER CONDITIONS. CUSTOMERS ARE ADVISED TO MAKE ALTERNATIVE ARRANGEMENTS."

"See," Leo says. "Told you, so let's get out of here."

"We can't leave her here, I'm not going without her." She snatches at Leo's rucksack, trying to get it off him.

"Stop making a scene and let go of my bag, Paris."

They stand face to face glaring at each other. Paris looks away first. She turns to me. "You'll be okay, Rose?"

I nod 'cause I can't talk. She stretches out her hand to try and hold mine. Leo grips her arm tight and pulls her through the door.

I don't want her to stay, but I don't want her to go.

I can't stay in this cafe forever.

I don't know where to go.

All my trains have gone.

I'm stuck.

six

Paris and Leo stand outside the cafe window. They look cross at each other. Paris is waving her arm up in the air. Leo picks up his rucksack and walks off with Paris holding onto his coat. He pushes her off him. She watches him go.

He keeps on walking and vanishes 'round the corner.

I hold my bag on my lap and rest my hand where Jack's cards are. Jack wouldn't leave me all by myself.

Paris comes back into the cafe dragging her rucksack behind her. She sits on her bag beside me. For a long time she doesn't say anything. She sniffs a lot, so I give her a tissue.

"You need to blow your nose."

"Ta." She looks at me. Her eyes are red.

"You can't stay here, Rose. I said to Leo, it wasn't right abandoning you, with no trains. Come to Gaz's place and keep warm, then you can party and crash at the house with us. It's only up the road...you can get the train tomorrow."

I shake my head. "Nothankyou. It's ten bits before the two. That's too early for a party."

Paris smiles. "What, you serious? It's never too early to party. Come on, you have to come—where are you going to go if you don't?" She looks up at me so I can see into her eyes. "Please come."

"Nothankyou... Leo doesn't want me."

"Yes, he does. Leo will LOVE you once he gets to know you."

I shake my head. "Leo's mean. Jack's never mean to me."

Paris bites her fingernail. "He's not like that, really. You see it's all my fault, I get silly and say stupid things that make him angry, so I have to find Leo and say sorry. He's nice really, I promise you he is."

I try and work out what I am thinking in my head. I wanted Paris to go away before. But I didn't want her to go. I want to go with her now...but I don't...I have nowhere to sit and wait for the rest of the day and the night...I'm NOT going home to Henley-on-Thames. If I do, Dad will stop me finding Jack. I will never see him again. I want to find Jack. I don't want to think of "never again." It's too sad. I have to be with Jack, and Jack has to be with me. I have to go with Paris.

Paris looks at me like our dog when she wants a treat.

I stand up. "Will you take me back to Victoria Station in the morning, please?"

"Of course I will—so you're coming with me?"

"Okayyes."

She punches her hand in the air. "Go, Rose!" She puts her

rucksack on her back. I get my stuff and follow Paris out of the cafe.

Outside, she folds her arm in mine and walks me along the road. She keeps falling about and not walking in a straight line.

"I can't walk my feet as fast as yours."

"Sooorry." Paris sing-songs along. "I'm excited! I love parties and I LOVE the snow. When I was little, I used to stick my tongue out and catch the snowflakes on my tongue because I thought they were ice candy from the sky."

She puts her tongue out now. "Go on, you do it."

"It's too cold, my teeth have the shakes. And my bag is hurting my arm. Wherearewegoing?"

"Right, then right again...I think." She bites her lip between her teeth. "There's a kebab shop on the corner..." She crosses her arms and buries her hands under her armpits. She looks left and right. "Got it! Over there—where that taxi has stopped." She points her finger past my nose. "See, by that yellow and red light. Come on!"

She grabs my bag and swings it along. I'm too tired to ask for it back. I stick my hands in my pockets and follow her snow footprints up to the house.

The door is wide open and the inside light shines onto the path. It's covered in rubbish peeping through the snow. Some grown-up people stand outside smoking. One of them is the tallest man ever. He's only wearing a T-shirt and jeans. He has Popeye arms. And a spider painted on his head. It makes him scary.

"You're such a stoner!" Paris shouts to spider man.

I step backward. "Idontwanttocomehere." I try and take my bag back from Paris, but she won't let me. She swings it over her shoulder, and it hits her rucksack on her back. She falls backward. She lies on the ground and giggles. Her legs kick in the air. "It'll be f...fine. Don't l...look so worried."

"Iwanttogohome."

The big man helps Paris up. He looks over his shoulder at me. "Hey dufus, you coming in or what?"

An ice wind blows up the path making me shiver. "My name is Rose, not Du-fuss."

He laughs, but I know it's a wrong laugh. He picks my bag up. "Nogivememybagback!"

He doesn't hear me. I run after my bag into the house.

The house smells like Mum's bonfire when she burns all the leaves. It makes my eyes sting. It's dark in the hall. My bag is sitting on the bottom of the stairs. I hug it to me. When I look up, I can see a girl through a doorway with long, long hair in fuzzy blonde ropes. She's dancing all by herself, her arms swaying above her head. Her arm shadows look like dancing snakes on the wall behind her. The girl opens her eyes and sees me. We stare at each other.

Paris barges past me to the girl. "We need to look for Leo, have you seen him?" she says to her.

"No, babe. He's probably in the kitchen getting some gear from Lenni."

80

"Cool, thanks hun. Hey, Lily, this is Rose. OMG! You've both got flower names—how cool is that? Rose is crashing the night here."

"You're a scream, girl, always bringing home strays. You like dancing, Rose?" She twists her arms around her body and jiggles her hips, making her red ballet skirt rustle. Her nose diamond sparkles and winks at me.

"I want a nose stud."

Lily drops her arms and comes over to me. "I could do it for you, babe, I have a spare stud. I can do it with a needle and an ice cube."

I hold my nose tight.

Paris laughs. "You look like a ghost. It doesn't hurt, you should do it, it would look so *amazing*." She drags me into the kitchen.

"Nothangyouverymuck."

The kitchen is old-fashioned, like my grandma's kitchen in her holiday cottage in Cornwall. But hers is clean. This table is covered in bottles and spilled drink. A broken glass lies in a puddle of red.

Paris pulls a long, fat cigarette out of someone's mouth and takes a huge puff. After a bit smoke rolls out her nose in a curl. She waves the big cigarette at me. "Here, try it, babe, you'll love it. Ha ha! You can take your hand off your nose now; no one's going to pierce it. Go on, have a drag of this, everything will look beautiful." She shuts her eyes and takes

81

another big breath of smoke. She holds it in for ever before blowing it up to the ceiling.

"Smoking kills."

She takes another big breath of it.

I want this place to be over. I can't see anything beautiful. I want to get to tomorrow-day so I can get my train. I don't want these people. I don't want this kitchen. Or a party. It's still day time. Even though the snow clouds have made the sky dark. People should be at college... 'Cept I'm not. But it's different 'cause I'm going to get Jack.

I make my mind up.

"I'mgoingbacktoVictoriaStation,Paris,thankyouverymuch."

"No, no, no, come on, we've got to find Leo."

"Idon'twanttofindLeo. I wanttofindJack."

I'm too stupid to do this. I hide my face in my hands. When I open my eyes again, I want to be with Jack. Safe in my Henley-on-Thames. And not in this not-me place.

Someone folds their arms 'round me. Like Jack does. It doesn't smell like Jack, so I move back.

"I don't want a hug."

Paris sniffs. "Sorry, I wanted to help."

"Why did you help Rose?"

"I felt good helping you, like, I'd done something, you know...good."

"Rose isn't a stray dog, girl, you've got to stop and think." Lily walks into the kitchen. She rests her hand on Paris's shoulder. Then she talks to me. "Maybe you should ring your parents?"

I shake my head no. "I have to find my Jack. He needs me." I can hear my voice getting shouty.

Lily frowns. "It's okay, sweetie. It's okay; we can take you to the station in the morning. Paris is right about something, you can't sit all night by yourself at Victoria. You can chill in my room if you like?"

Her eyes are more blue than Jack's. "Okayyesthankyou," my mouth says before I mean to say it. I don't want to stay in a room I don't know.

In the background some rapping music starts. If my brother Ben plays it Dad shouts at him to turn it off. I think of home. And Mum. And my bedroom. Then a picture memory of Dad comes in my head.

"Where are you going, Rose?"

I pull my hat down over my ears and tuck my scarf ends into my coat. "To see Jack."

"But you just saw him at college and then at the cafe afterwards. Can't you live without him for longer than two hours?"

"I have lots of hours I don't see him."

"What about your homework tonight?"

"It's Friday, Dad."

"And?"

"Everyone goes out on a Friday."

83

"Who's everyone? Every Tom, Dick, and Harry?"

"I don't know them."

"It's an expression, Rose, it means—oh for goodness' sake, it doesn't matter what it means. When are you going to do your homework then? Remember you're working at Waitrose tomorrow and then we're seeing Grandma on Sunday."

"I know that, Dad. I did all my homework in the cafe when I waited for Jack today."

"He's a bad influence on you; you used to take such care over your college work."

"I'm top of the class after Lou."

"And that's another thing, you never used to answer me back until he came on the scene. You'll be shouting at me next."

"Ben shouts all the time and so do you."

Dad frowns. He opens his mouth but no words come out. He looks very silly. My phone pings.

"Jack's outside." I get excited in my stomach. "Bye, Dad. BYE, MUM."

"Bye, Rose," Mum shouts from the kitchen, "I'll see you at the back of the cinema at ten fifteen."

"'kay!"

Dad looks even grumpier. As I shut the door I hear him say to Mum, "She needs to cool it with that boy."

I don't think Dad ever wanted Jack and Rose. I don't want to see my dad. 'Cause then he'll put a full stop to Jack. I have to stay here so I can get to Brighton tomorrow.

"Rose?" Lily waves her hand in front of my face. "I'm talking to you, where did you go?"

"In my head."

She smiles. "Come on, I'll take you up to my room." She has to shout in my ear, 'cause the music's got louder. It's blocking out everyone's words.

Paris takes my hand. "I'll take her, I'm going upstairs to look for Leo anyway."

"Don't just dump her if you do find him. She looks worn out."

"Course not. Come on, hun."

"My bag!"

"It's in the hall—you can grab it as we go past." Paris tries to pull me along behind her.

Lily stops her. "Let go of her, girl, she's not a child."

Paris drops my hand. "Sorry, babe, I'm a bit hyper."

Lily shakes her head. "Go on, Rose, I'll come up in a bit."

I follow her. I see my bag and pick it up. We have to step over a lady and man kissing. Jack and me kiss like that in his bedroom at his house or under the willow tree on the park bench. Paris opens one door but Leo isn't there. I'm glad.

Some boys and girls are sat in a circle 'round a lamp. I think it's a lava lamp. My mum had a lime-juice green one. Grandma found it in her attic and told me Mum had it at university.

"Hey, come and join us."

85

I hold onto the back of Paris's jacket, so I can be close up to her.

My ears are going to burst with all the shouts and loud music. It hammer-bangs through me. I want to find Lily's room so I can hide. And just be with Jack in my head.

"Where is he?" Paris kicks the wall. "He's got to be here somewhere...I know!" She bangs on a door with fuzzy windows. "LEO! Is that you?" She rattles the door handle and presses her nose against the glass. "Leo, are you in there?"

"Who's Leo?" a man shouts back. "I'm trying to shit here."

"Let's try the attic," Paris sighs. "That's Lily's room, so I don't think he can be in there but he's got to be here somewhere." My legs hurt and my bag is getting too heavy to carry up more stairs. But I don't want to leave Paris. And she said she's taking me to Lily's room now.

I have to stop to get my breath at the top. I get a lot of in-fections on my chest. It makes my breath struggle sometimes going up hills and big stairs. Paris opens the bedroom door. Two people are on the bed. They only have clothes on their top bits, and their legs are stuck together. I don't want to look. Paris can't stop looking. Her mouth is frozen in an O.

Then she screams. "You bastard! How could you?" Her face is squeezed up with hurt. "You PROMISED!"

"What the fuck?"

Leo jumps off the bed. "Paris, wait, I can explain, babe." His hands cover up his man bits.

I look away.

"Just fuck off and leave me alone!" Her mouth makes a pain noise.

I cover my ears up. I don't know what to do. "Wehaveto-GOParis."

Leo tries to grab her with one hand but she slaps him away. His face looks ugly with angry. Paris pushes past me and runs out the room and down the stairs. I run after her.

Leo shouts, "You leave this house, we're done!" My bag bump, bump, bumps on the stairs.

Paris pushes everyone out the way and races out the front door. I run up the path after her, slipping and sliding. I don't think she knows I'm with her any more. I'm too out of my breath to shout to her to stop. My chest feels tight and burny. I keep running, I'm scared to get left on my own.

In front of me Paris drops down onto the steps of a big, big church with lots of towers. I run over to her. I can't speak until I've got myself together again. I'm shaking all over me.

"Are we...going in here?"

Paris looks at me with surprise. "Rose."

"It's t...too freezing to s...sit here." I wag my finger at her. "You'll c...catch your death of cold."

"So what? If I did die nobody would care." She shuts her eyes.

I don't like her saying that. It frightens me. I want my mum. She'd help Paris, 'cause that's what she does.

I'm lost and iced up. I can't move my fingers. I clap my

hands together to wake them up. It hurts. I get a crying lump in my throat. "Paris, let's find a warm place...pleasethankyou."

She rests her head on the metal fence, but doesn't answer me. I hear music floating out from the church. I go and peek through the door. It's the tallest room I've ever seen. Paintings shine like jewels on the walls. They are lit up by hundreds of candles. Two baby angels with tiny wings fly across the roof.

I take a few steps in. I feel very small. Above my head, Jesus watches me from a red and gold cross. He looks kind and sad, both together. I want to smile and cry, all at the same time. An old man sits on a long chair with his head bent over. He's whispering to himself. I think he's saying a prayer to Jesus. I sit on a chair by myself and ask Jesus on the gold cross to get me safely to Jack.

"Rose! What are you doing in here? Let's get going."

"Shush!" The old man frowns at her.

Paris is hugging herself with her arms. Her lips are blue at the edges. "I'm starving, bloody come on," she says very loudly.

"Language, please!" The old man stands up very tall. "Please show some respect. You are in a house of God."

"House of miserable old sod, you mean. Come on, Rose, let's get out of here." She turns her back and leaves.

I take one last look at the baby angels and follow her out.

"That was mean," I say.

"Don't get all goody-two-shoes on me. Let's go window-shopping now, and then there's a twenty-four-hour McDonald's near the cathedral. We can chill there tonight, eat tons, and keep warm. Let's get a taxi."

"Burgers make you fat."

"Great!" She waves her hand in the air. A black car with a yellow light on top drives up. Someone shouts, "PARIS!" We both look round. Running toward us is Leo.

"Paris! Come on, babe, what you doing?" Paris looks at me and back at Leo.

"Babe, this is fucked up, come here."

"Wait there, Rose." Paris goes over to him.

I don't understand. Leo is badbadbad.

The taxi driver sticks his head out the window. "You getting in or what, love?"

He reaches his arm out the window and opens the door. I slide onto the seat, putting my bag next to me. Outside, Paris shakes her head and walks back over to the taxi. Leo stops her and holds her face in his hands.

"Hurry up!" the taxi man shouts out.

Paris looks from Leo to me and back to Leo. Leo kisses her and won't let go. I get a knot inside me. Then Paris pulls away and comes to the taxi. I move up on the seat and let the knot go.

Paris opens the taxi door. "You get going, Rose. Here." She throws some money onto the seat. She speaks to the taxi man. "Take her to Victoria Station, please."

"Iwanttogowithyou."

89

"I can't." Her voice is small and wavy. She won't look at me.

I watch as Paris and Leo walk away. Her head is on his shoulder. I want to shout at her to stop it. The taxi drives out into the traffic. I watch as Paris vanishes in all the people.

I'm muddled and angry-sad. At her going with a bad person. At leaving me on my own. When she promised to look after me. I'd never do that to Lou. Or any of my friends... But Paris wasn't my friend. I wish I could see Lou now. She's my best friend in the whole world. Apart from Jack. Her eyes are nut-brown with dots of gold. When she smiles, they light up and make me smile too. But she's a long way away. I'm on my own, and I have to work it out all by myself. I want to cry. I have to be brave.

"You all right, love?"

I see the taxi man's eyes in his driving mirror. "Yesno. Yes." "Sure?"

"I'm going to Victoria. I'm going to be with real Jack."

"Right-o, love, as long as you're meeting someone there."

I rest my hand where Jack is safe in his pocket. I feel stronger. But my hand is shaking like a leaf.

I fall back in the seat and shut my eyes. I can work out what to do all by myself.

I can't make my hand sit still.

Dear Rosie

  Im angri all the time here. Thats
crazi isn't it? Im suposd to get beter.
I havnt even seen my kownsler yet
cuz shes skeeing. That made Mum
mad. Did I tell u my mate Sebs got a
dent in his hed from wen a car drove
over him? He got noked off his bike.
He sed he used to be reerli clever. I
think he still is. I wori u dont luv me
ennymore, cuz its been 8 days since
I herd from u, but Im going to keep
riting becuz it feels like Im talking
to u. Seb sez Im bonkers talking to a
bit of paper. Dont giv up on me, Rosie.
I'll get home to u as soon as I can and
meet u at our tabel. Dont forget
the marsh-melloes on my chocliti!
  Luv Jack X

Rosie Tremayne

61 Cromwell Avenue

Henley-on-Thames

Oxfordshire RG96 2LD

seven
december 12th

The cafe on platform seven is open 'til midnight, but
you can't stay on Victoria Station after that. A train lady told
me. It's four and halfway 'round the clock now. The day has
run away from me. It's been a for-ever day.

I try and eat my egg sandwich, but I can't swallow it. It's
all dry and curly-up at the edges. I spit it out into my tissue.
It's the mint-smell one. Mint always makes me think of
Grandma. Grandma loves old-fashioned glass mints with a
polar bear on top. It's not real glass. She says "they're clearly
minty" in a funny voice whenever she eats one.

She likes telling me what to do too. Grandma would tell
me to put my thinking cap on. When I was little, I thought it
was a real cap.

I think I have to ring Mum 'cause the trains aren't coming
back today.

I don't want to go home. Not when I've just started. I got
away from the scary house. I can't give up. But I've run out of
clever. Stupid Rose is sitting here.

Grandma would be very cross with me, if she heard me say that. "*Head up, shoulders back and don't give up. You can do anything, Rose.*"

But I can't find Grandma's thinking cap. It's hiding from me.

The old lady sitting at my table looks over her magazine at me.

"Are you okay, dear?"

"Okaythankyou."

"Are you on your own?" I nod.

"Have you got stuck?"

"All my trains are snowed up."

"Is anyone coming to meet you and take you home, your parents or someone who looks after you?"

I blow my nose and swallow down my sad. "I'm going to call my mum."

"Good. Now, now, don't get upset. You'll soon be home."

"Jack will think I don't love him."

"I'm sure Jack, whoever he might be, won't think that at all."

"Really?"

"Of course! Dear me, it's a beastly afternoon. I'm waiting for my son to pick me up, he should be here soon."

She smiles at me, which makes her eyes apple-pie crinkle 'round the edges. Just like *my* grandma.

"What a pretty butterfly brooch you're wearing. Such a lovely blue."

"Thankyou. Jack gave it to me. He told me he loved me for the first time. And I loved him back."

93

"That makes it a very special butterfly then."

I nod. "Jack's mum made it in her jew-el-ry workshop. Jack painted a picture of how he wanted it. So she could copy it. Jack's the best artist ever." My words start to shake when I think of him.

"He sounds like a very talented young man." She gets a little gray book out of her bag. "I call this my boasting book. That's a photo of my son on his wedding day, he's six foot three!" She passes me the book. "It's hard to believe because he was such a scrap of a thing when he was born. There he is as a baby, his father said he looked like a little hairless monkey."

"When I was born, I was the size of a bag of sugar. My heart had a hole in it. After lots of operations, my heart got better. Then all of me got sick and I nearly died."

"You poor thing. That must have been so traumatic for your mother."

"What's tror-matik?"

"It means something is very difficult and upsetting. Do you have any brothers or sisters? I always wanted to have more than one child, but it wasn't meant to be."

"I have a brother, Ben. He was a BIG surprise for Mum and Dad. I didn't know much about him when he was little 'cause I was in hospital all the time. He just got bigger every time I saw him. When Ben was six, he fell down the stairs and hurt his back."

"Goodness me, as if your parents didn't have enough to cope with."

"It was Ben's turn to be in hospital. When he came home he lay on a made-up bed in the sitting-down room. For a long, long time, everyone was worrying about Ben, not me. Mum got me a nurse's uniform and a doctor box. I made Ben get better."

"That's wonderful, I'm sure you were a huge help. I think Ben was lucky to have you."

"He was. I didn't like Ben being ill...but I liked being important."

"I can understand that. How old is Ben now?"

"Only fifteen but he's the size of a barn."

The lady claps her hands and laughs. "Just like my son, David! Built for rugby, which he loves."

"Ben too! He plays for Henley Hawks youth team in Henley-on-Thames where I live. Sometimes, when he's not FaceTiming Sophie Baxter, he swings me 'round with one arm and makes me laugh. Sophie Baxter is Ben's girlfriend. Dad thinks it's cool Ben has a girlfriend. I'm sixteen and ten months and Dad doesn't want me to have a boyfriend. That's not fair."

"Dads can be like that with their daughters."

"Another lady on the tube train said that." That makes me feel more happy.

"I remember my father was exactly the same as yours. He hated Eddie, my husband, well he was my boyfriend then but he became my husband. Father said he wasn't good enough for me and he tried to keep us apart."

"That's what my dad's doing! He thinks my boyfriend, Jack, is a bad in-flu-ence. But my granddad didn't want Dad to marry my mum. He told Dad to keep away from her. Then Dad got very cross and threw a cricket bat and it hurt Muffin's leg. She had to go to the vet."

"Oh dear, that's not very good."

"Noitisn't. But Dad still got married to Mum. And I want to marry my Jack."

"Nothing was going to stop Eddie and me; when you love someone that much, as you do when first you fall in love, you feel you can *conquer* the world."

I want to ask the lady why she wants to put a conker nut on the world but her phone rings. Her face happy lights up. "David, thank goodness. Outside by the where? The Tourist Information Office. How do I— Side entrance, opposite platform eight. Okay, darling, yes, yes, I'll be careful. See you soon."

She stands up to go and stops next to me as she pulls her gloves on. "You make sure you ring your mother right away now. I'm so sorry, I didn't ask you your name."

"Rose Tremayne."

"That's a very pretty name. My name is Margaret. Now you need to get home as quickly as possible, Rose, you really shouldn't be on your own like this, not with this terrible weather. I'd hate to think of you getting stuck here. I shall ask a member of staff to come and help you while you wait for your mother, then I won't worry about you." She tucks her black dotty scarf into her coat. "Let me tell you something before I go; my father grew to love my husband, Eddie, even though he never said it in words."

I smile at her.

She rests her hand on my cheek. "Bye bye, dear, it's been lovely passing the time with you. I'll get the staff member to come and meet you in here."

I wave as she walks away. I'm glad she's going 'cause I need to leave before the staff comes and finds me. And I need to remember what she said. Side exit. Opposite platform eight. Side exit. Opposite platform eight. Tourist Information Office. I know those places. They tell you lots of things. That's where Grandma took me when we came to London. I know what I have to do.

I've found my thinking cap.

It's stopped snowing, but the cold bites my ears. The cars are wrapped in clouds of smoke, and their lights are shivering in the water on the road.

I can see the Tourist Information Office. The windows are all steamed up, but I know the white "i" on the blue square.

It's busy inside. Lots and lots of young people are crowded 'round the desk, all talking at once. I wait quietly at the side for my turn. I hope they hurry up. It's getting later-on, and I want to get moving on for the next day. And Jack.

The lady in charge claps her hands. No one takes any notice.

She stands on a chair. "Quiet, please! If everyone could listen, PLEASE! Due to the terrible weather conditions a lot of people are in need of accommodation. We have a list of cheap hotels, B&Bs, and youth hostels that my colleague, Denise, is going to hand 'round to you all now. The address, telephone number, and nearest underground station or bus route are printed clearly next to each venue in blue ink. Please note that Oxford Street YHA is full to capacity already."

A short, dark-haired boy raises his hand. "Excuse me, please, which is nearest hostel to the Victoria Station?"

"Let's see...number five on your list, Earl's Court, four stops on the District line, westbound. Five minutes' walk to the hostel from there. It's open twenty-four hours a day, but even so, I'd get there as soon as possible."

"The District and Circle line is closed," a red-haired girl shouts.

Everyone starts talking at once so the lady on the chair claps her hands again for silence. The red-haired girl carries on talking until someone tells her to shush.

"Thank you, the District and Circle line has now reopened."

The lady handing out the list gives one to me.

"Canyoushowm— can you show me the nearest place to Victoria Station that the dark-haired, short boy said, pleasethankyou verymuch?"

She looks at me in a strange way. "Earl's Court, it's a youth hostel." She puts a line under it with her pencil. "D'you know what that is?"

"My friend Jess at Henley College goes to youth hostels."

"Does she? That's nice."

"Can you tell me the under-the-ground train again, pleasethankyou?"

"District line...four stops...westbound. The District line is green. It's a little walk from there, so are you traveling with anyone?"

"No."

"How old are you, love?"

"I'm sixteen and ten months."

"Really?"

I push my shoulders back and put my head up. "I'm in-de-pen-dent. I'm going to Earl's Court. District Line. Green. Four stops, west moving. Okaythankyou."

The lady walks off shaking her head. I can see her talking to the other lady and pointing at me.

I think I need to go. I think she doesn't believe I'm sixteen and ten months, but you should never tell lies... That makes my face glow red.

The dark-haired, short boy is going out the door with another boy. "*Dépêche-toi! Allons-y,*" he says in an impatient voice.

I follow behind him into the cold. I don't look back.

eight
december 12th

I follow the boys to the underground.

I stand on the train holding very tight to the silver pole. All I can see are the buttons on people's coats. I turn in a circle to face the doors and don't look down the gap.

As the doors shut, the red-haired girl from the Tourist Information Office pushes on to the train with some other girls. They're all laughing. One of them is looking at her mobile. "Just checked," she says, "Earl's Court YHA is very near the tube station and it only takes five minutes to walk there."

"Great, I'm frozen."

"Shit! That's awful."

"What?" the red-haired girl asks.

"Fourteen-year-old girl jumped in front of a train. She died instantly; that's why the District and Circle line was shut. Oh no! They don't even know her name...that's so tragic."

My head can't take this in. I feel sad inside and outside. Why would you jump in front of a train?

I hope it wasn't this train that hurt her.

Where did her name go?

Her mum and dad will be broken up... I must text my mum when I get to the hostel.

I'm very squashed on this train. I don't mind this time. It's nice and warm after the frozen streets.

"THIS IS EARL'S COURT. STAND CLEAR OF THE DOORS, PLEASE. THIS IS A DISTRICT LINE TRAIN TO WIMBLEDON."

I follow the girls when they get off. I heard them talk on the train. They said they were going to my hostel. I have my pleased face on, I can tell. I'm using my brain.

I don't think the girls see I'm with them. They stop to throw snowballs at each other. One hits a car window. The driver beeps his horn. The red-haired girl runs and skids along the pavement. Her legs fly up in the air and she lands on her back. Her hat comes off, and her hair is spread out across the snow.

"You all right, hun?" Her friends help her up, and one of them brushes the snow off her back.

I pretend I'm doing up a lace on my boot. I'm pleased I'm thinking so hard.

"Come on, let's get going." They walk on, arm in arm. Everyone is quieter now. My feet are so heavy, I can hardly move. This day is going on and on. It should have been done ages ago.

We turn down a street that reminds me of one in Henley-on-Thames. It makes a lump come in my throat. That's a lot of lumps in one day.

The girls stop outside an old house lit up in every window. The roof vanishes into the sky. I stand in the shadow of a wall. Four large trees guard the outside. Their branches are bent down with snow, which looks yellow in the lights from the windows. Some steps go up high to the front door. The girls hurry up the stairs.

"Careful!" someone shouts. "They're very slippery in places."

I walk up the steps holding on to the edge of the wall at the side. I stop at the top, too nervous to go in. I don't know these places or what to do.

A boy with a gray beanie, like Jack, stands behind me. "You goin' in?"

He reaches over my head and holds the front door open for me. I go through.

Inside the noise fills my ears up. A man behind the desk waves a little red book in the air.

"Make sure you have your ID ready because it will save a lot of time. There is a line, you all know what a line is, so *try* and form an orderly one. Have you got any ID?" he says to a girl, in a tired-out voice.

She shakes her head and holds her hands up in the air.

I know ID. That's who you are. I look around me. The girl with red hair gets her passport out, but I don't have that with me. Dad keeps it safe in his office, in the third drawer down in his desk.

102

I keep moving forward in my line. I hope I get a bedroom, as I can't sleep outside.

A lady, who looks like my friend Ati from Waitrose, pushes through everyone with a mop, wiping up the snow water on the floor. I move back and smile at her. She stops and looks at me, frowns, and clicks her teeth. I can feel my smile falling. She swings the mop around the floor and over my feet before moving away.

I don't understand mean people. I heard my mum's friend talking in the sitting-down room when I was twelve and three bits of the year. She said it would have been best if I hadn't been born. Mum got really cross, and Mum never gets really cross. Mum said she couldn't believe she could say that. She isn't Mum's friend anymore. I felt sad all over. Most of her friends are lovely. Though Mum doesn't speak to Uncle Tony or Mrs. Carney at number thirty-three any more. They said hurting things about me too. And I was standing next to them. Mum told me I'm very important.

"Hey, are you okay? You need to move forward."

"Yesthankyou. I'mokay."

The girl who spoke has a big blue sweater on. It's the same blue as my old primary school uniform. Her face is covered in freckles, like my brother Ben. He hates them.

I'm next to see the man at the help desk. He has hair longer than mine, which touches his middle. The front bit is pulled back. It sits in a bun on top of his head.

"Hi there, you have ID?"

"My passport is at home. In my dad's office."

"Right, are you with anyone I can speak to?"

"I'm with me. I'm going to Brighton but all my trains are canceled."

"I see... How old are you? You have to be sixteen to stay at the YHA."

"I'm sixteen and ten months."

"Any way to prove it? Driver's license?" He snorts and clears his throat. "Student ID...perhaps? You *have* to have some proof of who you are or I'm afraid we can't let you stay here."

I remember my student card from my college, which is in my purse, and feel happy. The man looks at it very closely.

A real phone rings on his desk. "Where are you? I can't cope, it's worse than the first day of the Christmas bloody sales here. Okay, just try and get here ASAP." He slams the phone down. "Sorry about that. I guess that's all okay then... cool." He hands me my ID back. "Do you want a bed for eighteen or private room for forty-nine pounds? You can pay by cash or credit card."

"A bed, please. Is that by myself?"

The man laughs. "Not at that price. You'll share with four to six other people, all girls of course. Can you pay?"

I look at him and put my eyebrows up. I give him a twenty-pound note, and he puts the change in my purse. I don't want to be in bed with strangers, but it's better than having to go home. Better than no Jack.

The front door opens and a snow-blowing wind rushes into the room. A big crowd of boys and girls come in talking in words I understand, but they sound different.

The man helping me groans when he sees them.

"Here's your key to your room. Ground floor, room six, down there on the left. Bathroom opposite with self-catering kitchen at the end of the corridor. Cafe with snacks at the other end of the corridor, to the right. Grab the bed you want as soon as you get in there."

"You haven't given me a key."

He picks up the white card on the table. "This is your key *card*; use it like a credit card in the door. It accesses all other floors as well." He looks over my head at the person behind me. "Who's next?"

"Okaythankyou."

It isn't okay. I have a key that looks like my money card. I feel too tired to keep my thinking cap on. Room six. I shut my eyes for a moment and see me in my bedroom at home. P'raps my home bed is better. Mum is tucking me up and stroking my head with butterfly fingers. My mum. She will be frightened when she can't find me at home today, at evening seven on the clock.

"Can you not stop there, please? You're blocking the bloody way! Oh, sorry, I didn't realize you... I mean—sorry." The girl

105

picks up her bag and walks away. I don't know why she was sorry. I follow where the man at the helpdesk pointed. There are so many doors, and all the numbers are dancing around in my eyes. When I find my room I'm pleased, but then I can't see where to put the card key. I want it to be easy. I'm cross and upset that opening a door is too hard for me. I will never be in-de-pen-dent. I throw the card on the floor.

"Hey, you dropped your card. Can I get it for you?" The girl with the Ben freckles bends down and picks it up. "Here, let me show you, these things are tricky—there's a knack to it." She opens the door then pulls it shut again. "See? You have a go."

I take the card and push it down in the slot like she did. The door opens when I turn the handle. As I stand up straight, I feel like I'm spinning around.

"Whoa, I've got you. You look shattered, come and sit down."

She takes me to a bed that squeaks when I sit on it.

"Lie down until the dizziness goes. Let's take those boots off."

I sit back up. I need to text my mum. To tell her I'm safe. "I'm okaythankyou. I can do my boots." I push her hand away.

She looks a bit cross. "Hey! I was just trying to help."

"I'm grown up now. I can take my own boots off."

"Sure, I get it."

She doesn't sound sure. She half smiles at me. "Well, I'm going to have a shower. Perhaps I'll see you later in the cafe."

She opens the door and starts to go through, but turns around instead. "I know you want to paddle your own canoe, as my grandma says to me, but it makes people feel good to help."

The door clicks shut. I'm happy she's gone but I feel a bit wrong. I don't understand why she thinks I want to go in a canoe. I don't like them.

I walk 'round the room. There are two bunk beds squashed up against the walls. And my bed at the side. The floor is like the bathroom floor at Grandma's. It looks like tiles, but they're not real. It feels sticky under my boots. In the corner is a sink with a mirror over the top. The glass has a big crack in it. That's bad luck. The sink has a hair in it. Mum would get the bleach out. It dissolves grease and dirt so you can remove tough stains in the kitchen and bathroom. Mum uses it all the time.

Mum!

I get my phone out the front pocket of my bag. It takes forever to undo the buckle as my fingers are falling over each other. The front glass on my phone has gone black. I push the top button down but nothing happens. I shake it up and down. It stays black.

My phone has died.

I go through all my bag in all the pockets to find my phone charger, but it's no good. I didn't think like a grown up. I don't have my charger.

I'm for real on my own now. No Mum. No Grandma.

No anyone to get me.

nine

december 12th

Crying won't sort me out. I've cried two times already
and it's ri-dic-ulous. It won't make my phone work. I need to
have a grip.

All my numbers are in my phone. Maybe I can remember
Mum's number if I look inside my head. I sit on the bed and shut
my eyes tight, but nothing happens. I can't remember anything.

Don'tpanicRose. I need my messy head to go away.

If I can't call her, I can't tell Mum that I'm okay. She will
be *beside herself.* She will be scared-sad.

Ben probably won't notice I'm not there. His face will be
stuck onto Sophie's on his laptop screen.

I don't care what Dad thinks 'cause he stole my Jack from
me. I need Jack. I get my photo of him out of my bag. My
hands are shaking, making Jack's face tremble. I bring the
picture up to my face and try and get him to help me.

I feel calmer. Jack stops shaking in my hands. I hold his
picture-face against my ear. I listen. I shut my eyes to imagine
us both in Brighton.

We will be holding hands on the beach. The sea wind will be blowing across our faces.

Jack's fringe flies over his eyes. I reach up and push it away from his face. He takes my hand and kisses my fingers.

"You're frozen like ice," he says.

Then he opens his coat and wraps me up with him. We stay like that for a long time. We don't see the waves washing white foam over our feet.

After a while we walk along the water's edge, finding shells curled under the stones. Jack picks up a twist of seaweed and circles it 'round his head. He lets it go, and it flies through the air before splashing down on the water and rolling with the tide.

Jack turns and smiles at me. "We can go to the beach when I see you tomorrow," he whispers in my ear.

My eyes fly open. I can get a train tomorrow. The snow will melt off the train lines. It's not forever until tomorrow. It's only one sleepover.

"Not forever," Jack echoes in my head.

I pick my phone up. There is an idea I can't make into a shape. I'm about to give up trying, when I get it! If I tell my mum where I am, she will come and get me. Then Dad will stop me seeing Jack ever again.

I look at the black phone glass. I can see my face smiling on it. It's good that my phone didn't work.

Fingers crossed. Please, please let the snow be all melted tomorrow. Then I can be in Brighton in one hour and one minute. With Jack. And I can find a phone and let my best mum know I'm okay.

I find Jack's card with the name of his house in Brighton. I trace my finger over the words. Manor House Farm. It's not a farm for animals. I think it's a people farm, for people who need help. I run my finger over the shooting star Jack's drawn on the front of the card. We saw one once.

Hey Rosie
Its nite time and thats wen I mis you most. I was looking at the stars with Seb. Ther wer hundreds of them. Lots mor than in Henley. We shudnt hav gone outside but we needed a smoke. I love it out here at nite. I feel so small and yet so BIG. Do v remember when we stade out late and sor a shooting star? It was imense. Ware r u now? Can u see the moon? I can see a ship on the see far away in the moonlite. Its the size of my little fingernail. Thats crazy! Y don't u rite? I can't bare anuther day wivout u.

I LUV U. Jack xxx
Seb thinks v look cute in vr piktur. Here is my adres agen in case u lost it. Manor House Farm, Woods Lane, Hassocks, Brighton, BN6 7QL. It's the 1 paynted wite with see-green shuters like ur eyes ☺

Rosie Trem

61 Cromwe

Henley-on-

Oxfordshire

Jack's drawn a little cartoon house in the corner. It stands on the top of a hill.

Outside the door, I hear people talking. Then someone pushes the door open and tumbles into the room.

"Sounds like they're having a real *jol* next door. Mine's the top bunk? *Ja*?"

"*Ja, ja*, just don't roll over the top in the night. What's happened to Maryke? I thought she was right behind us?"

Two girls stand with their backs to me. They talk like me, but they don't sound like me. They must be the girls who came into the hostel when I was paying for my room.

One girl takes her coat off and throws it onto the top bunk. My mouth feels dry, and I can't swallow.

"Taryn, help me with this damn rucksack, it's stuck."

"Ag, shame."

At that moment, the door opens again and another girl comes into the room. "Sorry. I was talking to this cute guy." They all laugh very loudly.

"PleaseSHUSH! You're very noisy. Pleasethankyou."

They stop and look at me.

The whole room has gone quiet.

"Hi, we didn't see you there."

One of them steps in front of me. I feel very small. I can see right up into her nostrils.

"What...is...your...name?"

Her nostrils go in and out as she talks. One of the other

girls, whose hair is almost white, smiles at me and bends down to talk to me. She has winter-sky eyes. "Where...is... your...carer? Should...you...be...here?"

"Why are you talking so slowly? And in that funny voice?"

All the girls look at each other and burst out laughing again. I join in.

The girl with almost-white hair stands up. "Do you mean our accents? It's because we're from a country called South Africa. This is Lindi, this is Maryke, and I'm Taryn."

Maryke looks grumpy but Lindi and Taryn smile with all their white teeth showing. I smile back.

"My name is Rose Tremayne. I'm going to Brighton. Jack is there."

"That's nice for you. What a pretty name. Who's Jack?" Taryn glances at the other girls and pushes her eyebrows up.

"Myboyfriend."

All three of them hold their eyebrows up this time. "Well, that's lovely," Lindi says in a squeaky voice.

"Shame." Taryn walks over to her bunk bed.

I don't know what's a shame but I'm glad when they all stop staring at me and start to unpack their rucksacks. They sound like seagulls screeching at each other. I lie down on my bed and stick my fingers in my ears.

Why did the trains have to go away? Snow makes me happy at home. This snow makes me fed up.

I wrap a pillow around my head and think about Jack. He

promised to take me ice-skating in the Christmas holidays, to London's coolest ice rink. His mum took us before, at the beginning of November. It was in front of a big house that wrapped all around the ice, with hundreds of windows. The garden was turned into an ice lake. We were so excited.

"Take my hand, Rosie, I won't let you fall."

Jack stops my feet slipping away on the ice. We hold onto each other, trying to stand up straight. People fly by on their skates, their scarves floating out behind them. They make it look so easy. My boots are strange on my feet. Heavy and awkward. I'm clumsy all over.

Jack laughs at me. "You have to move your feet from side to side, don't try and walk on them."

He slides across the ice getting faster and faster. Racing away from me. His head held up high. His hair blown back by the wind as he skates. I watch him moving in and out of the people, like a dragonfly darting in and out of river reeds. He spins in a circle and waves to me from across the ice. I let go of the side to wave back and nearly fall over. A lady catches me and helps me up just as Jack shoots past, spraying us with an ice shower. He stops and turns back. He holds onto me and kisses me. His lips are snow-cold on mine.

"Come on! You can do it." He drags me out into the middle of the ice.

I copy what his feet are doing and move forward. Right, left, right, left. I hold his hand tight. Slowly, I start to slide across the ice without falling. But I make Jack go back near the edge, just in case. He slips his arm around my shoulders, and we move our feet together. We're dancing on the ice. My heart sings inside me. I look up at Jack, and he shouts to the sky, "Go, Rosie! I knew you could do it!" He twirls round me, clapping his hands and bumps into a man with a little boy.

"Watch what you're doing!" The man tells him off.

"Slow down, Jack," I say. "Look at the house!"

It's pink all over, but the windows are shining in gold. The Christmas tree at the end is twinkling with silver lights that dot the skaters. The house changes to blue and the ice becomes the sky under our feet. White snowflake lights pattern the floor, turning slowly in time to the music. I turn with them...

"Watch it, Taryn!"

The girls are getting louder, and I'm hot and sweaty under the pillow. I want to go back to the ice-skating in my head. The girls are too shouty. I feel all fidgety, even though I'm so tired. I sit up and get more Jack cards out of my bag and spread them on the bed.

Maryke passes a bottle of Coca-Cola around. Everyone I meet seems to like Coca-Cola, but fizzy drinks are very bad for you. They're full of sugar. Six teaspoons in every glass.

Maryke says something that makes Taryn burst out laughing. Her drink sprays out of her mouth all over my cards.

"Oh no! I'm so sorry."

As she gets up to come over she slips and the bottle splashes more Coca-Cola on them.

"MyJack!"

I see Jack's words spreading in a puddle. I try to push it off. Taryn grabs the cards and rubs them on her jeans. "I'm sorry, I'm so sorry."

"Getoffgetoff!" I can hear myself screaming. "MyJackisgoingaway!"

"Ag! What is she saying? Tell her to stop, Taryn, or they'll think we're doing something to her."

Taryn tries to help me but I push her off. "Leave my Jack alone!"

"Shush, sweetie, shush, I only got a couple of them a bit wet."

I wave my card in front of her. "It'sallmyJack. He's washed a...w...way."

"No, no, look, he's fine, he's just a little smudged."

"Don'ttouchmyJack!"

Taryn snatches her hand away. "I won't, I promise. Lindi, go and get the guy on reception, eh?"

"J...Jack is r...rubbed out."

"Shame. It's okay."

"What's she on about?"

"Shut it, Maryke." Taryn picks up my hand and strokes her finger in a circle on my arm. I don't like it. I rub where she touched me.

Maryke kneels in front of me. She's all blurry. "Do you

have any more Jacks in your bag? Maybe you could put these Jacks on the radiator and find another one to hold?"

I wipe my eyes and sniff. I want them all to go. Taryn is hiding the bottle under the bed. Maryke goes to the bathroom. She comes back out trailing something behind her.

"Here's some bathroom tissue to blow your nose, it's a bit long, sorry."

Lindi walks through the door with the reception man with the bun on his head. She points at me. Pointing is rude.

The man kneels down in front of me. "Hi again, my name's Rick. You okay?"

I shake my head. "Jackgotwet."

"So I understand, I think. The young lady here says that perhaps they're being a bit big and noisy for you."

"Yes."

"Um...look; I think it might be best if I call someone, your parents or a carer, maybe? I'm snowed under, no pun intended, but maybe you could give me a number to call? Do you understand what I'm saying, Miss—"

"Tremayne. Rose Tremayne. There isn't any snow on you."

"Yes, um, actually that was just an expression."

"I know those. My mum likes expresshuns."

"Talking of Mum, do you have her number so I can give her a call as I'm kinda pushed for time here?"

"I don't have her phone number. It went away when my battery died."

"You don't remember it?"

"No. And I don't have to remember it. I press MUM on my phone."

"Okay...well, we need to find you a place to stay, Rose."

"I have a room. Rose paid—*I* paid my money."

"Well, um, we can refund it, you know, give it back."

"I don't want it back, thankyou. I have to get to Brighton tomorrow."

"Right you are then, so I think the best thing I can do is move you upstairs to a private room. I have a big line waiting at the desk so I don't have time to do anything else now. The private rooms are cool."

"You said a private room costs a lot of money. I need my money to find Jack in Brighton."

"Okey dokey, no problem as it will be at no extra cost, so we can get you settled. Can I carry your bag for you?"

"Nothankyou. I can manage." Then I decide to give it to him 'cause people like to help. "Okaythankyou. You can."

Rick holds out his other hand to help me off the bed. I take it and stand up. I pick up my cards and hold them tight. I can hear a bell ringing outside the door.

"All right, I'm coming!" Rick shouts.

I turn and wave to all the girls as I go. They smile and wave back.

"Sorry about Jack!" Taryn shouts after me.

When the door shuts, I hear them all burst out into laughter. I don't mind.

I spot the girl with freckles and the blue sweater leaning against the wall outside. I go up to her. "I have a private room. All to myself. No extra cost."

"Go you."

We high-five, and I walk to the desk with my hand tingling.

We pick up my new plastic key card at the desk. Everyone is trying to talk to Rick all at the same time. A red-faced girl with lots of spots keeps ringing a bell on the desk by thumping it with her purse.

"Will you please stop ringing that bloody bell!" Rick grabs it and throws it in the trash.

Everyone is very loud and very snappy in London. They use a lot of bad words. I can't wait to have my all-by-myself room. I can be with Jack. In my head. No one can take him away.

ten

My new room is big with a window overlooking the back garden. It's nicer than the other room and smells like Febreze Cotton Fresh Air, so all the tough odors have gone.

I have my own shower that no one else can use, and it's shiny clean.

The walls don't have any pictures on them like my home bedroom. It makes the room a bit lonely. But I have a very big bed! And the duvet is pea green. I like peas. My stomach is hungry and grumbles at me. I'm not going downstairs. I don't want to meet anyone again.

All my brave has left me.

I put my cards on the radiator. They start to curl up at the edges, and it feels like Jack is safe and warm in the middle. I want to talk to him so much. At night, I play his voicemail over and over so I can go to sleep with his words. But 'cause my phone died, I can't hear his voice now.

The window is covered up with mist, so I wipe it away with the toilet paper Lindi gave me. It leaves bits all over the glass, so I wipe it with my sleeve. The room is warm but the glass is snow cold. The lights from the house make ink-shadows of the trees across the ground. The tops of the benches look like they have Christmas cake icing on them.

I can't see any stars, just the shape of the moon hiding behind the night clouds.

I wonder if Jack is thinking about me. I want to let him know I'm going to be in Brighton tomorrow. And that nothing matters but us. He is in my head and all of me.

I reach out to touch the moon where it shines on the glass. Once, Jack said he wanted a pizza the size of the moon. I shut the curtains. Thinking about pizza makes my stomach moan again. I have a coconut bar in my bag. It sticks in my throat, and I have to get a drink of water from the sink tap. The water hurts my teeth.

I decide to get ready for bed. It's not my bedtime as it's only six o'clock and five bits past. But I want to get to Jack quicker.

The tap shudders and whistles when I turn it on again, like the one in the girls' toilets at Henley College. College seems so far away from me. Lou will miss me. I wonder who pushed her wheelchair for her at college today? I'm sad I can't talk to her 'cause I'd have to tell her where I am, and her feelings will be hurt. My phone is out of battery anyway. My Rosie face in the mirror looks disappointed with me.

But Jack will be over-the-moon happy when I see him.

I wipe the toothpaste off my mouth and check my teeth are whiter than ever before.

I lie down on the bed and curl myself around my bag, making sure the badges are on the other side. I stroke the soft fur away from my face. I think of Winniebago, who makes me feel calm. She has lots of white fur that fluffs up like a lion mane 'round her head. She always knows when you are sad. She followed me everywhere after Jack was taken away.

I shut my eyes and listen to the laughter coming from downstairs. My eyes open and shut. The tired falls down from the top of my head to the bottom of my toes.

I wake up later, and I don't know this place. I'm wrapped 'round my bag, and the fur is tickling my nose. Slowly, I start to remember the room and where I am. The light around the door shines brightly. Then part of it goes dark. The handle of my door moves down...down. I grab my pillow and hold it tight. I can hear someone stopping a cough. Then I hear a burst of angry air hiss behind the door. I can't shout for help. My mouth is scared shut, and my eyes can't move away from the handle. But I want to bury myself under the duvet and be safe. The handle moves slowly back up.

The dark goes away, and the light is all around the door again.

I'm shaking. Someone whimpers. It's me. I slip under the

covers, taking my bag with me. No one can see me now. I lift the duvet up in a little tunnel so I can look along it and watch the door.

I don't know what the time is, but it's gray night in the room. I can hear the radiator click like my one at home. My nose is stuffy. I stretch my leg out and rest it on a colder part of the bed.

I remember the door.

It's tight shut and the light is in a yellow line all the way around. I throw the cover off and make myself go and check the door. It doesn't move. I let out a big sigh. P'raps last night wasn't real. P'raps it was a nightmare.

I open the curtains and make a circle space for me to see through the mist. The sun lights the bottom of the sky, turning the black to purple. My favorite color. It makes me feel good about today.

It hasn't snowed anymore. Little feet have walked holes across the garden making dot to dots. I follow them with my finger on the window. It leaves a snail trail on the glass.

My trains will be back. I feel butterfly wings inside me. They are more excited than me. I open the window and shout out to the morning, "I'm going to see Jack today!"

A dark shape runs across the garden and disappears. I can

hear it scratching around in the bushes. My breath puffs out fog in front of my face. I clap my hands to catch it but it jumps through my fingers. The cold air makes my nose run. I don't want to catch a chill and I have to get a move on. Jack needs me.

I close the window and get ready for the day.

I'm going to wear the earrings Jack got me. They have peacock feathers that tickle your face. Jack says they match my eyes.

Mirror Rose smiles at me. "Not long until Jack."

I pack my bag carefully and make sure everything is there. I make my bed up and wipe 'round the sink with some tissue. I'm ready for breakfast.

There's a knock on my door. I don't know anyone to knock. "Hi," a lady voice calls.

When I open the door, the girl with the freckles is there. She has a black sweater on today. It's all baggy. She's smiling and holding a tray with two muffins and two mugs piled with marshmallows.

"Look, I got breakfast for us."

Behind her a voice calls up the stairs, "Maddie, is that you?"

She starts to come through my door.

"I think that voice is talking to you," I say to the girl.

She shrugs. "I don't know him."

"Hey! Maddie! It's me—Jed."

She raises her eyes up to her eyebrows. "Take that, please." She hands me the tray and goes to look down the stairs.

A head appears at the top of the stairs with round glasses on his face. "Maddie! Didn't you hear me just now?"

"Do I know you?"

"Yeah...you're joking, right?"

Maddie doesn't answer. The boy pulls at his chin. "We, like, spent some time together yesterday? At the Mex Bar." His voice falls quiet.

"You must have got me muddled with someone else. I'm super busy right now, Reg."

"Are you crazy? What do you mean? We had a bite, drank tequila... We were going to Madame Tussauds today... And it's *Jed*."

"I. Don't. Know. You. You obviously drank too many tequilas." She comes into the room and shuts the door. "What a moron. Here, give me the tray back and bring that table round so we can sit together. Great room." She walks 'round looking at everything. She opens a door. "You got your own bathroom. So cool. I had to share mine with a bunch of losers."

"That boy looked very sad, Maddie."

"It's not my problem he's a complete knob. And my name isn't Maddie, it's Mia."

I feel all wrong. "Knob" and "loser" aren't nice words. Ben uses them all the time.

She puts the tray on the bedside table. "Come and sit with me." She moves my bag onto the floor and pats the bed.

I slide my bag over to me and push it under the bed.

"You want some muffin?"

"Yesplease."

"Chocolate orange or blueberry, I'm cool with either?"

"Chocolate orange, please. I don't eat cake 'cept on special occasions. I watch my weight. I don't care today."

"Absolutely! Who cares about stupid diets? God, you don't need to worry. Is hot chocolate okay?"

"Yesthankyou!"

"Don't you just love cream and marshmallows?" She scoops a large spoonful into her mouth. "What did I say? You've got the biggest grin on your face I've ever seen."

"My Jack loves marsh-mellows."

"You are so sweet! Who's 'my Jack'?"

"My boyfriend."

"Wow! Lucky you. No, put your purse away, this is my treat."

"Thankyouverymuch."

I don't know why she's treating me. I don't know her. She's very, very kind.

"Don't bounce up and down too much; you'll spill your drink."

I spoon some marshmallows into my mouth. Mia cuts up her cake with a plastic knife. I check the bed clock on the table. Nine-o-four. I'll be with Jack before the morning is over. My heart does a flip-flop.

"Hey, I can't believe we haven't swapped names. Mine's Mia."

"Iknowyousaidthat. I'm Rose. Rose Tremayne."

"Pleased to meet you, Rose Tremayne." Mia points at my

mug with her teaspoon. "You'd better catch some of that cream that's spilling down the side of your mug. So, what are you doing today?"

"I'm going to Brighton. To be with my boyfriend, Jack."

"I'd LOVE to go to Brighton. I've heard it's super cool. D'you want to try some of this blueberry muffin?"

"Yesplease." Mia breaks off a bit and passes it to me.

"Here." I hand her my muffin to bite.

Her nose crinkles. "Yuck! No thanks."

"Are you scared you'll catch my germs? Mum says people are scared of what they don't know. I don't want anyone to be scared of me."

Mia looks at me with her mouth open. "God, Rose, *relax*. I can't stand chocolate orange, that's all." She pushes her plate away and tosses her hair back over her shoulder. It makes her hair-parting move to the side of her head. "What are you staring at? Didn't your mother tell you that staring at people is rude?"

I'm all mixed up, and my cheeks have gone pink. I look at my lap. Mia said she was cool with both cakes...my ears must have got it wrong. When I look back up, Mia goes over to the window and looks out. She writes something on the glass, I think it's her name. Then she rubs it out with her sleeve. She turns back to me. Her hair-parting is back in the middle of her head.

"Cheer up, Rose, no harm done, but you shouldn't jump to conclusions."

"Sorry. My grandma told me not to jump to con-fusions," I say in a quiet voice.

"No probs...what's this?"

"My Jack card. It got wet when some girls put Coca-Cola on it. It's gone curly on the edges."

She drops it onto the radiator top but it falls down the back. She leaves it there. "You ready to go?"

"Yesthankyou." I get up and save Jack from behind the radiator. I brush the dust off and put him on the bed next to me.

"Oh, sorry. Have you got everything?"

"My train ticket is in my bag. And my money. And my Jack cards. I have to go to Victoria Station."

"I checked the internet before breakfast, and most trains are running now—supposedly. Anyway, rush hour is nearly over so we can get moving. Put your money away, you have to be careful. You can't keep waving it about, sweetie. I had fifty pounds stolen from my rucksack in the last hostel I stayed in."

"That's veryvery bad! You mustn't steal. Do you go to lots of Youth Hostels?"

Mia gets her phone out her pocket. "Hmm?"

"Someone tried to get in my room last night. I don't think it was a bad dream, but I told me it was."

"Sure."

She's not listening to me. I unzip my bag and put my money back. "There! My purse is in the pocket inside my bag. Jack is looking after it."

Mia laughs. "Are you hiding him in there?" She pulls my bag over to look.

"No. He sent me cards to let me know about him." I zip my bag up and slide it back under the bed. "Jack loves me."

"Ah, that's so sweet. D'you have a photo of him?"

I have to open my bag again. Mia bends down to look. I pass my picture of Jack to her that I keep in the secret pocket.

"He's cute," she says, handing it back to me.

I kiss Jack before I tuck him away. Mia checks her watch. "Areyouokay, Mia?"

"I'm good; I just need to get going. You too, if you want to get to Brighton before it snows again. Why don't you go to the bathroom then we can make our way to Victoria Station together?"

"I don't need a bath. I had a shower when I got up."

"I mean go to the toilet. You don't want to use the ones at the station. They're gross. I'll go first then you can go."

When Mia comes back, I go for my wee. I have to make one come, 'cause I don't really need to go. When I come out, I can't see Mia. I go and look out the door but she's not there.

I eat more muffin but my tummy says I don't want it any more. I pick it into crumbles and make it into little hills.

The bed clock on the table says nine and four six now. I can't wait any longer. I want to get to Jack as fast as possible. I've had enough of this place.

Mia has forgotten me. Maybe I took too long trying to make a wee and she had to run for a train. P'raps she was cross with me. I'm mixed up in my head now and I can't sit still. I pick my Jack card up. It's number six. The last one Jack sent. It has a drawing on the front of a sad Jack face. He's crying. In the corner is our little blue butterfly.

I messd up. I didnt want to tell v. Dont be sad with me. I had a bust up with Seb. He sed yood get bored of wating for me. He sed yood be siting at our tabel with sum one else. I went cracy. I didnt hurt him even tho I wanted to. But I broke my room up. They took me to the kwiet zone. I woz ther a long time. When I woke up my fase was stuk to the plastic on the flor. I sat and thort of v. Then I got mad at me. I wont see v if I dont get me togethur. Then I got upset. Why did my brane get hurt wen I woz born? I cride Rosie. Dont tell ennywon. I hav to get better but how do I do it wivout v?

Jack X ☹

Thers a litel blu butturfli on the wall. He shuddnt be ——

——ut him out the windo and sent him to v. Look out for him. He wil take care of v. Jack x

Rosie Tremayne

61 Cromwell Aven

Henley-on-Thames

Oxfordshire RG16 2

I *have* to get to Victoria. I'm not waiting for Mia. Jack needs me.

'Round the edge of the postcard there is some tiny writing.

> Thers a litel blu buturfli on the wall. He shudnt be awake yet. I put him out the windo and sent him to u. Look out for him. He wil take care of u. Jack x

I look 'round the room but I can't see him. I remember all the butterflies in the tunnel with the singing man. They flew off the picture and danced with me. They made me happy. I will look out for Jack's blue butterfly. It will help me find him. I smile and do my coat up. I check inside my head for the journey. Earl's Court. District and Circle line. Green line. Four stops to Victoria. I can remember the way to the tube station.

It's easy.

eleven
december 13th

I'm standing by a red postbox. I didn't see it last
night. It must have been hidden in snowflakes. I don't know
which way to go. A man with a dog in a green coat is coming
toward me. "'Scusemeplease. Can—"

He walks on with his head down. The dog tries to say hello
to me. The man drags him away, making the dog yelp. His
bottom leaves a path in the snow.

The houses down here aren't looked after. They look at
me with their window eyes. One of the eyes winks at me. It
makes me shiver. I walk up the road and see a little park. I
go in there to think. The cold is making my head not work.

I can see some swings. The wind is pushing them backward and forward. They squeak and groan. They are in pain.
They look so lonely. I want to sit on one and pretend I'm a
little girl again. Then all the big things I have to think about
would be gone. I'd kick my legs up to swing higher and higher
so I could sit on a cloud and be safe.

I walk along the path a bit. Someone has swept the snow

away. It's piled up at the sides. In the middle of the path is a little statue. I brush the snow off it. A lion looks at me with a sad face. His ears have gone. I think he's sad because he can't hear any more.

I find a bench and make myself be a grown-up person. I clean it up and sit with my bag on my lap. I'm wasting time being this Rose again.

I can ask someone else how to get to the station.

I can wait here for someone to come.

My nose is running. I get a tissue from my bag and pat the purse pocket to check everything is there.

It *was* fat and poking out.

It's flat now.

I unzip it.

Only my Jack cards are in there.

I rub my eyes and look again, but my purse and my tickets have vanished.

I throw everything out onto the snow. They must be in the big part of my bag. I pick up my clothes and turn them all inside out. I shake and shake them, then throw them back on the ground. They're getting wet but I don't care. I check all the pockets again.

Inside and outside.

My purse has gone.

My money has gone.

My phone has gone.

132

My tickets.

Gone.

"Nonononononono."

"Hey, *dziecino*, hey, hey. What is it?"

"Mystuffsallgone."

"Don't cry, *dziecino*, tell Janek what has happened." He starts to pick up my clothes.

"NO! Don'ttouchmystuff!"

"They're getting ruined, come, let me help you."

The big, gold-coin ring on his finger gets caught on some sparkles on a T-shirt. He pulls it off. The sparkles scatter across the snow.

"There, we fold this up and put it in your bag like so and I shake the dirt off, then we dry them later. One more, see? It's good you are calming down now. Blow your nose, you will feel better."

He puts my bag next to me on the bench and hands me a white hanky.

"Blow! Fantastic. No, no, you keeping it now. Let me wrap my scarf around your neck, you need to get warm, yes?"

It smells of stinky aftershave and smoke. He sits down next to my bag and takes out a cigarette.

"Tell me what is making you so upset."

My words are stuck inside me. I just want my things back. I think Mia was pretend nice. I think she took my things away. I want my Jack. Not this man wearing sunglasses in

133

the winter. He has little holes on his face, like my dad's work-boss. His hair is blond with gray bits at the side. It goes past his collar.

His match hisses.

"What is so terrible that you cannot talk? What is your name? That is a good place to start."

"R...Rose."

"That is a beautiful name. I am very pleased to meet you, Rose, my name is Janek." He takes his glasses off and smiles at me. "Calm down, Rose, you are not helping yourself. Janek can't help you if you can't tell him problem. This is better, now tell me what has caused all these tears."

"My p...purse has gone. My t...ticket h...has gone."

"You are sure is correct?"

I nod.

"Where are you last having these things?"

"The hostel. I know they were there. Rose put them there. IhavetogettomyJack. Ihaveto...get a train."

"Don't get all upset again, Janek will help you. Tell me what is this train you get?"

"To Brighton. Where Jack is."

"Who is this Jack?"

"My boyfriend. I HAVE to find him."

"Then find him we will, my *aniolku*."

I open my mouth, but it doesn't say anything. It just opens and closes.

"You look like a little fish I kept as a child." Janek puffs his cheeks out and pop, pop, pops his mouth. He sees my face, throws his head back, and laughs. He has a pointy tooth at the top. "*O mój Boz̒e.*" Janek wipes his eyes. He re-lights his cigarette, and I watch the smoke curl out his mouth and 'round his ear.

I put my serious face on and look straight at Janek. "You will help me find my Jack? Swear promise?"

Janek throws his hands up in the air, which sends me backward. "Of course! Did Janek not say he would help you?" He puts his hand on his chest where his heart is. "Cross my heart and hoping to die. Is that not how you swear promise in this country?"

The sun pushes 'round the corner of a cloud and makes Janek's hair shine like the gold angel wings in the church.

"Come! We will find this Jack together."

In my head my mum is saying, "Don't talk to strangers. Don't ever go anywhere with someone you don't know." But lots of people have talked to me and been good. Lawrence. The lady at the station in the orange bobble hat. The lady at the cafe like my grandma. The lady with the baby like me. Janek isn't a stranger 'cause I know his name. Janek is taking me to Jack.

He picks up my bag and I follow him out of the park.

12th December

Im going to keep writing evn tho I dont
know if u see my cards. Seb sed ur mum
and dad mite not let u have them. I sor my
kownsler today. Her name is Mrs Evns. Shes
got ENORMUS tits. She woz nice and gave
me a yelo notebook to rite down my feelings. Eksept Im alowd to paynt al the monsturs in my
insted so I can paynt out al the monsturs in my
hed. But I CARNT paynt wivout u. Mrs Evns
arskd me how I kopd b4 u. I told her ther
wozunt a b4 Rosie. No 1 gets it. I told her
I hav to speek to u. She wont let me hav a
fone. I rifusd to talk arffur that Seb sed its
mi folt I smashd my fone. and I hav to suk it
up. Im not talking to him now ithur. Evn tho I
no hes rite. I sat on the gardun gate
arfturwrds and looked at the clowds. I cudnt
see dragens or swans or fish like u. Just a
poodul. Plese rite.
Jack X

Rosie Tremayne

61 Cromwell Avenue

Henley-on-Thames

Oxfordshire RG6b 2LD

twelve
december 13th

"Put that thing down." Janek has a grumpy dad face.

I hold my bag tighter and look at him through the handle space. I don't know why he's like that. He pushes his hair up at the front and makes his mouth move upward.

"Sweetie, I'm sorry, Janek is tired. Come now, don't look like that, please come into my house."

His face is smiling, but it doesn't look right.

"Come meet Lisette. She take care of you, not this grumpy old man, yes? Lisette? I bring someone to meet you. Lisette!"

A girl brushing her long black hair comes to the top of the stairs. She's in a T-shirt and pants. The T-shirt has Tinker Bell on it and it only just covers her bits.

Janek pushes me forward.

Her mouth falls open. "What the fuck?"

I don't like that word. It's badbadbad.

"Look after her and settle her in." Janek pulls me by my sleeve toward the stairs and turns to go.

"But I 'ave to get ready for later and I don't want to be left with *that*."

"It's your lucky day, *skarbie*, you get to do both."

"She can't have Jaycee's bed."

"Jaycee? Jaycee? Where is she, eh? I'm not seeing her. Give this girl the bed and quit whining, I have things to do." He disappears through an open door.

I feel weak.

The girl sniffs. "Come up, then. You can walk?" She looks mean.

The stairs are jiggly. The carpet is broken up. My boot gets stuck, and I fall on my bag. The girl thumps down the stairs and grabs my arm.

"It's that door up there, to the right—if you know what right is? What's with the tongue thing? It's gross."

She drags me up the stairs and through a door. She points to one of the beds. "Just push the clothes off the bed onto the floor. Go on then!"

She sits cross-legged on her bed and picks up a pink, spar-kly mirror. She has makeup spread all over the duvet. She starts to clean her face with a baby wipe. It leaves orange all over it. Her face is very white underneath.

The room is small. The wallpaper is falling off by the door. The window is closed but I can feel cold air on my face.

Somewhere far away is Jack. I wish fairies were real and I had a magic wand 'cause then I could wave it and fly to him in one bit.

I watch the tears dropping on my jeans.

"Christ, stop snivellin', you only just got here. Why don't you take that coat off?"

"I don't want to take my coat off 'cause I want to go and find Jack."

"Tough shit, you can't."

I don't know why she is being so rude. I'm not going to look at her.

The duvet is covered in little ponies with rainbow manes. They're for babies. A big brown stain spreads over some of the ponies, making them hide.

"Here, put that down." The girl tries to move my bag. "I'm tryin' to help you, you can't sit in your coat all day. Why's everythin' purple?"

"I like p...purple."

"Hold your arm up." She yanks the arm of my coat.

"Ow! You'rehurtingme."

"Don't be a crybaby, just give us your other arm."

I don't like the way she's leaning over me. Her T-shirt falls forward. She's got a tiny blue butterfly painted on her chest.

"What you starin' at now?"

"You've got our butterfly!"

"What you on about?"

"Jack and me saw the butterflies at Chester Zoo. A blue one landed on us. It was special. Then Jack gave me one. Look." I show her the brooch on my coat she's still holding.

She shrugs her shoulders.

"Then Jack sent me a little blue butterfly on my postcard. He found it on his wall. In his room in Brighton."

"You're crazy." She drops my coat on the floor and jumps back onto her bed.

I smile inside me. The butterfly will take care of me. I pick my coat up and put it on the bed next to me. "Why d'you have a blue butterfly on your chest?"

The girl is rubbing more orange on her face. I don't think she heard me. Then she turns 'round. "It was somethin' me and Jaycee got done together. She's my best friend. That's her bed you're sitting on. We was in Hyde Park boating on the lake. We weren't s'posed to be there; we should've been picking up some stuff for Janek. This blue butterfly landed in the boat. It were so beautiful. We ain't never seen nothin' like it before. Jaycee said it must've escaped from Battersea Park, where they've got that little kids' zoo. After, we saved up and both went and got a butterfly tattoo, in the same place, to remind us of when we was happy."

"Do you think our butterfly was the same one?"

Lisette snorts. "Get real." She turns away.

I don't like this room. It's very messy and covered in litter. There are lots of fizzy drink cans lined up on the carpet, which is all worn out. We don't have those drinks at home.

It smells like the changing rooms at Topshop in here. I don't want to stay...but the butterfly is here. And all my stuff has gone.

"What's your name then?"

I don't want to talk to her but Mum says I must always be polite, so I tell her, "Rose Tremayne."

"Mine's Lisette, though that's not my real name of course."

"That's silly."

"Only if you're an idiot like you."

I was so polite and she's rude. I pick my bag up and look at all my stuff. It doesn't make me feel better. It makes me feel worse 'cause I want to be with real Jack. Or everyone I love. I can see Lisette in the mirror on the wall by her bed. She's putting too much makeup on and the blue eye color has gone up to her eyebrows. She has clown eyes. She was pretty before she did that. Now she's drawing a big black line 'round her eyes. She looks back at me, so I turn my face away and find Jack's sweater he gave me so I can hold it.

"What else you got in that bag of yours? It's stuffed. You been shopliftin', Rose?"

"No! I know what that is. There were some bad students at my college. You mustn't steal. You'll get put in prison... I need to find my Jack."

"Who is this Jack? What's he got to do with anythin'? You're not makin' any fuckin' sense."

"That's a very bad word."

"Fuck, fuck, fuckety fuck. It's only a fuckin' word." She turns her back on me.

"Jack and me are going to get married."

Lisette spins around. Her mouth is wide open. "Are you *allowed* to get married?"

I shove a dressing gown off the bed and cross my arms very tight. I don't want my lip to wobble, so I bite it.

141

She sees me and looks down. When she speaks it's hard to hear her.

"I don't mean nothin' and I ain't goin' to get in an argument with a learning difficulties person."

She wipes her nose on her arm. She picks up a brush and puts pink on her cheeks. She looks really silly. I did make up like that when I was playing dressing up.

"Where's this Jack person then?"

"Brighton. I need to go there. Now."

"What part of 'you can't' don't you get?"

"Why not? Janek said I could."

"Janek says lots of things but it don't mean they'll come true."

I can't work out these words and what she is saying. But I don't get a good feeling about them.

Lisette is putting some big, big gold circles in her ears.

My mouth falls open. They're touching her shoulders.

"What's up with you? You look dopey—oh, hang on, that's 'cause you are." She laughs loudly.

I do a Mum frown.

"What?" She sniffs at the air and then sniffs her armpit before squirting some stuff on them that smells like bubblegum. She waves the can at me. "Cat got your tongue?"

"There aren't any cats."

Lisette laughs again.

"I'm ignoring you. Like Mum said. Ignore bully people then they'll go away."

"Whatever." Lisette draws 'round her lips with a red pencil. I count the badges on my bag and pull out the tangles in the fur with my fingers. Lisette tries to do a bracelet up with one hand. It makes her cross. She throws it on the floor.

I pick it up and give it back to her. "I can put it on for you."

She snatches it back. "No, ta. Don't look like that. I don't wanna wear it now. Tell me what's goin' on with you then." Her words are less shouty. "Why's this Jack person in Brighton?"

"He got sent away."

"Why?"

"He gets angry. Sometimes he breaks things up. He doesn't mean it."

"Sure, Rose, that's what they all say."

"You sound like my mum."

"I wouldn't know how to sound like a mum."

Lisette opens a drawer and finds a mascara stick. She points it at me as she talks. Her voice is hard. "After a bloke's right-hooked you and left you with a split lip, he'll come crawling back, beggin' you to forgive him, promising he'll always love you; says he'll change. But take it from me"—she bangs the mascara on the bed table—"he won't."

"Jack won't ever hurt me."

"Yeah he will."

"NO HE WON'T!"

Janek bursts into the room. I fall back on the bed. Lisette jumps up and stands like a soldier.

"*Kurwa ma´c*! I leave you five minutes with her, Lisette, and you've managed to upset her. You're supposed to be helping her settle in." He snatches her mascara and throws it on the bed. "Go get her some food and a proper drink!"

I put my hands over my ears and shut my eyes. "TakemetoJacktakemetoJack."

Someone taps my knee. Janek kneels in front of me. "Enough, baby girl, we give you hot meal."

"I'm not a baby! I'm sixteen and ten months."

Janek laughs.

"It's not funny. I'm all grown up. You promised to take me to Jack."

"And I will, but first we must look after you."

"I want Jack. You—"

"Shush, shush, shush, you do as Janek says and you will be fine. That is right, Lisette...? I said, that is right, isn't it, Lisette?"

"Yeah, sure."

Janek walks out the room. As he goes past Lisette, he slaps his hand on her bottom.

You shouldn't touch people's bottoms.

"Let's eat." Lisette's voice is sulky. My brother Ben is good at sulky voices.

"I'mnothungry. I had breakfast with Mia. Lunch is at one o'clock."

"You eat when you can here." She rubs her arms hard. "It feels like a fuckin' goose just walked over my grave."

5th December

Im in the shed. Need to think wich isnt eesi. My angri kiks evrithing out my brane. I no I hav to get beter. Seb sed its up to me nobodi els. How cum Seb gets to be so smart wen hes got a hole in his hed? Its kwiet in here. It smels of oil and rust metel. My torch is makin weerd shapes on the wals. I can see a spyder spining on a bit of thred. Do u remember wen we got stuk up between the lornmoer and the old nusepapurs? Wen we wer hiding kissing? U taystd of strorberis. Then v sor a big spyder and went crazi. I skwoshd it for u. I got upset agen tonite. Seb fownd me and gave me a rag to blo my nose on. The smel made me sneeze. We sat and watchd the spyder makin a web and had a smoke. Im in my room now. Wen I go to sleep Im going to pritend u r nxt to me.

Sad Jack xxx Im not going to stop riting to u.

Rosie Tremayne

61 Cromwell Avenue

Henley-on-Thames

Oxfordshire RG96 2LD

thirteen
december 13th

There's a girl standing at the sink, with white hair.
It's dark at the top. She's eating pizza from a box and pulling
a long bit of cheese from her mouth.

Lisette runs over to her. "Courtney! Babe, where you been?"

"Hey, hun."

The two girls hug each other and squeak like mice.

Lisette stands back and frowns. "You seen Jaycee or heard
anythin'?"

"Nah. Quit stressin' about her, she'll be with Mani or
somethin'."

"But she didn't say nothin'."

The blonde girl picks up a slice of pizza and stuffs it in
her mouth. She talks with her mouth full of food. "She'll be
back soon and then you'll be moaning 'cause she's nicked all
your makeup."

A bit of pizza falls on the floor. The girl sees me over
Lisette's shoulder.

"Who the fuck's that?"

Lisette crosses her eyes and puts her tongue out. "Some stray Janek has dumped on us. Says we got to look after her, settle her in. It's a piss-take."

"Yeah it is; where the fuck did he find her?"

"God knows, but she's here and now we've got to bloody take care of her—for what?"

"What's he want someone like *her* for?"

I'm *not* a stray. I don't want them to look after me. I'm more grown-up than them.

"But she's, you know..." The blonde girl holds her hands up in the air. "She can't do nothing, I mean that's sick."

"It's all sick, Courtney."

"Yeah, but with a handicap person, even Janek ain't that perverted, is he?"

They are very rude 'cause they are talking about me. When I'm next-door to them. And Lisette didn't tell me who the blonde girl was. I just heard her name myself. I don't understand that per-ver-ted word they used. But it sounds wrong.

I feel floaty. The girls are fading in and out. I try and find something to hold on to. Lisette makes me sit down. She doesn't do it nicely.

"Thought you was goin' to conk out."

"What's...per-ver-ted? I want to know, Lisette, please."

"My name's Lisette, not Lee-set. You don't wanna know what PER-VER-TED means, do she, Courtney?"

Courtney shrugs. "Means Janek is a dirty bastard."

"My brother Ben doesn't wash."

The girls hold each other, they are laughing so much.

"Why are you *laughing*?"

"Shit, Rose, dirty don't mean you don't wash, not here it don't anyways!" Courtney shrieks and makes me jump.

I put my hands over my ears. I want them to stop. I make Jack come into my head but those noisy girls get in his way. They stand by the sink blowing smoke at each other and flicking ash onto the dirty plates. That's so yucky. Courtney's jeans have lots of holes in them. I can see her bottom when she turns 'round.

"Your jeans are rude," I tell her.

"Sexy you mean."

Courtney wiggles her bottom at me. I don't think she has any knickers on. You only do that when you are in your pajamas.

Idon'tlikeher.

Courtney stops texting, picks a bit of tomato off her pizza and chucks it at Lisette. Lisette throws it back and it lands in Courtney's hair.

"Oi! Sod off, Lisette, I've just washed it."

"You started it... Your roots need seein' to."

"Your face needs seein' to."

Lisette sticks her finger up at Courtney. Dad got very cross when Ben did that to him.

I wish I was with my friends at Henley College. We don't throw our food like babies.

Courtney walks up to me. "Why've you got that face on? You look like you're chewing on a fuckin' wasp."

I bury my face in my arms. I don't want these girls. They're whispering to each other, but I can hear them. I DON'T WANT THEM.

"She won't last, babe."

"Yeah, Janek will—"

I block out their voices with my fingers in my ears and go inside my head to a happy picture. I choose when Jack took me to the fairground. I press my ears harder and make the memory come.

The air smells of fried onions and smoky burgers. We walk in and out of different music. Each tune plays louder than the next. Somewhere a bell clangs and a child squeals with excitement. Jack shouts to me above the noise. I put my hand on his arm, and it feels warm where the sun made it pink earlier. I stand on tiptoe so I can reach his ear to hear me. He smells of summer. He turns his head as I'm about to speak and stops me with a kiss. His lips are soft and taste of ice cream. There are lots of people pushing past us, but I feel like we are the only ones here. His hand rubs my back and touches my skin where my shoulder is bare. Jack smiles down at me and says, "I wish we were alone."

Something thumps on the table making me sit up straight. A voice says, "Wakey, wakey!"

My fairground picture runs away from my day dream. Courtney is sitting on the table with some cans of beer next to her. It's not beer-drinking time.

Courtney takes a gulp from her can and burps loudly.

"That's a pig noise."

"Are you sayin' I'm a pig?" She bangs her can on the table. It splashes up everywhere.

"I'm glad you getting to know each other, girls."

Janek has a different shirt on. It's black and shiny. His hair is brushed right back so I can see a diamond in his ear. His perfume smell is so strong it makes me sneeze. He takes Courtney's beer and drinks from the can.

"What's up with you, Courtney, Lisette? Where are your manners? Where is drink for her?"

"My name is Rose."

"Sure it is, baby."

"I'm not a baby."

"*Kurwa*, is she always like this?" Janek shakes his head making his ear diamond catch the light. "Lisette! Get her some juice."

"I like juice."

Janek smiles showing his pointy tooth at the top. "You're really going to like this juice, my *aniolku*, my little angel."

Lisette hands me a glass full to the top with orange. I take a big gulp. It tastes different to my home orange.

Janek holds his drink up in the air. "Welcome to our family. *Na zdrowie!*"

Lisette puts music on. It's one of my favorite songs. It's called "Happy." It makes you smile even when you don't want to. She and Courtney grab hands and dance together. They bump their bottoms together and against Janek. He talks on his phone with one hand on his other ear. When he's finished he shouts above the music, "The guys will be here in an hour or so."

"Christ! Why so early today? We only just got up."

"It's still breakfast."

"You're always moaning, you two, come on, it's nearly the lunch time, so smile, show me those sexy moves."

My glass is empty but I don't remember drinking it. Courtney fills it up. They dance around the table. The room starts to go 'round and 'round with them. I can't stop it.

Someone near me shouts, "Watch out! She's going to—"

fourteen
december 14ʰ

"WhereamI? WhereamI?"

"Shu' up."

"WHEREAMI?WHOPUTMEHERE?"

"Me an' Courtney, now shu' the fuck up."

Something hits me on the head. It's a toy rabbit. My head thump thumps. Pictures punch in and out of it. My stomach squeezes tight. Stuff gurgles up.

"Not over Jaycee's bed, you loser!"

Lisette shoves something under my mouth. I grip it until all the sick has gone.

"For God's sake, all over the bed. It stinks."

"Getitoffme! Getitoffme!"

"YOU get it off. Why should I clean up your mess? It's my bedroom that's rank 'cause of you."

"I want my mum."

I pull the curtain 'round me 'cause the duvet is covered in sick and hide in the dark. It starts to pull away from me but I hold on tight.

Lisette hiss-whispers at me, "That ain't gonna get this shit cleaned up, so get up! If Janek sees this he'll go crazy."

"You can't see me! You can't see me!"

"What? Stop that baby chantin'. Stop it! Janek's room is above ours. Please don't wake him up. I don't want nothing to happen to us."

The curtain is pulled out of my hands.

"Rose needs a hospital."

"What d'you expect if you knock back vodka like that?"

"Rose didn't know. Rose might die."

"Don't be a drama queen. And. Keep. Your. Voice. Down," she hisses. "Believe me, you don't wanna see that man angry."

She looks behind her at the door. Her eyes are wide. And full of frightened.

A tear rolls down my face. "RosewantsJack."

Lisette throws her hands in the air. "What's with the 'Rose' shit? Stop actin' like a toddler."

"I'm not a toddler."

"All you do is whine, so just get out of bed and clean up this puke. You ain't got Mummy to run after you now."

Lisette stands with her hands on her hips. Her face is full of cross. Her eyes are full of tears. She lifts up her big T-shirt and wipes them away. Her legs are very thin.

"Is it today still?"

"Of course it's today."

"When I arrived day?"

"For fuck's sake—oh, I get it, no it's next day. You slept for hours, all the rest of Saturday and all night."

"I vanished a day. Nonono. I was going to Jack."

"Go and clean up, your smell makes *me* want to vomit."

I don't move. I think I'll do more sick if I move.

Lisette grabs a can of orange by her bed and drinks. "Sit in your puke if you want to." She climbs back into her bed and pulls her covers up to her nose.

I look down at my front and I start to really cry. I can't stop. Lisette gets her pillow and puts it over her face.

I hurt all over and inside. I open my mouth and do loud crying.

Lisette throws her covers off and smacks her hand over my mouth. I choke. I can't breathe.

"Shut it, Rose, I ain't telling you again. *You'll...wake... Janek* and then we're done for. Didn't you hear me before?"

She takes her hand away and puts a finger to her lips. Her face is worried white. We look at each other. All her cross-patch has gone. Her hands are shivering, so I take one and squeeze it. My mum does that to me.

"Go and wash, you smell really gross." She pulls her hand away and pinches her nose. She wrinkles it up. "You got wash stuff? Great, take that dressing gown on the floor if you like, while I deal with this lot. I'll go chuck it in the machine... Why are you standing there, starin'?"

"Tosaythankyou."

Lisette goes pink. She starts to roll up the sick.

I see me in the mirror by Lisette's bed. I can't believe it's me. My eyes are red, and my hair has bits of sweetcorn in it. And there's tomato sauce on my cheek. I don't want to find Jack like this. I'm a nightmare.

Lisette goes out the room with the sheets, holding her arms out in front of her. I keep staring at this Rose I don't like. I can't stop.

"Move it, I feel like shit." Lisette gets back into bed and curls up in a ball. "Bathroom's on the right just down from this room." She pulls the duvet over her head.

I go to the bathroom and splash cold water on my face. I'm so thirsty I drink from the tap. I get a picture of Mum inside me. I could ask Lisette if I can ring my mum. To tell her I'm okay. On her phone 'cause my phone got lost with my money and my tickets. But I haven't seen Lisette's phone. Or Courtney's. I can't remember Mum's number anyway. And I don't want Mum to take me home. I have to get to Jack. Janek promised he'd take me to Jack. I try and get rid of Mum in my head. She would be so upset to see me like this. I slept in my *day* clothes. I'm not going to do that again.

I'm so happy Jack can't see me like this. He wouldn't want to go out with sick-covered Rose.

I must clean up and get to Brighton. Everything will be all right. I wonder what he is doing, and if he is learning not to lose his temper. I want that more than anything. Then we can be together in Henley-on-Thames.

He wouldn't believe me in this house. He would say it wasn't a Rosie house.

My sick smell stops me thinking of Jack. This bath is disgusting. It has a brown ring around the top, and the paint is missing on the side. I try and rub the yucky brown away with toilet paper but it won't go. My head is in a drum roll. I have to hold onto the sink so I don't fall over. I must get ready to go. After I wash, I will find Janek. He can take me to Jack. He promised. On his heart.

I stand in the bath and use the hand shower to clean myself. I watch as all the mess washes away. I think and think.

I think Janek shouldn't promise on his heart. Promises should be real.

fifteen

"She's been a long time, Court, I hope she hasn't drowned."

"Hope she has, you mean."

Courtney is horrible all the time. I don't say nasty things to her. She's sitting on Lisette's bed and blowing lines of smoke up to the ceiling. She jumps when I come into the room.

"Shit, you look like ET in that."

I put up the hood of the dressing gown down. "What d'you mean?"

"Nothin'. Come on, babe, let's go chill downstairs 'cause I don't wanna see *that* naked." Courtney grabs Lisette's hand and pulls her off the bed.

I'm left on my own. I'm happy I'm with just Rose.

A can of Coke by the bed is smoking. It looks like a snake twisting out of the hole. I'm so tired and sickie. I can't be. Today I get the train.

I find my tablets for my headaches and finish up my bottle

of water in my bag. I get dressed in Jack's best sweater he gave me. It feels like he is holding me all around.

I go downstairs to the kitchen. I hear Lisette's voice saying something. I stand in the doorway. There are lots of bottles on the table. And messy pizza boxes.

Lisette's fridge gazing. That's what Ben does. It makes Mum ir-ri-table.

"Oh, it's you." She frowns. "The kettle's over there if you want it. Can you use one? Don't touch Danka's coffee in the white pot."

"Who's Danka?"

Lisette points over my shoulder. "She is."

A beautiful lady floats across the kitchen floor. She's holding a pale pink cigarette with a gold end. "You have light, Lisette?"

The lady sits down on the edge of the table. I can't take my eyes off her. She's Snow White in my old story book. She's wearing a shimmery red dressing gown, covered in painted birds. She has night-black hair. It touches her bottom.

Lisette takes the lady's cigarette and lights it on the stove flame before passing it back to her. She takes a big puff which makes her cough and cough.

"Smokingkills."

She doesn't hear me. She rubs between her eyes and gets up and walks away. "Bring me coffee, darlink."

Her voice is deep and papery. Her dressing gown flutters out behind her as she goes into the next-door room.

158

"That lady is beautiful."

"Yeah, she is. Don't go pestering her. Danka likes to keep to herself first thing."

Lisette comes over and puts a spoon under my chin, pushing my mouth shut. "Put your tongue away."

She looks unkind again. I'm going after breakfast.

I don't think I want any breakfast.

"Are you gonna come *into* the kitchen or what?"

"Does that lady live here?"

"Yeah."

"Is she your mum?"

"Don't be stupid! She's Janek's girlfriend."

"You look like her."

Lisette looks pleased. "Here, I'll find you somethin' to eat to soak up the alcohol." She opens a cupboard and grabs a packet of Coco Pops. "Sit down and put that bag of yours out the way before I chuck it in the trash. Ha ha, you should see the look on your face. Don't worry, I won't touch your precious bag."

She puts a bowl in front of me. The spoon follows, clattering on the china.

"Well sit down then."

"Where are your mum and your dad, Lisette?"

She makes a lot of noise stirring the coffee before saying, "Talk proper. I told you before it's LISETTE. Don't you ever learn?"

159

"I learn lots at Henley College... Where are your mum and your dad?"

"I don't have a mum and dad. *Okay?*"

"Why are you in this house? I don't understand this house."

She turns to me. "Who does?"

"How old are you?"

"What's it to you?"

I look at my soggy Coco Pops. Everything I say is wrong. Not like in Henley-on-Thames.

I glance up at her from underneath my fringe.

"Stop lookin' like that, Christ, I'm fifteen. Happy now? Fifteen last March."

"My brother Ben is fifteen and he has to go to school. How can you be here then?"

Lisette shakes her head. "I don't know where the fuck I'd begin."

sixteen
december 14th

Lisette has gone to be with Danka and Courtney in the sitting-down room. Courtney didn't say hello as she walked past me. She took the cigarette from Lisette's mouth and pulled her away. I'm glad.

This cereal tastes dusty. I eat it 'cause my stomach is empty, and I need to stop it spin-drying. The television is on in the other room. I like television, but I'd rather stay here. I have to plan my journey. By myself.

I get my photos out of my bag and lay them on the table.

Seeing them makes me Rose again.

My brother Ben smiles at me. His freckles have grown because it's summer in the picture. Dad used to tease me and say he drew them on Ben's face with a crayon. I can see Mum behind my brother in the picture. I've put a bit of sticking plaster over Dad's head, 'cause I don't want to see him. Mum's curly gold hair is tied up in a green scarf that matches her eyes. She doesn't smile with all her mouth 'cause she has a crooked tooth. I think she's beautiful.

All my other pictures are of Jack. His hair is curly like Mum's, 'cept his is the color of dark chocolate. He has eyes that are forget-me-not blue. They are my favorite flower. They grow at the bottom of Grandma's garden by the honeysuckle. Jack has a tight white T-shirt on in my last photo. He's tanned from being on his friend's boat on the River Thames.

"Wow! He's cute!"

"Givememypictureback!"

"No need to spaz out, I was just lookin'."

Lisette hands me my photo back.

"That's Jack," I say proudly.

"You are *kiddin'* me! He's hot, but he ain't got that Down thingy has he?"

"No."

"Why does he go out with you?"

I throw my spoon on the table. "He loves me."

"I didn't mean it like that." Lisette eats cereal straight from the box. "Sort of, what's up with him then? He's been sent away, right?"

"His brain got hurt when he was born."

"Shame. What a waste."

Courtney shouts from the sitting-down room. "What you doin', Lisette? Get your butt in here."

"Hang on!" She stuffs some more cereal in her mouth.

"Will you take me to the station, Lisette? I'm going to Jack today."

"No!" Coco Pops shoot out her mouth. "You can't ask that 'cause Janek will—"

"Janek will what, *suko*?"

He's leaning against the door. Lisette goes up to him and places her hand on his chest. He has hair curling out the top of his shirt. She picks up the gold cross on a chain round his neck and reaches up and taps him on the end of his nose with it. I don't like looking at them. But I can't stop.

"Janek...will...*what*?" He takes his cross back and moves her fringe out of her eyes with it.

Lisette talks in a funny, little girl voice. "Janek will want me to buy some clothes for Rose so she can look pretty at the next party."

He tucks his necklace down into his shirt. "Get me coffee."

Janek walks past me but I grab his sleeve. "We go to Jack today?"

"What is rush?" He pulls away from me. "You stay and have good time; Lisette will buy clothes to party."

"Nothankyou."

"You will stay as long as I say, *kochanie*."

"Nothankyouverymuch."

He walks away but he turns his head. "You do as Janek say, baby, then everything will come up Roses!"

He laughs and laughs as he leaves the room.

"Did he make a joke, Lisette?"

She looks at me and doesn't say anything. She shakes her head. "Don't know why he's laughing."

"He promised he'd take me to Jack today. Hepromised hepromised."

Lisette flaps a tea towel at me and puts her finger on her lips.

"Come in here, both of you," Janek calls from the other room.

"I don't want to go in there."

Lisette looks right in my face. "Don't you get it? Just do as you're told if you don't want us all to get hurt."

"Whywouldweallgethurt?"

"Where's coffee? Are you picking the bloody beans?" Janek shouts from the other room.

Lisette picks up Janek's cup and pushes me in front of her. I don't want to be with him. I don't want to be hurt. I don't want anyone else to be hurt. There is a lump of scared inside me. It was hidden by getting to Brighton and Jack. I knew the scared was there, but I didn't pay attention to it. I can see it now and I feel sick from frightened.

Janek waves a hand at me. "Sit." He doesn't look. He points to an old armchair. I sink down into a hole and my legs stick out in front of me.

I don't think Janek is going to take me to Jack. He wants to forever keep me. I don't know who can help me. Not Courtney. Not the beautiful lady. I don't know her. Lisette can be mean. But inside-Lisette is kind. She could help me get out of the house. In secret. I shiver.

I look at the television to block out the not-good pictures running in and out of my eyes. It shows some people icing a

Christmas cake. I do that with Grandma. I can't look anymore. I don't want to fall into pieces.

Danka picks the varnish off her nails. There is a pile of
little red bits on the carpet. Janek tries to kiss her but she
pushes him away. He puts his hand inside her dressing gown.

I want him to stop. "Leaveheralone!"

Janek knocks his coffee over. "*Kurwa!*"

Danka sits up and looks right at me. Her eyes go big. "Why
is this girl here?"

Janek waves his hand at Lisette and Courtney. "Clean this up."

Danka turns to me. "I have a brother like you, back home
in Poland. I miss him very much."

A phone rings. Janek stands up and goes into the kitchen.
Lisette and Courtney are wiping up the coffee. They whisper
and keep peeking at Danka. She's holding her head in her
hands. The television carries on icing the cake.

"Pay attention! Pete is coming tonight. Lisette, go get
clothes for Rose, something sweet and pretty, not these, what
do you call them, motor-biker boots?" As he talks, Janek kicks
my purple Dr. Martens with his foot.

"Ilovemyboots."

"Sure you do, baby, but no one parties in ugly boots. Come,
don't look like that, you be pleased, yes? Every little girl wants
princess dress. Lisette, get shoes too."

"What size?"

"Why you ask me? You know this stuff." He takes a big,

big pile of money out of his pocket and gives some to Lisette. "And get something sexy for you."

"Woohoo, shopping. Can Court come too?"

"No, she watch the girl, so go shop-shop, shop!"

"Sorry, Court. What's your shoe size, Rose? Three?"

"Two and a half. I like my boots."

"Yeah, but who don't love new shoes? Reckon you're a dress size six-to-eightish?"

I don't answer. I don't want baby shoes or a princess dress. I don't want another party. Lisette shrugs and skips out the door.

"Hey!" Janek calls after her. "You watching how you behave, don't be drawing the attention to yourself. And no disrespecting the neighbors...or the shopping staff."

Lisette sticks her head back through the doorway. "Yeah yeah, I know. We ain't got neighbors anyway."

"We are having neighbors on the left side. No cheeking Janek or I'll send Courtney out instead."

"Bye!" Lisette shouts and we hear a door slam.

I want to go with her. But I don't want shopping. I want Victoria Station. Circle line. I don't know how many stops. I try and work it out but I don't know where this house is.

Courtney bangs 'round the room picking up all the mess. She sends me hate-eyes.

I want to go outside and ask a nice person for help. But Courtney won't let me. And Lisette told me Janek would hurt me if I go.

Janek is whispering in Danka's ear. He stands up and says to me, "Stay in that chair until I telling you otherwise."

His tongue licks his lips.

In my head I get a picture of Kaa the snake. In *Jungle Book*. He sing-hisses in my ear.

I make myself as small as I can.

seventeen
december 14th

It's just me now.

I throw the cushion away from my face. It smells of old wee and smoke. I can't rub it off my face. I twist my bottom round and the armchair squeaks. I hold my breath. Janek told me not to move.

The chair is broken. I stick my finger in a hole and pull out some stuffing. Dust goes up my nose and in my mouth. I want a drink of water. But I must stay here. Janek might come back.

I shut my eyes, then everything will vanish.

I can hear something bump. It's coming from the ceiling. I put my fingers in my ears but I can still hear it. I bury my head down in the seat.

Bump, bump. Bump, bump, bump.

I don't want to look…but I have to. I peep up at the ceiling. Janek shouts out. It sounds silly. I laugh. I'm too loud! I look at the door. Please don't open.

The door is scratched up. The paint has gone browny-yellow. It looks sticky.

Someone has drawn on the walls. That's naughty. There are three ducks flying up the wall. The little one has a broken wing. His head is pointing down. He's falling from the sky.

My leg has gone fuzzy. I can't get up and walk it. Jack would rub it for me. He'd make all the pins and needles go away.

I don't know if Jack knows I'm lost. He'd come and save me. He'd take me away from this badbad house.

I don't think Jack will find me.

eighteen
december 14th

"She's still asleep, thank God."

Lisette and Courtney are sitting on the floor with a pile of colored bags between them. I wish I was asleep. I'm just pretending. I don't want to talk.

"What d'you think of these, Court?"

I peep through my half open eyes. Lisette is holding up a pair of tiny silver shorts.

"Cute, Christmas-y. Do they even cover your butt? Can I borrow them?"

"Fuck off, I haven't even worn them yet."

My eyelids shut them out again.

"Christ, she's dribblin', go get a tissue, Court."

"You get a tissue 'cause I'm not touching her slobber."

That girl really hates me. I don't know why. Mum says people haven't learned enough at school. I wish Mum was here to tell her that. My mum will be upset. I've been gone two whole sleepovers now. I think she will be crying.

I need to work out getting out of this house but my body

wants to sleep. My head still hurts too much to think. That's from the drink last night. Ben's head hurt for ages after he drank Dad's whiskey. Dad said it served him right.

It's hard to shut these girls out. Their words push into my ears.

"She's gonna find out soon enough, ain't she?"

"Not from me, babe, 'cause it's wrong, ain't it?"

"Why are you bothered about some nobody, Lisette?"

"She ain't like us, she don't deserve it."

"What d'you mean? You've changed your tune."

"Chill, Court, here have some more drink. Ain't Rose got enough problems bein' a Down person?"

"You've got the problem, I don't get it."

"It's like, like—"

"Like fuckin' what?"

"I'm buying this party dress that should be for some cute little kid on Christmas Day and—"

"What are you on about?"

"I'm tryin' to tell you, you stupid cow. Oi! Don't throw Doritos at me. That purple party dress, Court, I hate it. I hate what it means and bein' part of this mess. She, Rose, ain't got a clue about any of this shit. The games. The men. The sex. She's innocent, right? She's everythin' we're not, everythin' we lost. If Rose gets hurt, then it's like, like we lose everythin' all over again."

"You've lost it."

"Who's going to hurt Rose?"

171

"O-M-G! You nearly gave me a heart attack. How long you been listenin'?"

"Who'sgoingtohurtRose?"

Courtney gets up and knocks Lisette out of the way. "I ain't doin' this, you sort it."

I stand in front of Lisette. "WHO'S GOING TO HURT ROSE?"

"No one is goin' to hurt you."

"I'mnotstupid. I'mnotstupid."

"Okay, okay, stop stressin', you're doin' my head in."

"I don't want to be hurt. I want Jack. I w...want my mum."

My frightened takes me over. I grab the TV controls and hit them against my head. I want to knock the scared out.

"Rose! Stop! What you doin'? Stop hittin' yourself and give me those TV controls. Give me the bloody controls! COURTNEY!"

"For fuck's sake, Lisette, get her to shut up."

"I'm tryin' but she's gone spastic."

Courtney slaps me. It knocks my breath out of me. I fall to the floor. Tears run out of my eyes.

Shehitmeshehitme.

I don't want to be Rose any more.

Lisette lifts my face up by my chin. "What's Janek goin' to say when he sees her like this, Courtney? He'll kill us."

"Us? I don't give a shit about her. You sort it since you care so much about her all of a sudden."

"Courtney, please?"

172

Courtney pushes past us. At the door she turns 'round and says in a small voice, "She's gonna ruin us, babe."

Then she's gone, slamming the door shut.

I shiver. I can't stop. My teeth are chattering together.

"Rose, we have to go up to the bedroom, 'cause Janek will be back soon."

I shake my head.

"Yes, Rose, if Janek sees you like this he'll—"

We hear a door shut near us.

Lisette grips my shoulders. "It's too late. He's home."

nineteen
december 14th

We hold tight to each other and watch the door. We can hear someone moving toward us. The door knob turns. We both gasp.

"Danka! What's up?"

Danka is crying, but she isn't making any noise. She's clutching a newspaper to herself. It's squashed up in a ball.

Lisette leads her to the sofa and sits her down. She goes out of the room and shouts up to Courtney, "Courtney, quick! Danka's crying."

Lisette kneels at Danka's feet and tries to take the newspaper away but she won't let go.

Courtney runs into the room. "Is she okay? Danka never cries—what is it?"

I move 'round and watch as Danka holds out the broken newspaper. I can't see what it says.

I hold onto the back of the sofa as my legs can't stand up.

Courtney snatches the newspaper, flattens it out, and starts to cry.

Lisette grabs the paper. Her mouth drops open and she screams. "Jaycee, Jaycee. No, no, no."

Courtney hits the wall with her hand. "She wouldn't kill herself, there's no way she'd throw herself in front of a tube train! Sh...she..."

Lisette throws the paper on the floor. "*He* did it... That bastard Janek made her so bloody miserable. He made her starve herself when she weren't even fat! And he always made her go with Pete, who she hated. And she was s...sweet and k...kind.'

Danka folds her arms around Lisette.

"She weren't w...worthless, were she, Danka?"

Danka shakes her head and pulls Courtney into her arms too.

It makes me sad they are sad. I don't feel right watching them. I don't like the things they are saying.

As I go into the kitchen, I hear Lisette whimpering like my dog when she's hurting. "He did it. He did it."

I put my hands over my ears, but I can still hear them. I need water, but I can't turn the tap on.

I'mscared. I need to work out what Janek did. I know it's important.

My face is hot and burny where Courtney hit it. My heart is beating on my face.

IcantthinkIcantthink.

My purple bag is tucked under the table. I pick it up and hold onto my Jack. A cold wind blows into the kitchen from somewhere. I put my bag back and follow the air out of the kitchen. The front door is open.

No one is watching me. Janek isn't here. I get my brain to work.

I run up the stairs and look for my coat and hat. I trip on the rug and hit my elbow. I'm clumsy 'cause I'm rushing. I don't have time to rub it better. My clothes are sticking out from under the bed. My arm gets stuck in my coat sleeve. I want to cry. I swallow it down. I don't bother putting my hat on. I squash it up in my bag. When I lift my head up, Lisette is standing in the doorway. Her eyes are red and puffed up.

"W...what you doin'?" she hiccups.

"RosegoingtoJack." My words flutter in my mouth. "Please-letmego."

She shakes her head. "You'll never get away on your own."

"I have to. Janekbad."

She nods. Then she sits on the bed and picks at the duvet. "This cover must 'ave been quite pretty once." She gets up and paces.

I step back. I'm too jellylike to run past her.

She kicks a sneaker at the wall. "I'm coming with you. Let's get out of this shit hole."

I don't know why she says this. I can't sort her words out. "Why are you coming with Rose now?"

"One of my best friends died 'cause of how Janek is."

My brain can't get these words. They're too wrong. "We must go to the police."

"No, never, we'll all be done for. I'll take you to Victoria and you can get to Jack."

"Wherewillyougo?"

"I don't know, anywhere but here—as far away as possible."

I sit on the bed to help my frightened stop. I press my hand on my chest to stop the thunder.

Lisette is pushing clothes into a plastic bag. "Get in the fuckin' bag," she mutters. She keeps dropping stuff on the floor. "Shit, shit, shit." She leaves it there. She picks up some bits of makeup and sticks them inside a shoe. "Christ, I need a cig." She picks up a pair of jeans. Some coins fall out. "Yes! I've got that shopping money from Janek." She takes it out of her back pocket and waves it at me. "I didn't spend it all, so we can use it to get away."

"That's stealing."

"What else we gonna do? A fairy godmother won't come to rescue us. Come on, we gotta get out of here before Janek gets back, I don't know how long we've got. Courtney's lookin' after Danka, just pray she don't come out and see us, so *don't* make any noise."

"My bag's in the kitchen. I ran to find my coat and left it. It has all my Jack in it."

"Shit! Okay, okay, I'll get it."

We tiptoe down the stairs. I wait by the door. My heart has moved up to my ears. Every bump echoes in my head. I hop up and down until I see Lisette coming out with my bag. I grab it and hold it tight.

177

Lisette gets her coat but doesn't put it on. She looks out of the open front door.

"Let's go."

We burst out and don't look back.

It's started to rain. Cold water runs down my neck. I blink to get the wet out of my eyes.

My feet don't want to move fast, but I keep going. I won't stop until I can't see the house.

My chest hurts from running-walking. It always hurts when I have lost all my breath.

Houses go past. A white van on the road. Green Mini. Silver car. I check behind me. Please don't let them follow us. Lisette is in front of me. I watch her ponies' tail bounce up and down. I see the red postbox that I saw before near the park. I stop to hold the pain in my side. My head sweats.

"Don't stop, we gotta keep movin'." Lisette runs back to get me. Her breath huffs out clouds.

In the distance I see a bus. Buses take you to places. I run across the street without looking. A car honks at me and a voice shouts, "Idiot! I could've killed you!"

"Watch it!" Lisette grips my arm. "Look—we can get that bus up there if we hurry, but be careful."

The bus is getting bigger. And bigger. We're nearly there. One more road to cross. We just stop in time as a black car with black windows pulls up.

I make me slow down. My face looks back at me from the

car window. I smile at me 'cause I'm nearly at the big road. The black window of the car slides down. I see a man with very white teeth. One of them has a sparkle.

"Fuck!" Lisette screams. "Run!" She snatches my bag from me and runs up the road toward the bus. "Run, Rose, run. Run for that bus."

I try and keep next to Lisette but she's too fast. I look back and see the black car driving up the road. The man leans out the window and shouts at us.

"Lisette darlin'—hey, wait! Come back here, bitch!"

Lisette puts her hand out. I grab it and we run together.

Her breath pants in and out. I can't get my breath in. The bus starts to move again.

Lisette shouts, "Jump!"

We throw ourselves onto the bus step. I grip the handle tight. Lisette bends over holding her stomach. I cough and cough. The black car is stuck at the corner. It honks its horn. Over and over. I watch as it gets smaller.

Lisette starts to laugh-cry. She stops herself. "We gotta h... hide out."

"I don't want to play hide-and-seek."

"No, we're not playing a game, this is for real. I'll explain after I've paid. Go and sit down at the back and keep your head down."

I sit down and rest my head on the seat bar where no one's sitting in front of me. I'm shaking in every bit of me.

"You okay, love?"

A lady on the other side is looking 'round at me. I nod 'cause I can't make any words come out.

Lisette smiles at the lady. "She's my sister. We had to run for the bus. It's best she don't talk 'cause of her asthma."

"You don't look like sisters." The lady frowns at Lisette.

"Course not! Anyway, she's my stepsister and my stepdad is a ginger."

"It's nice you look after her." The lady turns back 'round.

I whisper to Lisette, "I don't have asthma."

"You do now. You wanna get to Jack, don't you?"

"YesIdo."

"Then just do as I say."

Lisette sticks her bag under the seat in front. I hold mine tight. On my lap. Lisette rips a bit of fingernail off and spits it on the floor. "We gotta lay low... No, sit up, I didn't mean that, just listen to me. That guy in the car, that's Pete."

"Pete? I don't know that name."

"Yeah you do, that's who Janek—look it don't matter, he's evil, you don't wanna know him. He's gonna tell Janek about us, so we gotta hide from them."

"Nohide."

"Yes hide. If they find us...shit, I've had it, you just 'ave to trust me."

"Why can't we find a police man? You can always ask a police man."

"Get real."

"IwantJack."

"I know. What d'you think I'm trying to do?"

I won't look at her. I press my face against the window glass. Rain trickles down making everything wonky.

I watch the shops pass by. Another bus stops next to ours.

A little boy with a Batman face waves at me. I wave back. "Who you wavin' at?" Lisette looks worried.

"A Batman boy."

"Well don't, we gotta stay invisible. We've already had that old girl checkin' us out thanks to you. Where's your hat? Right, put it on properly and pull it right down. What are those two police doin' there?"

I can see them underneath a tube station sign. They are giving people bits of paper.

Lisette chews another nail. "We'll 'ave to get off at the next stop. Look, tuck your hair into your hat, all of it. That's it."

My brain hurts. I wish I could talk to Jack. I count the badges on my bag. To stop me thinking Jack things. The badges bring home back to me. Dad buys me a new badge every time he goes away for work. I have twenty-eight. I did have thirty-two but Winniebago ate some.

"Don't go to sleep, we have to get off here. Come on."

I won't let her take my bag. I walk behind her. I'm falling into black-sad. I'm never going to find Jack. Or go home. I'm going to be lost forever. Lisette is talking to me, but I don't want her to.

"Rose, you 'ave to listen, I know a place we can stay, just for a bit, then you can get to Brighton... Promise."

I stop walking. "I don't like promises anymore. They aren't real here."

Lisette carries on walking. She calls over her shoulder. "We need to get off the street. I know a person who'll help us. Courtney, me and Jaycee go there...went there, to get our nails done." She swallows. "Her name's Telah, she runs a beauty parlor and she knows Janek, knows what he's like."

We walk and run along the street. The rain is bigger now. It's snapping back off the pavement. My jeans are cold-soggy. Lisette is quiet. She looks up and down all the time. Her hair is flat on her head.

When we get to a busy road full of people she slows down. "Not far now, thank God."

We go past a shop with fruit and vegetables. They're piled in hills on a table. A man with a big beard tries to stop Lisette.

"Hey, darling, any bowl one pound only. Come, you like? You give me your number, yes?"

"Get off me!"

She pushes him away. He falls back on the table. Oranges bounce onto the ground and roll into the road. The man shouts at her and waves his fist. I don't understand his shout-words.

"Down here, it's the shop with the bottle of pink nail varnish outside."

The bottle is huge and sparkly. It isn't real. Lisette looks up and down the road again. Then she pushes me through the door. It rings a bell.

"Telah, I gotta talk to you."

A tall lady with lots and lots of baby plaits looks up at us. She looks like a model lady in a magazine. "Hi, honey, am I expecting you today? Oh my, what's up, sweetie? Who's this? Please excuse me, Dolly," she says to the large lady sitting with her. "Put your hand under the nail drier, darling, I won't be a minute."

Lisette turns to me, "Go and sit at the back 'round the corner, go on, go."

I want to stay with Lisette. But she has a do-as-you're-told face. I sit in the corner and watch them. They have their heads together and they're whispering. Telah has a frightened face. It makes me more frightened. Lisette is tugging at her T-shirt. Telah shakes her head a lot. Her beads clatter together. I give up looking. My eyes are too tired.

I'm too knotted up to think here. I'm happy I'm not in the bad house. I'm sad I'm not on my way to Jack. I don't want to play hiding. I'm scared I'll never get home... I can't talk in my head about nevers. 'Cause I can't bear to never see Jack again. I'll fall into pieces.

Lisette comes over to me. "We can only stay here for a couple of hours. Telah don't want no trouble, says it's too dangerous as Janek knows we come here. We can rest in the storeroom downstairs, and she'll get us something to eat.

She thinks you should go to the police...and go home to your family."

I think of Mum and Ben and home. In my head I say YES. 'Cause I'm scared of Janek. But my heart shouts NO! I say it out loud. "NO! If I go home, Dad'll never let me see Jack again. Ever."

"It ain't right you bein' here."

"You promised Rose. You. Promised. Me."

"Yeah, I *promised*. Promises don't count when you got Janek after you."

Telah comes over with a set of keys. "Let yourself in. Don't make any noise. I'll be down in a bit." She sighs and pinches the bit between her eyebrows. "Lord, I must be mad."

The room is small with lots of shelves. Full of nail varnish stuff. Lisette puts her bag on a shelf and gets some towels and puts them on the floor. She pats next to her. "We gotta make a plan, Rose. I don't wanna go to no police station with you, they'll start askin' questions, so you're gonna have to go and tell someone you need help and get them to take you."

"Not home. Not now. I find Jack."

Lisette kicks the wall with her foot. "Do what you fuckin' want then!"

I cover my face to block her out. We don't talk for a long bit.

"Won't your mum be worried about you?"

I don't want to look at her yet. My voice comes out in a whisper. "Yes... But Jack makes me Rose."

She sits with crossed legs and takes money out of her pocket. She counts it up. Then she puts some in front of me. And some in front of her. "Stick that in your pocket."

"That's bad money."

"You want to get to Brighton or what? How else you gonna pay?"

"Rosedoesn'tknow."

"Rose better get off her high horse then and go buy a ticket to Brighton and find Jack, but don't go blaming me if it goes wrong. Remember, none of this, me, the house, Janek, happened. You got that?"

"Rosegotthat." I feel grandma old. I pick up the money. I put it down. I pick it up and stuff it in my pocket.

The door opens and Telah brings in a plate of sandwiches and some bottles of water. "Here, eat this. It's getting dark, so you can both go soon." She checks her watch. "In about half an hour, at five, okay?"

"Yeah." Lisette swallows. "I'm sorry."

Telah turns to me. "Honey, I don't want to know who you are or how you got here but I don't want to see you mixed up in all this. Go home, sweetie, stay there, and never come back." She goes out the door. It clicks shut.

Lisette passes me the plate. "Here you go, I'd vomit if I ate anything."

"You should eat. It will give you fu-el."

"Ha! Who says that then?"

185

"My mum."

"Tell me somethin' nice," she takes a bite of sandwich, "aboug your Jacg."

"Don't talk with your mouth full."

Lisette rolls her eyes around. I think for a bit. There's lots of nice to tell. I think of our favorite place to go. I turn the picture of it into words.

"We love the river. The one in Henley-on-Thames. Where I live."

"Sounds posh."

"We take my dog, Winniebago, with us."

"That's a stupid name; ain't that one of them caravan thingies?"

"It's *not* stupid. Dad wanted a camper-van. But he got a dog."

"I'd want the dog, as they love you, no matter what."

"Winniebago loves everyone."

"What she look like?"

"She's white with brown ears and brown splodges. She has big black eyes. Her tail is like a helicopter."

"What is she—Staffy, pit bull?"

"A Jack Russell. With fluffy hair. Jack thinks she should be his dog as she has his name in her. We take her to feed the ducks. 'Cept Winniebago likes to eat the bread herself. Then we go to the cafe and buy ice cream. Even in the winter. We both like mint with little choclet bits. Jack eats faster than me and tries to eat mine too. Winniebago gets the end of the cone.

"After that we walk to the willow tree. Down by the old bridge. There's a bench hidden underneath it. The willow branches reach over the top of us. We sit there for ages, watching the boats through the gaps. If you shut your eyes you can hear the wind singing. And the tap, tap, tap of the branches on the river water. Winniebago plays hide-and-seek with the ducks. I put my head on Jack's shoulder."

Lisette's eyes are shut. Her mouth is a bit open. I fold my arms 'round my legs and rest my head on my knees. I want to be under the willow tree. Kissing Jack. That's what happens next.

"Don't stop, tell us more."

I sigh. "I'm too tired to tell more. When can I go to the train station?"

"Not yet."

"Sowhenyet?"

"Whenever. Just shut—did you hear that?"

"What?"

"Shouting." She looks very scared. Her hand squeezes my fingers up.

Above our heads we hear a muffled scream. Something hits the floor.

"Oh my God! Quick, Rose, pass me them keys."

I drop them and Lisette lets out a whimper of frightened. She snatches them off the floor and throws herself at the door. Her hands are shaking so much the key won't go in the lock.

"Got it," she says, falling to the floor with her back against the door.

Upstairs has gone quiet. Lisette crawls over to me on her hands and knees. Her eyes are huge.

"I think it's him, Janek." A tear rolls down her face. It falls on my jeans.

"Nononono."

"Shush." She puts a finger on my lips.

I hear thud, thud, thud, thud, thud, thud. The handle of the door goes down. I wrap my arms around Lisette. We bury our heads into each other.

Someone kicks the door. "Open this." It's Janek.

The door explodes. I hear screaming. It's me.

"Well, well, well. What have we here? How very cozy." He stands in front of us. I can smell his aftershave.

He crouches down and lifts up Lisette's chin. I don't want to look at him.

His voice is soft and gentle. I open my eyes.

"Hasn't Janek looked after you, *kurwo*? This word is meaning the whore, because that's what you are, yes...? Answer me."

"Y...yes."

"Good. Then Janek is not understanding this running away from him, and stealing of his property." He turns to look at me and smiles. "Was I not good to you, *dziecino*, my baby?" He strokes his finger down my cheek.

188

I want to rub and rub it away. I must be still. I sit on my hands to stop them shaking.

Janek clicks his fingers making us both jump. "We will talk about this more at home."

He pulls Lisette to her feet. She's shaking all over. Janek picks up my bag and waves it in front of me. I try to jump up and catch it. He laughs and holds it higher. Then he swings it over his shoulder. I follow behind him up the stairs. He keeps his hand on Lisette's back. She's holding her bag tight to her. Her head is down. Black tear dots appear on the stairs.

JackJackJack, I say in my head. MyJack.

The shop is dark. We kick broken bottles as we walk through. My foot slips on something wet.

"Not that way, the back door." Janek moves Lisette round. "You, go in front now and don't make a noise."

We go through a small kitchen with a table. Telah's sitting on a chair. Her head is resting on the table. She's asleep. I hear Lisette sob.

Janek pushes her forward. "Keep going."

The back door is open. We walk down a little road between two high walls. It smells of dog toilet.

A big man with no hair and wolf eyes blocks the end of the road. He turns when he hears us and holds his hand up. "Wait!... Okay, you coming now." He stamps his foot on his cigarette. It hisses in the snow. "Get in car. Hurry up!" He slams the door behind us.

Janek climbs into the front seat. "When we get home, you will go to bedroom. Then you dress for party. Then you have your bag back. Yes?"

I can't speak. I don't want to open my eyes 'cause I know when I do the bad men will still be there.

twenty
december 14th

I'm curled up on the bed. I don't care about my dirty boots. I have red nail varnish on the toe and bottom of one boot. People shout downstairs. Someone screams. I hear it even with my coat over my head. A door shuts outside the window. I sit up and peep 'round the edge of the curtain. The ugly man with wolf eyes looks up at me. I drop the curtain and sit as still as I can.

I'm not brave any more.

The bedroom door opens and Lisette shuffles into the room. Her hair hangs down over her face. She takes ages to sit on the bed. When she looks up, I can see her eyes have been forever-crying.

"I so wanted to get away from this... That ain't never goin' to happen now... Not for me." Her words are whisper-quiet.

She looks like she is going to talk more but she takes a big shuddery breath instead. She holds her side. Her knuckle bones are white. She lifts the edge of her top and wipes her eyes with it. Underneath it, I can see red marks with some purple showing through. All over her rib bones.

I fold myself up. After a bit a hand rests on my head. "Look, Rose, we gotta talk."

"Notalk. I w...want J...Jack."

"Listen to me, you wanna see your Jack again you gotta play the game for a bit longer."

"Rose not playing games."

"*I'm* not playin'. You see, you've gotta be grown-up."

I nod. She looks serious, like my mum when she talks about important stuff. Inside my head I put my mum's face on to her face, so I can listen.

"You gotta go along with what Janek says."

"Why? Badpeoplegotoprison."

"Well he ain't goin' anywhere, so you gotta do everythin' I say. You get your party dress on and 'ave a drink; but you just sip it, right? Most of all, smile at Pete. Nothin's gonna happen, okay? Nothin'. At first they just give you alcohol and drugs, and lots of presents like perfume and jewelery. You don't ask why, you just take it for granted, 'cause you ain't had nothin' like it before. It's ages before they want anything from you." She stops and swallows. Her eyes tear up again. "You keep smilin' at Pete, and I'll do the rest for you."

"NonononoIcan't."

"You've got to, babe, you've got to." Her words tremble. "Just pretend, then I'll take care of you."

I turn my back to her. I want to scream out loud, but I

mustn't. I hear Lisette sniffing. It turns into a big snort. Her head is buried in her pillow and she shakes and shakes.

I watch her for a bit. I don't know how to make her better. Or any of this. I go and sit next to her on the bed. I stroke her arm. I whisper words to her. I tell her some more about Winniebago and how she rolls over on her back, 'cause she likes to have her tummy tickled. After a while Lisette gets quiet again. She turns around.

"I like that."

"What, Lisette?"

"You strokin' my arm."

"My mum strokes my arm when I'm upset."

"I'd like your mum... She done good by you."

"Youcomewithme?"

Lisette laugh-cries. "I can't!"

"Janek BAD. Whydoyoustayhere?"

"I...ain't got nothin' else."

"You can share my family."

"Hah! I can just see your mum's face if you turn up with me."

"If you're not in love it's *bad* sex."

Lisette chokes. "I ain't gonna ask how you know that!" She fiddles with her earring. "You know somethin', Rose? You ain't stupid at all."

That makes tears in my eyes.

"Tell me more about your life, Rose, like before. That was good."

Her eyes are so full of sad, I start to talk. "Jack and me are going to have a winter picnic. On Christmas Eve."

"You can't have a picnic in the winter."

"Why not?"

"Dunno really—it's too cold for a start."

"Do you want me to tell you about it or not?"

"Yeah I do."

"Jack and me are going to sit by our river. You know, the one I said before. Next to the museum that looks like a ship."

"Course I know, except you didn't tell me about no ship bit."

"It's not a real ship. It's a museum building that *looks* like a ship."

"Cool...I'd like to see that."

"We'll sit under our willow tree. It's lost its leaves as it's winter." I stop as a big lump makes my words vanish.

Lisette sighs. Her eyelids have dropped down. "Don't stop."

I swallow and swallow. "I thought you were asleep."

"I was tryin' to see that boat buildin' and everythin'."

"Jack will put a picnic blanket on the bench. I'll have to shut my eyes. When I open them, he will be holding a white rose in his hands. D'you want to know what he'll say? '*It's a snow-rose for a special Rose, like you.*' All the prickles will be cut off with the cheese knife, so I don't get hurt."

"In your dreams!"

"Shush! Now I've lost the spot."

"Cheese knife."

194

"Okayyeah. After that, Jack will unpack the picnic. Everything will be white and sparkly. There will be big marsh-mellows with icing sugar dust that taste like, like— sugar pillows! And we'll have white chocolate cupcakes with silver stars on top. Jack will pop one in my mouth. Guess what?"

"What? Tell me!"

"They are going to sparkle on my tongue! Best of all," Lisette tries to sit up, "Jack will hold out his hand, and..."

"Go on!"

"Waitaminute, I'm thinking. I know, a little white sugar mouse will be curled up on it. With blue eyes and a pink nose. We can take it in turns to lick it."

"How very sweet." Janek leans against the door. He slowly claps his hands. "Time to get dressed. *Pospiesz się* ! Hurry up!"

He throws the purple party dress at me. It lands on the floor by my feet.

Lisette stares ahead without moving. I can see her earrings trembling.

Janek pulls her head round by her ponies' tail. "Tonight is good for me. Don't mess it up."

He slams the door after him.

I throw the dress across the room.

I hate purple.

twenty-one
december 14th

I look like a doll my grandma bought me when I was
six years old. My face is white. I have green eye shadow and
pink cheeks. I rubbed the lipstick off. My hair is in plaits with
silver ribbons at the end.

I want to rip the dress off and scrub my face clean. But
I must do as Lisette tells me and practice smiling... I'm just
showing teeth.

The dress is tight under my arms. The skirt bit sticks out
like a bell. Glittery, silver ballet shoes peep out the bottom. I
don't like this girl.

"I hate this Rose."

Lisette is next to me in the mirror. She has lots of black
eye makeup on.

"It's just dressin' up, Rose, remember? They're just gonna
look at you and give you stuff and pretend to be your friend. It's
sick but ain't nothin' more gonna happen. Not now. That comes
later when you've been spoiled lots...and they want somethin' in
return. You'll be outta here before that happens. Christ, I look

like a skull. I can't do anythin' more with this face." Lisette frowns at herself in the mirror. "You ready, babe?"

"I c…can't do this."

"Rose, you got to and I know you can do it. You told me you been on stage at college, so just pretend you're actin' now. It's what we all do."

"I'm no good at acting. Ican'tdoitlikeJack."

Lisette grips the edge of the sink. "Please, I'm begging you. I know Pete's gross, but I won't let him hurt you. I *promise*."

"Promises aren't real in this house. Remember?"

"This one is."

Her eyes look the truth.

I take her hand and we go out the door together.

twenty-two
december 14th & 15th

I sit in the corner, trying to hide.

Danka floats 'round the room looking after everyone. Three men sit on the sofa talking and watching Lisette and Courtney. They don't look at me. The young one with pushed back hair laughs a lot. It doesn't sound like a real laugh.

The nasty man isn't here yet. I hope he doesn't come. The wall clock says ten bits past the nine. The hands move very slowly.

Pleasepleasepleasedon'tcome.

The music is loud. It shakes through the floor up into my skull-bone.

Janek shouts from the kitchen. "Turn this music down, we not wanting the neighbors putting their noses in."

Courtney's orange lipstick is all smudged up. She's with a fat man. He's very old, and he has white hair that's yellow on the sides. Her pointy heel gets stuck in the carpet and she falls over.

Lisette dances with a dark man who has a gold ring on

his finger. He puts his hand under her skirt. That's wrong-wrongwrong. Lisette pushes him off. She watches me over his shoulder.

I want to run out the door, but my legs won't move. I want to block them all out with my Jack. But I don't want to bring him into this room.

Danka drifts over to me and wipes her thumb under my eye. She leans over and whispers, "Be strong, little one."

When she stands up, Janek has come into the room. He walks over to me. A bit of sick burns my throat.

"Pete will be here soon, so you smile, you play nice. You paying attention?" He holds a glass to my mouth. "Drink up!" Some spills down my chin. "Come come come, you not look, how you say here, down in the dumping place. You look after Pete, Pete will look after you. Ah, that must be him now. Danka, fill her glass and make sure she drink."

IwantJackJackJackJack.Takemehometakemehome.

Danka sits on the arm of the sofa next to me. I grab her hand resting on my shoulder. I can see the man with the sparkle in his tooth who drove the car come into the kitchen. I watch him through the doorway. He is pushing his finger into Janek's chest.

I scream in my head.

Janek comes into the room and switches the music off. Everyone stands in musical statues.

Janek is red in the face. "Get her out of here!" he hisses between his teeth.

I don't know who has to get out. No one moves but all the heads turn to me.

Janek shouts, "The streets are being searched by the pigs. Looking for runaway like her." He grabs Lisette by the arm. "You stupid bitch! She was seen on the bus. Now they are door to door searching all the area." His spit lands on her face. He turns and points at me. "Why you not tell me the pigs look for you?"

All my words are gone. Everything has gone.

"Courtney! Lisette! Up to room. You know story if you have to talk. I will answer door. Danka, sort the guys. You"— he stabs his finger in my chest—"are with me."

Ican'tgowithhim.

Janek grabs my arm and pulls me along behind him.

"You are hurting her, please, darlink, let me take her."

"Shut it, *suka*!" He slaps Danka's face. No one moves.

I start to scream. Janek holds his hand over my mouth. He growls as he takes me out of the room. He pushes me down on the floor and starts to pull away the wood bits under the stairs. JackJackJackJackJackJackJack.

"Get in!"

"Noooooooooooo."

Janek picks me up by my hair onto my feet. The pain shocks my mouth shut.

"You get in. You put blanket over you. You don't make noise."

He leans over me.

200

"Not...one...sound."

One by one the wood bits go back. The light gets smaller and smaller.

Black.

PleaseGodhelpme. Our Father who art in heaven. Harold be thy name. Forgive our daily bread... I can't remember the words.

It's so dark in here. I'm scared. Where are you, Jack? Why did you get sent away? I want to see happy pictures in my head. It won't work. Why did Jack hurt his teacher? I'm in this bad house. With badbad people.

What if I stay here forever? I want my mum. MumMumMum.

Something tickles my leg. Spiders! Don'tscreamRose. It will be okay. There aren't any spiders. It's the blanket tickling.

What's that banging? Up and down. Fast. Slow. Up down. Up.

Black. Somethingtickledmyleg.Pleasenospidersnospiders.

Jack. My Jack. I love you. You make me brave. I love you more than anything in the world.

WHY DID YOU HAVE TO GET SENT AWAY?

Why are there pigs in the street? Janek said pigs. Oink, oink.

I don't know why people want to hurt me. I'm kind Rose. I'm so hot. Something sticking in my back is burning me.

But I mustn't move...

It hurts.

Jack said on Henley Bridge, I can do anything I want to. He told me I was brave and strong. And that he loved me forever. I am brave and strong. Jack loves me forever.

Thumpdown. Thumpup. Thumpup. Thump...down. It's stopped outside me. I'm going to burst.

HE'S COMING TO GET ME.

A line of yellow hovers in front of my eyes. It gets bigger.

I bite my tongue. I taste metal.

"Rose, Rose?"

I stick my fist in my mouth. I mustn't make a noise.

"Rose, it's okay, it's Danka... Come on, sweetie, you coming out now."

Not safe. Everyone bad.

The blanket is pulled off me. I hold it tight and try and keep it over me. "Leavemealone!"

The light hurts my eyes. Danka is foggy.

"Let me help you. Please, you come out now, so I clean you up."

"Get off me! Leave me alone!"

"I'm so sorry you so scared. Poor, poor little Rose."

I'm all scrunched up. Danka rubs my legs, and I feel them buzz. It hurts to move.

"Come, little one, it's going to be all right; that's it, come out from that horrible place. Oh sweetie, you have lines of the tears running down your face."

I can't stand up. Danka sits me against the wall. I cry out as my back is burny.

"What is it? Is your back hurt?"

She pulls me gently forward and lifts up the dress. "*O jeny*, you have burn from the hot pipe. I get you cream."

I don't want her to leave me by myself.

"I not be long, I will just go to the kitchen and get the medicine. You will feel so much better, yes?"

I let her fingers go. I pull the skirt of my dress up to cover my face. I block all the pictures out my head.

"Here we are, you letting me put cream on these sore bits."

I bite the flannel Danka gives me to hold. She whispers to me while she puts the medicine on my back. It melts away the hot. She takes the flannel and washes my face. All the time she is trying not to cry. I reach out my hand to her face. "Is it n...next day?"

"Not quite but nearly past the midnight. It snows again."

"I go home now?"

"I'm so sorry, Rose."

My bag is next to me. "How did my bag get here?" I pull it onto my lap.

"I put it here, darlink, just now, ready for when you are going."

Someone comes downstairs.

"Stop making fuss, get that dress off her, and get her ready to go." Janek goes out the front door.

Danka holds me tight to stop me trembling. She starts to undress me.

I won't let her. "No! You can't see me with no clothes on."

"Here, I hold this blanket up and you do it yourself."

She gives me my Rose clothes. I pull the dress at the front.

Two buttons ping across the floor. "You help Rose. I can't get it over the burny bit. Pleasethankyou."

She lifts it over my head and drops the dress on the floor. She kicks it away. I put my Rose clothes on with shaky hands. "Now, you must put on hat and coat, because it's very cold outside."

"Youcomewithme?"

"I...I can't."

"Lisette come with me?"

"No, she cannot go with you. Look at me. You find your way home and go back to your family, you DO it."

"Findhome."

I let Danka do up my coat. She puts the sore cream in my bag. Janek comes back through the door. "We go."

I want to get out of this house but I don't want to go with him. I hold on to the stair post.

"Move now." His eyes make me do as I'm told. I let go of the post. I hear someone run.

"WAIT!" Lisette throws herself at me. "Rose! Wait!" She grabs me and holds me very tight. She slips something into my pocket. "Find Jack," she whispers into my ear.

Her T-shirt falls down off her shoulder. I can see her little blue butterfly. Its wings are trembling.

Lisette takes my hand and squeezes it. "You find him, Rose, d'you hear me?"

A tear falls down her cheek. I take my blue butterfly off my coat. To look after her. I know Jack won't mind me sharing it. Lisette holds it tight, then she wraps her arms round me in a for-ever hug.

Janek yanks my hood then kicks his foot out at Lisette. "Get back inside."

She doesn't move.

Janek talks behind me. "Walk to the car like you are with your daddy and wave as you get into it. You will smile."

Janek has his hand on my back. My bag swings beside him. I walk.

I turn and wave to Lisette. I can't smile. My mouth won't make the shape.

I store her picture face inside myself.

Janek opens the car door and I climb in. He soft-shuts it. He climbs into the driving seat and starts the engine. "There is a coat next to you, lie down and cover yourself."

ByebyeLisette.

twenty-three

The coat smells damp-moldy. It makes me sneeze.

"I told you to be quiet."

I want to cough, but I won't let me. I swallow and swallow.

I keep my crying in.

I hear music. Grandma music with lots of words you can't work out. And violins. I picture me on the sofa with Grandma. It gives me a little bit of strong.

I lift up a bit of coat. Janek has angry lines on his head. His phone rings. I don't know what he says. He shouts at the phone and throws it onto the seat next to him. The car stops. Janek thumps his hands on the driving wheel. "Come on, come on," he says through his teeth.

I hear a click. Then smoke rolls out of his mouth. The car shoots forward. I go with it.

"I tell you not to move, *kurwa*!"

I make myself into a ball. There are too many bad pictures in me. I want to make good ones. I press my fingers into my eyes to push them in. It doesn't work.

The car goes on forever. I get hot under the coat. I need water. I say everyone's name over and over. Jack, Mum, Ben, Lou, Jack, Jack, Jack. It hides all the awful.

The car starts to bump up and down. Janek swears, "Fucking road ruin my car."

The bumps hurt my head. Then it stops. I shiver and wait. A door opens and then another door. The coat is dragged off me. I wrap my arms round me and hold my scared in.

"A...am I at J...Jack's?"

Janek doesn't answer. He leans over me with his smoke breath. "Out."

I crawl across the seat. I stop at the door. My breath comes out in a cloud. When my eyes can see through the dark, everything is covered in snow.

Janek frowns. "Hurry up! Get out!"

I hide my face in my hands. I'm dragged out of the car. He pulls my hands away from me. I won't look up at him. The car lights shine on his snake boots.

Helpme.

Janek puts his face on top of mine. I try to turn away.

He holds my chin with his hand and makes me look.

"If you tell anyone about the house, or me, or my girls, I will find you. I will find your family, I will find this Jack and I will kill them, I will kill them all...and then I will kill you. You are understanding?"

207

"Nahnahnah." I try and get him off me. He lets go. I hear my mouth whimper.

"*Głupi* retard! *Dlaczego przeszkadza.*"

Janek gets back into the car and slams the door. The wheels squeal. Bits of ice fly into my face.

I watch as the red lights bend round the corner.

Janek is gone.

I stay watching, in case the lights come back.

In case Janek comes back to kill me.

I fall forward onto my knees. I wish I had a thinking cap to help me and keep me warm. I don't know where I am. I don't know how to find where I am. Idon'tknow.

I can hear water. It's so dark. In the distance, I can see the shadow shape of a bridge. There's a yellowy light glowing under it. I must walk to that light, but my knees are stuck in the snow. I'm too tired to stand up. My throat is sore.

I hear a car noise. I count out loud to block out the sound. Some wee comes out. It's nice and warm. I curl up in a ball where I am. My bag makes a pillow with all my Jack in it. I take his photo out of my pocket and hold it on my heart. I keep my eyes on the bridge light. I'll go there later. I'm too tired now.

Snow falls. It lands on my face. It covers me in a snow blanket.

twenty-four
december 14th

"**Good evening and welcome to Crimewatch. Our** first appeal involves a missing sixteen-year-old from Henley-on-Thames and I'm joined in the studio by Chief Inspector Tim Jones from the Oxfordshire Police, who's leading the search."

"Hello, Kate."

"Chief Inspector, Rose Tremayne was last seen two days ago."

"Yes, that's right. She left home just before nine in the morning on Friday, December the twelfth to head to Henley College. We're anxious to trace a person who was seen accompanying Rose at Paddington Station later that morning. Was that person you? If so we'd very much like to speak to you as you could provide us with valuable information. And today, someone fitting Rose's description was seen on the C1 bus heading down the West Cromwell Road toward Shepherd's Bush at approximately one o'clock. Were you on that bus?"

"Rose has Down syndrome, I understand. Has she disappeared from home before?"

"No, her family say this is completely out of character. However, she does have a boyfriend who's currently in Brighton and we believe that Rose is trying to make her way to him. Due to the heavy snowfall, we're getting increasingly concerned for her safety. And, as you'll appreciate, her family is desperate for news."

"Thank you. We're showing a picture of Rose on the screen now, anything you'd like to add?"

"Yes, Rose is just under five feet tall and was last seen wearing a black duffel coat, cream sweater, and black jeans. Two particularly distinctive items which I would urge the public to look out for are her purple Doc Martens boots and a fake-fur bag covered in badges, which is also purple."

"Thank you, Chief Inspector. If you see Rose or have any information about her whereabouts, please contact us here at Crimewatch or the Oxfordshire Police. Those numbers will appear at the bottom of your screen."

14th December

I carnt sleep. U r out ther all alown. U came to get me. My angri put u in danjer. I mite nevr see u agen. I hate me. I sor Crimewatch with Seb. It scard me. Crimewatch is reel. Peepel get ded. Then the polise came. I tride to hit the poliseman cuz he sed I coodnt look for u. Seb went crazy. He sed I was a wanky as I wasnt thinking wots best for u. He sed I shud be put in prisn to shut me up or Il lose the girl who luvs me. Tho fuk noes y she luvs me. I thru my shoo at him. Hes had enuf of me. And Iv had enuf of me. Im scard. I carnt shut my eys as I see u lying in the sno. Al by urself. Pleeze pleeze pleeze com home safe. Ur Jack X I wil keep all my cards to giv u now. So I can put them in ur hand wen I see u. Pleeze let me see u agen.

twenty-five
december 15th

I scream.

"She won't hurt you."

A square dog with pig eyes stares at me.

I push myself up to the wall. A boy squats in front of a big, big can with holes in the side. He feeds bits of tree into it and some newspaper. Flames burst out the top. The dog whines and pushes her nose against my leg. I push her away with my foot. She shuffles nearer on her bottom and fixes her eyes on me. I tuck my hands under my arms and hold myself tight.

I watch the boy closely. I don't want him to hurt me.

He's not big like Jack or Ben. His bird legs stick out from his coat. The fur on his hood has gone solid. He coughs and spits on the fire. It fizzles.

"That'sdirty."

He looks 'round at me. "Sorry, I'm used to being on my own."

He steps toward me. I bury my face inside my coat.

"I'm moving back. Don't be scared."

After two bits, I peep out to see where the boy has gone. The dog's nose is on top of mine. She licks my face. I think of my dog, Winnie, and I hold my tummy to make the hurt go away. I can't see the boy.

I'm in a tunnel. I can see sky out two ends. The color of pigeon wings. I shiver. It's damp and dark in here. The walls are old, and the bricks are slimy-green. Water trickles down the sides. The firelight makes shadow dancers on the walls. I look for a way to get out, but the dog sits in front of me. If I move, her eyes follow me. They shine with flames.

I'm too scared to move.

The boy's shape stands at the tunnel mouth. As he gets nearer, I see he has a broken bit of wood in his arms. He puts it on the fire. The flames spurt out of the can. Red sparks shoot up to the top. In the light I see the boy's white face. He has a few goldy-colored hairs on his chin. And a big spot. He scratches it, making blood come out. He wipes it on his coat sleeve and walks back toward the light. The dog follows him. I can't get up as my legs are too wonky.

"Stay there, Bella. I'm going to get some food." The boy walks away.

She comes back and lies across my feet. I'm stuck. Bella and me look at each other. I stay very still.

My eyes are getting used to where I am. I'm not in a tunnel. I'm under a bridge. I can see a river just past the fire-can. Sometimes a water drop splashes on my face. I can smell wet mud and dog. I try and think backward to how I got here 'cause my head can't think forward.

I rest my head on my knees and put my hands in my pockets, so the cold can't touch so much of me. My fingers feel something and I remember Lisette put money in my pocket. "Find Jack." Her share of money. Thankyouthankyouthankyou. I wish Lisette could hear thankyou.

I can't use it under this bridge.

Some voices speak outside. I look at the dog. She is showing yellow teeth. Don't be Janek out there. Don't be Pete. Notbadpeople.

The dog jumps up and runs toward the voices.

"Don't leave me, dog!" I shout. I squash behind the firecan as they might have heard me. I'm cross with me for being stupid. I cover my face so no one can see me.

A howl. One, two, three barks. Pleasedon'tbeJanek.

It's gone quiet. I don't know what's happening. I check between my fingers to see. The dog runs back in and licks my face. I burst into tears.

I cry for Jack. I cry for my family. I cry for all the hurting inside me. And all the scared. The dog lifts its head up to the roof and joins in with me.

No one comes. My crying becomes a sniff and a hiccup. The dog lies back over my feet. I'm stuck here again. My back burns where the hurting is.

The river slaps against the sides of the wall. I find a bit

of calm. I watch the river mist on top of the water. Like my Henley-on-Thames home. I get another crying lump in my throat. I try and push it down. The dog puts her feet on my knees and puts her head on one side. Her paws are gentle. She looks sad too. I slowly reach my hand out to touch her.

She's a mix-up dog. Bits of brown. Bits of black and white. Her legs are bendy, and her head looks too big for her. She rolls over on her back and puts her legs in the air. I rub her belly. My dog Winniebago loves that.

Jack loves dogs. Jack's face is getting cloudy in my head. The outside world has gone. The only world is under the bridge. There is no Jack. No Mum or Dad. No Ben. They've all gone.

I don't feel well. I'm shivery and my bones hurt. I slept on top of bumpy newspapers last night. I didn't feel the lumps 'cause I was ill, deep-sleeping. My bed cover was an old sleepy bag and some cardboard. It was warm. Even though I was sleeping outside. I don't know how long I've been here. It feels like forever long. But I know it can only be one night and a bit.

I try and look in my head again to see how I got under the bridge. The picture doesn't come. I see me standing in the snow watching Janek drive away. I feel sick seeing his face in my head. I feel cross I can see Janek and not Jack. Janek has rubbed him out. Badbadbadman. I must push Janek out. I love Jack. I shout it to the bridge tunnel, "I LOVE JACK" and the bridge tunnel shouts back, "I LOVE JACK...I love Jack...love Jack...Jack."

215

"I'll come and get you in a couple of hours. Mum and Dad are in the kayak and keeping an eye out. They're on the far side of the river at the moment. Me and the guys are river jumping on the other island. I can see you from that bank over there. Blow the whistle if you need me."

Jack picks up the whistle and blows it very hard. Ben puts his hands over his ears.

"Christ, Jack, chill. Only do that if you have to. Keep putting bits of wood on the fire, so it doesn't go out. Don't lean over it or go too near. I've filled a bucket with water in case you need it. Mum and Dad are trusting you, so don't muck up. Oh yeah—and don't burn yourselves."

"YeahweknowBen."

He jumps into the boat. "See you later."

Jack and me grin at each other.

"Woohoo!" Jack punches the air. "Look at that fire. It's ace." He picks up a stick and pokes it.

I put the blanket on a grassy bit. I sit down and watch Jack. His curls fall over his face. The sun catches gold bits in his hair. He stands up and stretches. His T-shirt pulls up and shows his tummy. It's full of muscle. I tingle inside me.

"I'm going to explore." Jack finds a big branch. He swings it at the grasses to make a path.

"Don't be long. I'm going to make lunch."

He turns to smile at me. Happy fills me up. I don't want to stop this moment.

217

I watch a boat row past. Circles of water plop onto the tiny beach. White foam bubbles on the edges. Two swans sail up and look at me as they paddle their orange feet. I wave to them. One opens its wings wide up. They crack the air. The wind touches my face.

"Hey, dreamer, where's my lunch? I'm starving!" *Jack throws himself down next to me. He lies on his back. A bit of grass sticks out of his mouth. I take it away. I lean over and kiss him. He pulls me on top of him and wraps his arms 'round me. The swan honks and honks. We fall apart laughing.*

"I bet that's your dad hidden in a swan costume," *Jack says.* "More kisses later." *He runs his finger along my lips.* "Maybe not, come here." *He holds my head in his hands. The rough bits on his skin tickle my face. I vanish into his kisses.*

Behind us, I hear the Henley-on-Thames paddle steamer boat as it chug chugs past. People cheer. Someone does a big whistle. Jack and me sit up and see everyone on the boat waving at us. We wave back. I can feel my mouth wide-split in a grin. My cheeks blush up. Jack gets up and does a jiggy dance. We hear laughter as the boat steams on its way.

Jack's tummy rumbles. We fall into giggles.

"Let's eat." *Jack pulls the picnic bag toward us.*

I unpack our food onto the blanket. "Mum's given us sticks of marshmallows to melt on the fire."

"Cool!" *Jack jumps up.* "Let's do those first."

"Save-oury first."

"Stuff that, Rosie. We can do what we want." *He takes a*

218

marshmallow stick and holds it over the fire. "This one's for you."

It sizzles and smells of burned sugar. I blow on it to cool it down. I hear a dog barking and wonder where it's coming from...

My eyes half open. In front of me a black nose fades in and out. My face is licked by a warm wet tongue.

"Go away, dog!" I bury my face into the cover pulled round me. "I want Jack back. You spoiled it up." Tears fill my eyes. I want Jack back. I want the island back. I want to go home. I hear a bark again. Not near. When I open my eyes properly, the dog comes back with the boy. He stays back by the wall. He smiles at me. He looks friendly, but I don't trust him. Janek smiled. But he was bad.

I watch him carefully. There's a bag in his hands. He puts lots more bits on the fire. Then chucks an empty burger box on. I can smell onions. My tummy hurts out loud.

"Hot chocolate?" He hands me the cup. "It will help warm you up. Try and eat this burger, you'll feel much better for it."

I'm so hungry I eat too fast. I don't like beef, but I don't care. Then I remember I should get a wet wipe out of my bag, to clean my hands. I'm too hungry to bother. The dog jumps on the bits I drop on the ground. She sits at my feet with her tongue hanging out. I give her my last bacon bit.

The boy takes his beanie hat off and scratches his head. His hair falls over his face. It's the color of the sun when it falls to the bottom of the sky.

He wipes his hands on his coat. "What's your name, then...? I'm Tom." He tucks his hair back into his beanie and pulls it down to his eyebrows. He has a fluffy bit on his chin like Lawrence had. "You'll feel better now you've eaten something. When was the last time you ate? It's okay, I won't hurt you... I can see you've made friends with my dog. Her name's Bella. Could you maybe tell me yours?"

The dog wags her tail at her name and goes up to the boy. He scratches her head.

"How long has Rose been here? How did Rose get here?"

"You slept through one night and it's now mid-morning-ish. Bella found you or you'd be buried under the snow."

Bella wags and wags her tail. She comes back to me and rests her head on my lap.

"ThankyouBella."

"So, what's the story?"

"I don't want to tell a story."

Tom smiles. "I mean, how come you're on the streets at night by yourself? You could've died out there. Hang on, you're shivering."

He puts the sleepy bag round me. I don't want him near me.

"Sorry, I'll move well away from you and stay here."

"Why are you helping Rose?"

"If you're on the street it's what we do, look after each other. I don't get how you're out here? It doesn't make sense."

I don't know how to make the words to tell. Telling it

220

makes too much pain. And I can't. Janek will get me.

Bella licks my face and curls up on my lap. She's very heavy. I start to talk a little bit, when I didn't mean to. It spills out my mouth. "Abadbadmangotme."

I hold onto Bella and cry.

"Bastard!" Tom swallows. He steps toward me. "It's okay, I won't touch you. We need to get you to the police... or hospital, Rose."

"No! I m...must get the train to Brighton."

Tom makes a cigarette stick, lights a match, and puffs on it. He kneels down near me. He reaches over and scratches between Bella's ears. "Don't you think you should go to the police?"

"Nopolice! I'm going to Jack. I want my Jack."

"You should go home to your parents first. You do have parents?"

I nod. My mum smiles in my head. Ben ruffles my hair. I even think about Dad playing Frisbee with me and Winniebago. My heart hurts. Then Jack brings a big sea-wave of love. And I know. "NO! Jack first."

"It sounds like you've been through, well I don't know what... Obviously it's bad stuff? Your parents must be going *crazy* with worry, and the police need to catch the man who took you and check you're okay."

"The bad man should be put in prison. He keeps girls in his house. I don't know what he does with their mums and

221

dads. He wanted to keep me too."

"Jesus, Rose, what the hell's been going on here?"

"But Danka put magic cream on my burny bit. Danka was a nice lady. And Lisette looked after me. And made me safe."

"For sure, but—"

"No, Tom, listen."

He looks at me with gentle eyes.

"Rose loving Jack makes Jack strong... Jack loving Rose makes Rose brave. Then Rose will be able to talk to the police."

"Wow, okay, I get it...but you should still go to the police as *soon* as possible and then home, for your sake...and the other girls."

"Roseknows. Why don't *you* go home, Tom?"

"I'm happy here."

"But it's dirty and cold and scary. And you haven't any family here."

"I have Bella, I have food, heat, books." Tom lifts up a black trash liner and underneath is a pile of books with worn out covers. "See, I have all the world I need under my bridge."

I want to cry again, but I can't explain it to me.

"I *choose* to be here, Rose, because here is far better than anything else I ever had."

I try and make a picture of this. I can't do it. Tom does a sad smile. I take a big bit of air in.

"I want to go to Jack."

"I just don't know, Rose."

"PleaseTom. I find Jack first."

"But you're vulnerable."

"I don't know that word."

"Um, more likely to be hurt."

I stand up tall. "Why? 'Cause I have Down syndrome? I am the same as you. I. Am. Rose."

Bella lets out a bark. Tom looks embarrassed. "I'm sorry, Rose, but this is difficult."

I look at Tom and try and get the words to help him. "Mum told me, 'Above everything, Rose, you are a human bean...we love the same...we think the same...and we are as important as each other.' The words in my head are the same as yours. Sometimes they just come out wonky."

Tom's voice seesaws as he talks. "Th...that's amazing. I get it, I really do, and it's not you who worries me so much, but everyone else. Oh crap, I'm not explaining this well. You did a much better job than me."

"IknowIdid. You could get hurt under this bridge. You are vun-rable."

Tom smiles and holds his hands up in the air. "Checkmate —you got me there. Look, give me a moment to think about all this."

He puts more wood on the fire and goes to watch the black river. Mist rises and makes a white scarf. It floats over the water. Tom picks up stones and throws them out to the middle. I hear them *plop* into the water. Then he sits with his legs over the edge. Bella snuffles over to him. She nudges him and whines. He strokes her big head. She takes his sleeve in her mouth and tries to pull him back. He stands up and comes toward me. He squats in front of me, keeping Bella in front of him.

"You'll need to disguise yourself or someone will recognize you. I'm sure your picture must be on the news or something."

"Why would *Rose* be on the news?"

"'Cause when someone goes missing, you know, doesn't go home when they should, the police help find them. For sure, your parents would have gone straight to the police when you didn't get back safely. Then the police get the newspapers and television to show a picture of the missing person, so they can, hopefully, be found. Someone might see your picture and it will jog their memory. Understand?" I nod. "So, that's why you need to get a disguise."

"Dis-scise?"

"Look like someone else, so they won't know it's you underneath."

"How can I do that?"

"Easy, I'll go on a night visit to the charity shops, get some different clothes."

"They won't be open at night-time."

"Doesn't matter because people dump bags of stuff outside

224

the doors in the evening. I'll get some things for you. All my stuff will be way too big for you and that would get you noticed."

"Will you be stealing clothes if the shops are shut?"

"Call it...borrowing. I'll go tonight."

I hold up my money. "I can pay."

"Where the fuck d'you get all that?"

"Everybody in the bad house used that word a lot. A girl called Lisette gave me the money."

Tom whistles. It makes Bella lift her ears up. "She must've risked a lot for that."

"I don't understand what you said."

"Lisette did good by you. Now hide that money away, you'll need that to get to Brighton."

"You won't tell the police man?"

Tom watches the fire before answering. "I don't think so." He throws the hat off his head onto the ground. He pushes his hair back with his fingers. "I don't know what to do."

"Please, Tom. Jack looks after me. He helps me read better. He helps me make my writing as good as his. He loves me with all his heart. He takes away the bad and makes me feel on-top-of-the-world Rose. If I don't have Jack, I will start to vanish like Tinker Bell. 'Cause no one believed in fairies. If I go home now, Dad won't let me see Jack ever again. I have to see him. Or Jack will vanish too."

225

I feel very tired after all my thinking. Tom watches me with his gray-cloud eyes.

"I've made my mind up; I think you should get to Jack BUT as long as you promise to ring your family as soon as you get there."

"I prom—"

"Shush!" Tom puts a finger on my lips. "There's a bike coming along the towpath, quick, hide under here."

Tom lifts up the black plastic and lies me down next to the books. He pulls the cover over me and tucks it up.

I'm in black dark. I don't like it. Janek made me go in the black dark. Something squashes up to me on the other side of the plastic. I can feel Bella's warm.

I hope she doesn't move.

twenty-six
december 15th

I know you can't hear me, Jack. I'm sending my *thought pictures to you. Through the sky and over the clouds. I'm hiding under black plastic to keep me safe. I can feel you here. Like you're with me. I lost you for a bit 'cause I was frightened. I thought I was going to heaven. A terrible man tried to hurt me. He pushed you out my head. But I got you back again. I'm going to be with you soon. I think about you all the time. In the morning when I wake up. And last of all when I close my eyes to sleep. And all the time in between. I am Rosie 'cause of you.*

I love u my Jack.

XXXXXXXX

In my head I'm kissing you.

15th December

Deer Rosie

U wont get this card. But I must rite it. I will giv it to u when I see u.

I am going to get beter. Life wivout u is not life. My anger has broken us up. U are wat I think about wen I open my eyes in the morning and when I shut them at nite. U make me strong. U make me want to be a beter Jack.

I luv u, Rosie.

Jack.

xxxxx

Theze are real kisses.

The litel blu buturfli is bak. He must hav got lost likke u. He landid on my hand. I told him to find u and bring u home to me. I held him up to the sky and he floo over the wintur sun.

twenty-seven
december 15th

"I want to go with you."

I'm in a panic. I can't stay on my own.

"Best you stay here. You're still in shock and we can't risk you being seen, we're lucky to have got away with it earlier when that cyclist went by. With that hair, you'd be spotted instantly. I have the same problem." He pats his head. "Except I'm a carrot top! So, keep your hood up, even under here."

"I don't want to stay on my own. He said he'd come and get me. The bad man said."

"He won't come back."

"Hehurtspeople. I...I c...can't stay here by m...myself."

Tom gets a black sweater out of a plastic bag and puts it on. "Rose, I won't let anyone hurt you and Bella won't let anyone hurt you."

"Tom?"

He looks at me with serious eyes. "You'll be okay if Bella stays with you."

"He'llcomeback."

"No he won't because it's too risky, you'll never see him again."

"Promise?"

"Cross my heart and hope to die."

Janek said that. He lied. Maybe Tom is bad. He crossed his heart. Like Janek. I don't know what to do. I don't want to be on my own here. He moves toward me, so I back up to the wall. Tom stops and moves back a step.

"You can trust me now, yeah? I know that's hard." His face crumples. I think he's sad. For a bit we just stand still and watch each other. Tom smiles a Mr. Cheeky smile. "If that man did come back, Bella would rip his bollocks off!"

"Tom! My brother Ben says that word... How would Bella know it was Janek's bol-locks?"

We both start to laugh. It echoes around the bridge tunnel and Bella barks and barks, joining in with us. When the laughing stops, I start to cry. I can't stay on my own under this bridge that sends our voices back to us. The noises sound spooky at night. You can't stop the ghosts reaching into your ears.

Tom takes my hand. "Don't cry, I get it. You can come with me, but you do exactly as I say."

Bella *gruffs* and turns in a circle, wagging her tail.

"We've got to do something about those purple boots; they're a dead giveaway. They're really bonkers! I've got an old pair of boots that are way too tight on me. We'll have to stuff the ends with newspaper, so it'll be a bummer to walk but it'll have to do. Let's hope we don't have to make a run for it. Here, push all your hair into my beanie, and I'll get the boots."

We walk along the towpath. It's not pretty like in Henley-on-Thames. It's lonely and smells of rotting vegetables. Like my dad's compost heap. The river mist has got inside my coat, and my teeth are banging together. It's clumsy to walk in the boots. Tom must be freezing 'cause I've got his hat and woolly scarf. Bella trots beside me. Her breath is coming out in little huffs of white. Tom kicks an old can out of the way and it clatters on the stony path. Bella picks it up in her mouth and takes it to Tom.

"Not now, Bella, go back to Rose."

She drops the can into the river and watches as it sails off into the distance.

"BELLA!" She comes back to me, tongue hanging out as she runs.

We go up some steps that are slimy-slippery. At the top, Tom stands under a street light. It makes his hair gold.

"Keep close to me and don't talk."

I stick my thumb up at him.

It's nice to see shops. Be on a street. I feel a bit of happy trying to push through my scared. 'Specially 'cause I see a tube train sign. I know I am nearer to Jack than I have been for a long time.

"All the charity shops are further down on the left. Bella will warn us if anyone is coming. Don't look 'round if a car goes by and keep your face down."

The first shop is Oxfam. I go into there a lot at home. I like vintage clothes. There's one box outside. It's got toys in. When I look at Bella she has a small, blue teddy bear with one eye in her mouth. She looks very happy with herself.

We stop at a shop I don't know. There are quite a few different bags. All full to the top. I stand by Tom in the doorway. He hands me a pair of sneakers that have lights in the bottom. They look my size shoe.

Tom whacks the shoes on the ground, turning the lights off. "Don't want to draw any attention to you."

Bella starts to growl. Tom pushes me behind him and stands up.

"Tom, mate. How are you doing?"

"I'm okay, Barney. What you up to, mate?"

"Tryin' to get me some booze, see my hands are shaking—you got any?"

"No, Barney, I don't drink, remember."

"Shame." He bends down and peers in my face. He has walnut skin and pinky eyes. He pats my head. "Who's this little feller, then? Don't be shy, say hello to your Uncle Barney."

"He's my cousin come to stay with me for a couple of days. Family trouble, you know what it's like."

"What's your name, sonny...? What's up, cat got your tongue?"

He smells bad. He has Janek breath, and he can't stand up properly.

A man voice calls his name from over the road. "Barney, come here."

"Trigger! Got any booze?"

He turns and sways out the doorway. Tom and I look at each other and sigh.

"Thank God for that. Luckily, he's too pissed to have a clue about you. I can't normally get rid of him that fast. He comes to mine for food sometimes and ends up staying a couple of days. Anyways, let's get a move on, Rose. We've got everything we need now."

A car goes past with very loud music shouting out the window. I can feel it jumping in my feet. Bella whines and looks up at Tom. The blue bear is still in her mouth.

Tom stops still and takes my hand. "There's a police car up ahead so I'm going to stay very close to you, like we're together."

"We are together, Tom."

"You know what I mean."

I don't, but I keep walking and not looking.

"Shit, that was tense. They've gone, let's get home. I shouldn't have brought you with me. They were clearly looking around. That big guy driving the police car looked right at me. I can't get caught up in this; I don't want them asking too many questions. I don't wanna go back to my parents any more than you." Tom looks sad and worried all at the same time. "Let's get home fast."

I stop and Tom keeps walking. I don't understand where we are going. Bella scratches at me with her paw... Then I get it. Tom means his bridge is home. I wish I could take him to my real home. But I don't think he'd want to come. Like Lisette. I hope she's okay. I hear Tom shouting for me to hurry from up the road. Bella runs after his voice.

I'm by a window of a house. I peek through the side so they can't see me. Two girls are on the sofa eating their dinner. The room is all lit up by a huge television. A man with gray hair fills up the screen. I can't hear what he's saying. Then my face comes up. My tummy does a loop and feels like it's been hit. Tom is getting smaller. I can't move from the window. It goes back to the gray man. Then I see a picture of my mum and my dad. I think Mum is crying and Dad is holding her hand very tight. I rest my hand on the glass 'cause I want to hold Mum. I'm so sorry, Mum. I wish I could hear what she is saying. Mum and I cry together. I feel the water running down my face.

"Are you okay?"

I jump in my skin and move away from the window. I turn and see a man and lady. The man stamps his feet in the cold.

The lady puts her hand on my shoulder. "Are you all right, love? You shouldn't be out on—oh my God, Derek, it's her, the girl who's missing. Look, she's there on the TV."

"I can't see anyone, just a bloke waving his hands about."

"She was there! Look at the girl in front of you."

My feet are stuck. My legs are stuck. My mouth can't shout for Tom.

"He doesn't look like a she to me. Where are the purple boots then?"

"Don't be ridiculous, Derek, give me your phone, now. I'm going to ring the police."

twenty-eight
december 15th

"Ben! BEN!"

I watch Tom running toward me. He called me my brother's name.

"I told you...to keep up...with me, Ben." He gasps for his breath.

The lady puts the phone by her side. "You know this girl—boy?"

"My bro...ther."

The lady looks from Tom to me and back to Tom. She's frowning. "What do you think, Derek?"

He takes her arm and pulls her along the street. "I think we need to go home—I'm tired and bloody freezing."

"But he looks just like the girl with Down syndrome on the television who's missing."

"They all look like that, Ruth."

She keeps looking over her shoulder until they go 'round the corner.

Tom rests his hands on his knees and groans.

"Rosesorry. Rose saw her mum crying on the television."

"Shush, you don't want anyone to hear you. Let's go, the sooner we're back under the bridge the better."

We walk back in silence. All my bits of happy feelings have gone. I don't want my mum to be upset on television.

Tom looks around him before speaking quietly. "You should ring your parents, Rose."

"I can't. The numbers went out my head when my phone died. And then I think a girl called Mia stole it from my bag."

"That's lousy. Try and get the numbers back. Think hard. How do you know where Jack is?"

"He's in my bag."

"Right, I know what you mean but you need to find real Jack as soon as possible, so we'll go in the morning."

We walk along in silence. I keep my face hidden. Bella has to run to keep up with us. My mum's sadsad face won't leave me. I hate it's my fault. I didn't want to make her crying-sad. Choosing is hard. Choosing means someone isn't happy. I wish everyone could be happy.

Bella is running ahead now. She can see the bridge. The fire is still glowing a little bit. I want to lie down next to it and go to sleep for a long time. When I wake up I want everything to be better. When you're grown-up, that doesn't happen.

"You climb in the sleeping bag, Rose, and I'll make some tea for us."

Bella whines at Tom. He tickles behind her ears. "Okay, old girl, I'll get you something too."

She turns in a circle, then walks over to me and drops her teddy bear onto my lap. I look at its little black eye shining in the firelight. Bella pushes the bear with her nose then looks at me.

"She's giving you the bear as a present, Rose."

I pick it up. It's all soggy. "ThankyouBella."

I know if I try and talk more my voice will choke up with crying. Bella curls up on my feet.

Tom hands me a mug of tea. It makes my hands feel better through my gloves.

"I want to hear my mum, Tom."

"You said you couldn't remember her number, Rose."

"No, I mean I want to hear what she said on the television."

"Maybe that's not a good idea because it will upset you too much, plus it's too risky. You're going to be with Jack tomorrow so you can ring her then, straight away."

"No! I need to know now. I need to understand her sad. Then I can make it right when I see her."

"Well...I have an old radio. The batteries are nearly dead so I can't guarantee anything. You'll have to wait for the next news slot, whenever that might be and I can't promise you'll hear your mum."

I nod.

Tom twiddles with his radio. It hisses and crackles. Someone talks. There's a buzzing noise that blocks out the words. Then it comes back again. I let the sound drift around my ears. Soft music plays without words. I like it. You don't have to think. It takes you away to different places.

Tom sits next to me and stares at the fire. Bella yawns and shuts her eyes.

"Whoa! Quick! News starting!"

Bella jumps up, wide awake, and Tom leans over and turns the sound up. The voice goes in and out, and then my mum talks out of the radio.

"Rose is a wonderful daughter. She's smart, she's kind...and very funny. We really need her back home. We miss...we miss her voice. The house is so quiet without her. Her smile lights up a room. There's such a big hole in the family. I go past her bedroom door and expect her to be there, but it's empty.

"If you know anything, anything at all, no matter how insignificant it might seem, please just tell us, or the police. She needs to come home; she needs to be looked after. We just want to know she's safe.

"If you're listening, Rose, we love you, darling, and we miss you so much. We can sort everything out. Home is where you belong."

Tom switches the radio off. Thoughts tumble-dry around my head. I have to go home to my mum. Mum is upset, like when Granddad died. And it's 'cause of me. It hurts my heart that I've made her that sad.

Dad's upset for me missing too. But he'll be more cross with Jack. He will say it's Jack's fault I'm lost, 'cause I would never have gone to Brighton by myself if Jack wasn't there.

Things will be worse-bad now. Dad will never, *ever* let me see Jack again. I am not Rose without Jack. Mum and Dad wouldn't have real Rose at home anymore. They'd have nothing-Rose. I have to find Jack. I have to be with him, like Mum has to be with Dad. And Mum is with Dad now. I love Jack as big as the uni-verse. I will ring Mum as soon as I get to the white house with sea-green painted shutters.

Tom opens his mouth to say something. I put my finger on his lips. He has a worried face. I shuffle up closer to him. I know he will good look-after-me. He slips his arm around me, and I drift off to sleep.

I can't believe it's me! Tom holds up a broken bit of mirror. My eyebrows are thicker and darker and all my hair is hiding inside a dark blue and green striped beanie hat. I don't have my Rose clothes any more. But I had to keep my jeans on. The pair Tom found were for six to seven years old. Bella is chewing them up. Tom had to help lift my T-shirt up. It was sticking to my sore bit. It feels better now it has more cream and some bandage on. I have a gray hoodie that Tom says is very useful 'cause I can make the hood hide my face really well. It's got "Jack Wills" on the front. I love it as I've got Jack's name over my heart.

I have the sneakers on my feet. I really don't like sneakers but Tom says I have to "suck it up." I know what that means as my brother Ben says it, but it's an extra silly expresshun. My purple bag is burning up on the fire, so that no one can find it. I took all my badges off and put them in my rucksack. They make me think happy memories. Tom doesn't want to get into trouble if a police person found my purple bag. I don't want him to get into trouble either. I don't like purple anymore, anyway. The fur has made black smoke that makes us cough. It makes my sore throat feel worse.

Tom got me a green rucksack with lots of pockets. Jack is safe inside it. My money is tucked in a zip pocket inside the puffing jacket Tom found for me. It makes me look fat. I'm glad I've got some nice Rose clothes for when I get to Brighton, 'cause I don't want Jack to see me looking like this.

"You ready, Rose?"

"YesIam. Putney Bridge. District line. Eight stops to Victoria."

I was so near to the Victoria Station.

"Remember, don't look back, keep looking forward."

"I remember, Tom. So the bad memories don't find me."

"Right, let's do this."

twenty-nine
december 16th

"Sit on that bench and don't move while I get your ticket." Tom turns back to me. "You're sure you don't want to go home, Rose?"

"I need to go to Jack."

"He's a lucky Jack."

Victoria Station is full of smiles. A Father Christmas hands out bags of shiny sweets. Standing behind him is a pretend snow bear that waves his giant paw up and down. Next to him is Rudolph the red-nosed reindeer. He has a very shiny nose.

A tiny brown bird lands at my feet. He hops around, pecking at the ground. There's a big, big Christmas tree in the middle of the station that touches the roof. It hurts my neck looking up. It has a white ribbon wrapped around it. It looks like toilet roll.

I shake with hot and cold. My neck hurts at the sides.

I can't be ill for Jack.

A big lady sits down next to me and groans. Someone sits

on her other side. I stick my hands in my pockets and watch the little bird clean its wing with its beak. It picks up all the crumbs the lady is dropping.

"Don't you want some muffin? You didn't have any breakfast."

"I'm fine, Mum, stop fretting."

The girl's voice sounds cross. I don't look up. They both might see me. I hope Tom hurries up. I want to move but I better not.

"I hope they find that poor mite on the television. Fancy getting lost in London. Anything could've happened to her."

I feel the woman looking at me. I tuck my chin into the top of my coat and pull my scarf over my nose.

"You all right, love? Terrible that girl missing, isn't it? She's one of yours, isn't she?"

"Mum! You're *so* embarrassing. Come on, we need to get our train." The girl stands in front of me. "Sorry about that, my mum doesn't mean any harm."

I don't say anything. They both walk away.

Tom comes up to me and hands me a ticket. "You have twenty minutes before your train leaves on platform nine. It takes just over an hour from here on the fast train."

I go to hug him, then remember I'm a boy. I thump him on the arm.

"Save your goodbyes 'til I'm putting you *on* the train. You won't stand out so much if you're with me."

"Thankyou."

243

Those are all the words I can say.

Platform nine has lots of people getting on the train. My stomach does a head over heels. Tom puts his hand on my shoulder. "Look over there!"

There is a group of young people with Down syndrome. Two helper people are making them line up and get on the train one at a time.

"They're like you."

"*I am Rose.* Remember?"

"Shush, you're a boy, *remember.* You're Ben and I don't mean you're all the same that way, I mean you can blend in, you know, not be noticed by anyone."

"Ohokayyeah."

"So keep near them but keep your head down. Obviously that group knows you're *not* with them, so keep a couple of seats back and pretend to be asleep if anyone talks to you."

I understand and I smile. "Today I'm glad I look the same as them. Ha! Mum would never believe it."

I hold Tom's hand tight. "Thankyou, Tom. I will never forget you. Ever."

I slip some money in his pocket. "No, no no, you'll need it."

I push his hand away.

"Thanks, Rose, now get on that train before it leaves without you."

He grabs me in a big hug. His eyes look bright. "Don't forget—go to the bathroom when you see the ticket collector coming. I know you're in disguise, but it's best to avoid people as much as possible."

I slip on to the train and find a seat right at the back, up to the window. I pull my hoodie up over my ears even though I feel hot and sweaty. It's hard to swallow. Tom waves and waves at me. Then he's gone, and I'm all on my own again.

thirty
december 16th

Clackety-clack, clackety-clack, clackety-clack. I love that noise the train makes. It's saying to me, *Clackety-clack, we'll get to Jack, we'll get to Jack, clackety-clack.* It makes me de-ter-mined. I learned that word from Tom.

Outside the window, towns and trees fly by in a hurry. London is behind me. Brighton in front. I'm excited more than scared now, even though my hurting head and throat are trying to spoil it. I can't wait to smell salt and vinegar and feel the cold sea wind on my face. I'll eat fish and chips and pink cotton candy. I like the way it melts on your tongue.

'Cept I won't have time for any of those. I don't mind. Tom gave me a tuna sandwich to eat. And I'm nearly with my Jack. I'll get a taxi in Brighton, to hurry me to him. Tom said not to get a taxi at the station. 'Cause police men might be on the station. Looking for me. He said there are lots of taxis near the pier. I hope he's right 'cause I don't know how he knows that.

Me and Jack went to Brighton when it was Easter. It was the *best* day... We've had lots of best days. Jack's mum took us, but she let us go off down the beach on our own. She sat on a picnic blanket on the stones. We had to keep her in our eyes. I can see the sea in my head picture.

The water is dark green, and the waves try to throw themselves up to the sky. Then the sea rushes up to the edge, crashing onto the stones. Jack says the waves look angry and that he must have waves inside him. He's all excited and runs down the beach, roaring at the sea like a lion. His sneakers get all wet, but he doesn't care. My hat blows off in the wind. Jack runs after it for me. The wind teases him and throws my hat in a different place. It's so funny.

We decide to go to the pier. Jack stops and points at the floor. "When I was little, I thought I'd fall through the gaps in the wood. My mum had to carry me over them." Jack picks me up and carries me along the pier. Jack's mum laughs and laughs. Jack stands on the railings and holds his hands up in the air and shouts to the wind, "I love you, Rosie Tremayne!" and I shout back, "I love you, Jack—FOREVER!"

"D'youwannacrisp? Saltandbingo?"

A round face with owl glasses looks at me. He holds his crisps in my face.

"Nothankyou. Go back to your friends."

"You'remyfriend."

"No I'm not."

He sits down and eats some of his crisps. "Areyouwivus?"

"Go back to your carer."

247

"Ilikeyou. Ohno! Charliespilledhiscrisps."

"Shush! I'll help you clean them up."

"What'sthatinyourpocket?Charliewantstosee." He pulls my blue Bella bear out of my pocket.

"Ohnobluebearonlygotoneeye. Bluebearpoorly. Charliegetabandage."

"No plaster. Charlie eat his crisps. I'll make blue bear better." I push the bear back down in my pocket.

"Crispsalldirty."

"Tickets, please."

I can see the ticket man's cap at the end of the carriage. I have to get Charlie back to his group. They'll see me and know I'm not with them.

"Charlie? Where are you?"

Charlie pokes his head 'round the seat. "Charliespilledhiscrisps."

"What are you doing up there? What did we say about sticking together?"

"I'mwivmyfriend."

"What friend?"

I bury down in my seat and pull my hood over my face and shut my eyes.

"Friendsleeping."

"Then leave them alone. Hurry up! We need to be together for the ticket collector."

Charlie pokes me. "Byebye."

I keep my eyes shut.

I can hear him being told off. The ticket man's cap is nearer up the train. I remember what Tom said about staying out of the way. I slip out of my seat and go to find the toilet. It's locked and my heart starts to *knock, knock* against my chest. Someone pulls the flush chain. They're taking forever and my heart is going to come up in my throat. The door opens. I push past the lady coming out. She tuts at me.

By the closed door I hear, "Tickets, please."

I splash my face with cold water. My legs have gone to jelly. Rose must be more careful. I must be more careful. The carer lady knows I'm not with them. And I don't have my own carer. Lots of people don't know we can be in-de-pen-dent.

Back in my seat, I put my bag next to me so no one will sit there. Tom told me to do that when I got on the train, but I forgot. I keep my hood up again even though I'm boiling up. My bones hurt. My chest hurts.

I watch the world go by the window. Walls with scribbles and giant rainbow words. Tall buildings with dolls-house windows. Speedy trains that lose their shape.

London disappears and fields grow outside the window. A row of little houses with straw caps. Wispy chimneys curling smoke up into the air. A lonely cow watches over a fence. Everything is brown where the rain cleaned up. After a bit the snow creeps back, hiding the fields in blue-shadow. White. White. White. Endless white taking me to the sea.

Gray sky falling down to the ground.

Clackety-clack. Clackety-clack. Take me to Jack.

thirty-one
december 16th

I got past the ticket man at the gates easily. I hid at the back of the group of young people with Down syndrome. I was so worried my heart nearly jumped out of my chest.

Brighton Station is lit up with hundreds of tiny blue lights. I can see Charlie try to pull some off a light post.

I need to find a toilet so I can clean up and wash. So I look nice for Jack. It's too busy at the station. And I can see some police people talking to everyone. Tom said they'd look for me at Brighton. I need to get away as fast as I can. But I must stay near the group. To hide myself.

One of the police men walks over to Charlie and takes the lights from him. He brings him over to his teachers. I'm nearly sick on my feet. I put my head down.

The carer lady takes Charlie's hand. "I'm so sorry, officer, he's a handful that one."

"Keep hold of him. We don't want any other missing kids."

"It's awful, isn't it? I wonder what could have happened to her? Her poor mum must be out of her mind with worry."

"We're handing out leaflets to everyone with Rose's picture and a description of what she was wearing." He hands one to the carer lady. "I'm sure we'll find her."

"I do hope so, the alternative doesn't bear thinking about, does it?"

My neck has a pain from keeping my head down. I have to take big slow breaths to stop me falling over. When I peek up, the police man is walking away. I swallow a sob.

I take a quick look 'round the whole station. I have a bad memory. I told Janek I was going to Brighton. I look for Janek in the crowd. He wants to kill me. Tom said he was just making it up to scare me. I don't know if to believe him.

I can't see Janek, but I hear the carer lady counting her group up. I have to move away. But I can't be on my own. I turn around and see a lady next door to me buying flowers. She has a baby in a buggy. I hold onto the handle and keep statue-still. The carer lady has stopped counting. I go back to the side of the group as she tells them all to be quiet. "We are going to the pier." They all cheer. "Please walk in a line behind me. I'll go at the front with my *Frozen* flag." She gives it a big wave. "Cindy will go at the back with her *Scooby Doo* flag."

"CharliewantScoobyDoobyDooatthefront."

"You would! Well, the girls and Matthew want *Frozen*; we'll swap to Scooby at the front later. If you hadn't wandered off on the train you might have got what you wanted when we voted."

"Matthewwantgirlyfilm."

"There's nothing wrong with that, Charlie. Are you listening to me? Charlie! Follow. The. *Frozen*. Flag."

Charlie does a big smile and a soldier salute. "Yessir!"

I can't see any toilet signs yet. We're nearly at the sea. All my bones hurt. Even though I'm hot, my teeth have the shakes. It makes a pain in my chest when I breathe. I often get this when I get ill. I've been in hospital to get better before.

I don't care. I can feel Jack is near.

As we get closer to the sea, the wind blows stronger. I have to push it hard away so I can walk. My eyes cry. But I'm not sad. I want to shout to the sea. "I'm here, Jack. I did it." 'Cept I can't 'cause people will look at me.

I can taste salt on my lips. And the vinegar memory of fish and chips.

The *Scooby Doo* flag bobs up and down further along the street. 'Round the corner, I see the pier. It sits on top of the crashing waves. White foam splashes up the metal legs. A pale sun peeps 'round a cloud. It touches the top of the round roof. It turns silver. My heart sings out loud.

I can hear fairground music. And dip-diving gulls. Three sit in a line on the back of a bench. One of them snatches at a little girl's cotton candy. Her mum pulls her away. The girl cries as her cotton candy is thrown in the trash. The gulls swoop. I start to feel like Rosie again. Real Rosie. I throw my hood back and close my eyes. I wish I could fling

253

my beanie away and let the wind blow my hair. Jack loves my hair.

It's his favorite color in his paint box. Chestnut Red. "Excuse me, dear. The rest of your group has gone down to the toilets. You don't want to get lost."

A lady in a green coat makes me jump. "Thankyou."

I bring my hood back up and have a stern word with me. I have to be more careful. I can't go in the toilets yet. I have to let Charlie and his friends finish first. I pretend to look in the gift shop. I pick up buckets and spades and a yellow beach ball. There are lots of postcards with pictures of the pier and the beach. I like the one of the pier in the sunset. There are some big cards with fat ladies on, in stripy swimming costumes.

I spot Charlie outside the toilets. He sees me and waves. I go behind the postcard stand and peep through the gaps. Charlie runs toward me.

"Charliedidawee."

"That's good. Bye bye."

"Charliegotweeonhishands." He rubs his hands on his trousers.

"That's not nice." I move backward. I can see his carer walking toward us. I try and shoo him away. "Please go, Charlie. Go! Shoo!"

His face looks hurt.

The lady grabs his arm. "Charlie! You don't run off like that, you didn't even wash your hands. I've had enough—oh, you're not with us, are you?"

I shake my head.

"Who are you with?" She frowns and looks 'round the shop.

Sweat-water pops out on the top of my face. I spot an old man looking at some sweets.

"Granddad!" I call and go over to him. I stand very close and pick up a bright pink stick of rock.

The carer lady marches a crying Charlie up the stairs.

My pretend granddad has something in his ear, but it's not an earphone. I give him an extra big smile when he sees me. He looks surprised. Then I walk out the door feeling very pleased with myself. My thinking cap is on the top of my head!

I slip quietly into the toilets.

It's not very light in here. I use the toilet to change. There isn't much room, and it's grubby. I squirt deodorant under my arms. It covers the old wee smell from the toilet.

I'm happy to get out of there. I squash my charity clothes into my rucksack. Like Tom told me. So no one finds them.

I have to go up close to the mirror to see me. I look gray-ill. I have shadow shapes under my eyes. I scrub my face clean. I brush my teeth two times. I don't want bad breath for Jack kissing. I brush my hair lots, to help it shine. I tuck it back up in my beanie. I hope I don't have hat-head when I see Jack. Ben teases me about that. I'm pushing the last bits of hair in when a lady with a small girl comes in. I look down into the sink.

"Mummy, why's that boy in here?"

"Never mind, sweetie, he's just made a mistake."

"Boys aren't allowed in the girls' bathroom."

"It doesn't matter, he's nearly finished, so just go to the toilet. Chop chop!"

The girl marches up to me. "You're not allowed in here. Go away!"

"Ellie! Toilet, now!"

The mum hurries her into a stall.

"Ow, you're hurting me. Why's he wearing a girl's top?"

"Don't be ridiculous, I don't want to hear another word from you."

The door bangs shut. I hold onto the sink to steady me. I'll put some makeup on in the taxi. I don't want anyone else to see me.

I feel better now I've washed and cleaned my teeth. I smell nice too. I'm wearing Jack's best of all top I got at the Topshop. The green matches my eyes. I quickly put my hoodie back on and run out the door.

I walk along the path by the sea. There aren't many people. It's too cold to be at the beach. I watch a black and white dog playing frisbee. It catches it in its mouth every time. I wish Bella was with me. I feel in my pocket for the blue teddy bear. My hand touches the bit of paper Tom gave me with the word TAXI on it, so I wouldn't get muddled. He told me to tell anyone who asked that I'm seeing my grandma. I will say "granddad" now, 'cause I found one in the sea-side shop.

There's a white sign with black writing on top of a post that says TAXI. There aren't any cars here. As I try and think what to do, a silver car pulls up with a yellow bit on top. It says TAXI. I want to cry, but it's not 'cause I'm sad. I open the door, push my rucksack onto the seat and climb in.

Jack, I'm nearly with you, I say inside me. I can feel him close to me. I'll run into his arms. He'll probably do a high five first.

"Hello! Anyone in there? Where to, love?"

I have the address ready. "Manor House Farm, Woods Lane, Hassocks, Brighton, BN6 7QL. Thankyouverymuch."

"You got money to pay for this? Gonna cost you twenty quid plus."

"Yesthankyou."

"Right you are, I just needed to check because I've got a cousin like you who can't do jack shit."

I don't understand that. He said "Jack" and a rude word, which makes me scared.

The taxi man is trying to find some music on his radio. He doesn't say anything else about Jack, so I uncross my fingers.

The taxi pulls out into the road behind a big orange bus without a roof. It's covered in bright paintings of ice-cream cones. Jack and me wanted to go on one when we came at Easter, but we had to go home. We ran out of time.

The radio plays pop music. I don't know the song but it sounds excited, like me. The houses and shops move fast past the window now. I wave them goodbye.

The taxi man is very happy. He sings in and out of the tune. His hair is blonder than my little cousin. His skin is very red.

"You on holiday then? Seeing relatives for Christmas?"

"Yes, I am, my boy— granddad."

I can see his eyes in the car mirror.

"You wanna go somewhere hot. I just got back from Lanzarote. Two weeks of sun, looked like a lobster after the first day. That's what you want—and plenty of booze. Didn't wanna come home." He whistles along to the tune.

Outside the car window, the houses go away. There's still snow on the trees here, but the branches peep through. The knot in my stomach starts to unwind.

My chest hurts, but it does that when I get a cold. I'll soon be warm with Jack. Jack, Jack, Jack. His name makes the clouds go away. I get my mirror and some mascara and blusher out of my bag. It's tricky in the car. It keeps going 'round corners. Last of all, I make my lips shiny pink. "Kissing pink," Jack calls it.

For the first time in a long bit, I wonder about Jack and his angry. I wonder if he has got better. It's so long since we talked, 'cept in my head. That kept me going to find him. I hope I've been helping him too. And that he remembers how much I love him. His face pops up in my daydream.

"I'm nothing without you, Rosie."

I know that really.

I open my eyes. There's no Brighton now. The road winds 'round and up. The town falls down behind us. I leave my pain in the bottom of my sneakers. I don't want it with me here in my head. I look up to my happy. With Jack.

"Not long now, love, just past this field and on for a mile. Look at the sea." He turns his mirror a bit. "Wow! It's so still. That's the calm before the storm, I reckon. It looks just like, um, like—"

"A sheet of tinfoil."

The driver slaps his leg. "Ha! That's it! I couldn't have said it better myself."

I look behind me. It's beautiful. A tiny sun winks on the water. The color changes from silver to bronze. I love everything. It's where Jack is.

We're going up a long, long curly road. I can see fields edged with orange-berry hedges. Snow sits in the lines where a tractor has dug up the earth with its wheels.

We're going very slowly. There's a big truck in front of us. The taxi man winds his window down, shakes his fist outside and shouts at the driver. "Idiot! Didn't you see the sign? No eighteen-wheelers! Are you a complete MORON?"

The car stops.

"Now what?" The taxi man hits the car steering wheel.

I'm near Jack. But I'm not. I don't want the taxi to stop. Come on, taxi man!

The music has faded away, and a news lady comes on. "*The search continues for Rose Tremayne, the sixteen-year-old girl with Down syndrome who went missing a few days ago.*"

The taxi man turns the radio up louder.

"*...to be reunited with her boyfriend. She has distinctive red-gold hair and green eyes. If...*"

The driver looks at me in his car mirror.

I try and stay calm. Lots of words come to me, but I can't say any of them.

"*...please contact Sussex police quoting serial number 1409.*"

The radio goes off, and the taxi man turns 'round. "All right, love, that's you, isn't it?"

I shake my head. The taxi man leans over and snatches the hat off my head. I try and grab it, but my hair falls out all around my shoulders.

"I'm gonna have to take you back to Brighton."

"Pleaseplease.No.Notnow.TakemetoJack.Ihavetofind-himpleeeeease?"

"I'm sorry, love. I gotta take you back. I don't have any choice."

"NONONONO! PleasetakemetoJack."

"I'm sorry. I'm gonna reverse at the farm track back there. I'll lose my job if I don't take you to the police."

"Jack is 'round the corner. He's veryverynear. Pleasetake-methere."

He shakes his head. "No chance, love."

I open my mouth to scream but it stays in my throat.

My head falls onto my knees.

I'll never see Jack again.

thirty-two
december 16th

"Shit! I don't believe it. Who uses a bloody RV in the winter?"

The engine goes off, and the taxi driver opens his door and gets out of the car. I sit up and look out the back window. The taxi man walks to the car behind. He puts his face in their window.

I'm sadder than I've ever been. Jack is near but I can't reach him. I let my eyes wander over the snowy fields to the endless line of the sky. I try to find Jack out there. I imagine him coming toward me with his arms out. Calling my name.

I tried so hard to reach Jack. I was nearly there. I didn't do it. The radio stopped me.

Dotted over the white snow are huge Swiss rolls of hay. Icing snow sits on the top of them. There's a gap in the hedge next to me. I can see a house on the hill. Where are you, Jack?

The taxi man said Jack's house isn't far. Is that Jack's house? It's white with green shutters...

Jack said on his card, *The 1 paynted wite with see-green shuters.*

I don't have time to check in my bag. I zip up my coat, open the door as quiet as a mouse, and slip out. I gasp as the ice-air hits my face. I don't wait to see if the taxi man heard me.

I slip through the gap.

I run beside the hedge where no one can see me. I run and run and don't look back. I run toward a Swiss roll. It's huge and I can hide behind it. My chest burns fire-hot. The rucksack gets heavier and heavier. I check behind me to see if I'm being watched, then cut across the field. I throw myself behind the hay roll and try and find my breath.

I shut my eyes and lots of tiny stars fall around me. I'm shaking so much my arms won't stay still. When I breathe more slowly, I peep my nose 'round the corner of the hay. I can just see the top of the taxi man's blond hair, turning from side to side. I want to throw up, but I swallow it down and count to ten. By the time I reach ten, the taxi man's hair has vanished.

I sit for ages and watch the world. The wind bites through my clothes. My face is frozen in a frown. I don't know how long to wait before it's safe to move. Big black birds are pecking at the ground. They look like witches making spells. A rabbit hops past me then sits very still, looking over to the gray water. I wonder if he thinks I'm a statue.

I'm so tired. My feet are stinging. My teeth won't sit still. I know I have to move before I am stuck to the snow and get Jack Frost bitten. I don't have a lot of time to reach my Jack. Everyone will be after me.

It's hard to stand up. I try and jump on the spot to make my feet wake up. I'm too weak. In the middle of the field I see a toy-size, red tractor. It gets bigger as I watch. I think it's driving toward some sheep cuddled together in the snow. I start to walk across the field. I know the tractor might see me, but I can't go back to the road.

It doesn't matter anymore. Jack is on the hill. I can fit his house into my hand, so I can't reach it before the tractor gets me. I put one foot in front of the other. Step after step. I'm dream walking. I keep going 'cause each step takes me nearer to Jack.

"I love you, Jack," I shout to the sky. It comes out in a croak.

I can hear the faint grumble of the tractor. The sheep move with it in a cotton-wool cloud. The tractor is as big as my rucksack now. It goes past the sheep and comes toward me. The sheep start to follow the tractor. I can hear their bleating mixed up with the rumbling engine. I stand still and watch as the noise drowns me out. Snowy mud sprays out of the big wheels and covers the sheep. I can see their black faces as they trot behind the tractor. I smell oil and mud.

I'm very small.

A man in a big woolly sweater sits up high driving the tractor. It stops with a shudder and a hiss and the engine cuts out. He climbs down the side and walks over to me. He tilts his head on one side and nods.

"You must be Rose."

If I try and speak, I will cry.

"I guess you're trying to get to Manor House Farm?" He points over to the white house with green shutters.

I make my words come out. "I w...want to get to my J...Jack."

A sob comes out of my mouth.

"Don't cry." He hands me a white hanky that smells of dog. "I'll take you in the old girl here. No point in going all the way back to the farm now. Might as well ring the police from Manor House Farm as it's the nearest place to here. You can see your boy and wait for your family there."

I can't make his words make sense. Then it comes in my head like the sun reaching through the clouds. I understand he is going to take me to Jack.

"Thankyouthankyouthankyou."

"Don't thank me, love, let's just get you safe."

He lifts me up into the tractor and puts a prickly blanket over my lap. I hear him talk outside before he climbs up next to me. He leans over and gets a flask and pours some hot drink into a cup.

"Here you are, get that in you, you look half frozen to death."

The tea is hot and sweet. I can feel it going into my tummy and warming me up.

"I'm Jim, by the way. Drink that up before we move or it will spill. Why are you laughing?"

"I know a Jim at my cafe in Henley-on-Thames. He's a lovely Jim too."

Jim laughs with me and starts the engine up. It roars through my legs and makes them wake up.

We drive over the bumpy field. The clouds break open and a bit of the sky peeps through. Then the sun appears in the blue gap and makes the snow glitter. We're driving over stars.

The engine is too loud to talk, but I don't want to. I say Jack's name over and over in my head. I'm more tired than I've ever been. And I'm more happy than I've ever been. Jack. Jack.

My Jack.

The tractor turns out of the field onto a road and then up a windy lane. Trees stand to attention all the way along.

"Nearly there, Rose, it's just around the bend."

I lean forward in my seat. We go 'round the corner past a huge tree with branches that touch the ground. The house comes into view. People stand outside. They start to wave.

I shake my head. "Why are they waving?"

"Because of you."

"How did they know I was coming?"

"I rang to let them know you were on your way just before we set off. Give them a wave, then."

"I can't see Jack." I lean forward to get the best view. I can see a boy with red hair like mine jumping up and down.

Then I see him. My Jack. He stands at the front, looking worried. He runs forward, then stops. Then he sees me and jumps up high and punches the air. I'm laughing and crying all at the same time.

The tractor *chug, chugs* to a stop.

Jim comes 'round to help me down.

I run into Jack's arms.

Then everything goes black.

17th December

My Rosie pleeze
pleeze dont di. I carnt
get the pikchur of u on the
strechur out my hed.

Thay carnt stop me commin
to the hospital to see u. Seb sez I
can go in the lorndri van in the morning. Hes
sortid it. Ill hide undr the sheets in the back.
I carnt get cort or Ill nevr see u agen. Seb
told me to proov I can be grone up and not
looze my tempa ennimor. I held onto mi anger
evn aftr thay took u away and left me bhiind.
When I get to the hospital Im grvoing to sit
outside ur room and wate. U hav to get
beter. I carnt sleep. Im scard. Its al my folt.

Luv u, Jack XXX

Its 4 in the morning. An owl floo
acros the moon. Its cold and cold
to me. Not long now Rosie. Not long.

thirty-three
december 17th

I can hear beep beep, beep beep. I don't know where I am. Blue light is wrapped around me. A shadow hangs over me and pulls at something on my arm. I can hear shout-words. It's Mum.

"Nurse! She's woken up and is trying to say something."

"It's fine, Mrs. Tremayne, we have it under control."

"Don't cry, Mum." I try to speak. My words struggle in my mouth.

"Hurry up, she's choking." It's Dad.

"If you could both please go out to the waiting room so I can remove Rose's intubation."

A face floats over me. It pulls at the thing in my throat.

I want to stop it. I try and grab it in my hand. Cool fingers hold onto mine.

"Don't touch, sweetie, it will be over soon and you'll feel much better."

A snake slides out of my mouth and plops onto the bed.

I cough and cough. My throat is on fire. "I know, it will hurt for a bit, Rose."

They give me some ice water through a straw. It helps put the fire out. My face gets wiped with a cloth. I can smell hospital smell.

The blue opens with a swish and lets in white light. It hurts my eyes. I shut it out.

When I open them again, Mum is smiling down at me. "Hello, darling." The sun rises in her eyes.

Dad gulps. A big hand closes 'round mine.

Mum gently picks up my other hand. "Welcome back."

"Jack?" I whisper. They can't hear me.

"Can I hug her?" Mum says.

"Of course," says the same voice as before. "Just be careful not to knock that IV drip out."

Mum laugh-cries as she gently curls her arms around me. A nurse in green pajamas peeps round the curtain gap. The other nurse goes over to her. They whisper together. Through the gap I can see a person on a bed all covered up in snake tubes. I think it's a lady. She looks very old. She has lots of wrinkly bits on her face, and her hair is snow-white. She makes a noise like my dog did when she cut her foot very badly. I don't like it. The nurse turns back to me. She smooths the hair off my forehead.

"Don't be frightened. There are a lot of silly noises on this ward, but they're nothing to worry about. Poor Mrs. Brown is very confused."

She squeezes my hand then talks to Mum and Dad. "Mr. and Mrs. Tremayne? Can I have a word, please?"

Mum doesn't want to leave me. Dad puts his arm around her. "Come on. It'll only take a minute."

"Dr. Jefferson will be coming to check on Rose in a bit, she'll be delighted to see she's awake and aware of her surroundings."

Their footsteps disappear. A door swings shut. All I can hear is the *beep beep, beep beep* of the machines again. And the old lady. I watch her nurse clean her up. The nurse has a summer smile.

I want Jack. Where is he? I found him, but he's gone. All I know is Jack. Tears fall out of my eyes and down my face. I can't move my hand to wipe them away. Where are you, my Jack? You must be sad too.

When I open my eyes again, Mum is next to me.

"You've been crying, my poor darling." She runs her finger along my eyebrows. Like she did when I was little. "I need you to listen to me, sweetie. Don't try and talk." I watch the little vein in Mum's neck. It sticks out when she's upset.

"The police would like to talk to you; not right now, only when you're feeling a bit stronger. Can you do this, do you think?"

I look away. Janek's face jumps into my head. I tremble all over. I can't make it stop.

"You don't have to do anything you don't want to. Dad and

I haven't given them permission to talk to you yet. Don't cry, Rose, please don't cry, it's okay, you don't have to do anything."

I bury my face in my pillow.

"Oh God, Mike. What do you think happened to her? And that burn on her back..."

Their voices move to a different place. I want to stop Janek in my head. I want him to go away forever. He's glued onto my eyes. I can't rub him off. My hands are wired up.

Mum and Dad stand by the window. They look old. Dad has baggy eyes. When they come back to me, I try and sit up.

"I want Jack." I sound like a frog.

"Your poor voice, but it's so lovely to hear you, darling."

"Jack?"

"Only family are allowed in here, darling." Mum sighs.

"Jackismyfamily."

Mum doesn't look at me. Dad is looking at the floor.

"Mum...? Dad?" I croak.

"Not now, Rose, you're too ill, we'll discuss Jack when you're better." Dad rubs his eyes.

We never talk about Jack. Angry-sad bubbles up. It pops before I can use it. I'm too sick to get it back. My throat is full of fire again. I don't want to swallow, but I have to. I cry more.

"Mike, why don't you go and get something to eat?" Mum says.

"Yes, yes of course, but I won't be too long. My little girl has only just woken up." Dad grabs his jacket and walks away. He smiles over his shoulder.

I want to talk to Mum, but I'm falling away from her into ill-sleep. She holds my head up and gives me some more ice water with a straw.

"That will help you sleep better." She strokes my arm and whispers to me. "Winniebago misses you so much. She's sat by the front gate ever since you went and she won't budge. Ben's had to put her food and water bowl outside, next to her."

"Inthesnow?" I whisper-croak.

"Yes, in the snow! Her water bowl had ice on it, but she still wouldn't move."

"She'llgetnew-monia."

"Ben made her a cardboard doghouse from an old box that he lined with a trash bag, and I put that old blanket of Grandma's over her. In the evening Ben carries her into the kitchen—or she'd stay there all night as well. Oh sweetie, don't get upset, you'll see her very soon."

I love Winnie. I miss her so much. I miss telling her my secrets. And her warm nose in my hand. I cry 'cause she sat in the snow for me. But I'm not just crying for Winnie. I'm crying for Lisette, as I wish Mum was stroking her arm too. She'd like that. And I'm crying for Tom and Bella. 'Cause they rescued me from the snow.

Mum doesn't talk for a bit. She takes away my tears with her finger-tops.

"DidBenmissme?"

"Of course he did. He's been even more grumpy than

normal and that's saying something. I found him on Monday sitting on his bed with your old Tigger in his hands. He said he was fine, but I knew he wasn't. He's stuck pictures of you up all over Henley, Caversham, and Reading. He wanted to go and look for you... Oh darling, you need to sleep, you look wiped out, and as always, I'm talking too much."

But I don't want Mum to stop talking. It blocks all the horrible out. My eyelids are heavy. I can't hold them up. I want to talk about Jack... I must see him. I want to tell him everything.

I hear Mum get up. Her skirt whispers as she goes past. The *swish* of the machines sounds like the sea... Jack and me by the sea. With seaweed wrapping our feet together. Pushing our toes into the sand.

Where are you, Jack?

I can hear Mum talking. I make my eyelids sit up. She stands in the doorway, holding it open. It's Jack's voice next to her. I struggle to get up. It's no good. Elephants sit on my arms and legs. I push past the hospital noises. I find Mum's voice again.

"Hasn't everyone got enough...plate? ...sneaking out your unit?"

I listen harder.

"...near Rosie. I won't be any trouble. Is she awake, Mrs, Tremayne?"

It's Jack. "Jack. JACK!" I shout. A wheeze of words comes out.

"She's very ill, Jack...waking up properly."

273

"I'll sit here and be good—I have to see her."

"Oh, Jack...not possible... Your mum's coming...and then her dad and I will have to see how she is."

"She won't...?"

I hear Jack's voice crack up. I can't bear it. I try and lift my body up. A tube pulls at my arm. Pain shoots up it. I can't hold me up. I fall back on the pillow.

"Don't even think that, Jack, have faith in her. We must all have faith, then Rose will do the rest."

"I can't bear it...I'll just sit in the waiting room. I promise I'll be good."

"Oh, Jack, I just don't know. Okay, perhaps...if your mum agrees...and I know it would help Rose a lot—"

"What's *he* doing here?"

"Calm...Mike! Stop...ing—"

"I'm NOT having him near Rose."

I want Dad to go away. He can't stop me and Jack. Not now. I can see Jack. He's so near. Dad's pushing him back. "No, Dad, stop it!" Why can't they hear me?

"Please, Mr. Tremayne, let me see her. I love Rosie. I'm staying good, I—"

"Ha, you don't have a clue what that is. Haven't you caused enough trouble? We don't want you here."

"Nonononononono. NONONONONONO." My voice won't shout. Only in my head shouts.

"Mike, please. It's what's best for Rose...surely five minutes—"

"Over my dead body!"

"Keep your voices down! This is the ICU, please show some respect for the patients' safety and privacy."

I watch as the nurse shuts the door on them all.

"Please don't take my Jack away," I whisper. I make my head sit up. I see Jack at the round window. His eyes catch mine. Then he's gone.

Again.

The nurse stands by my bed. "I'm going to do a few checks, then you can go back to sleep." She tucks a stick in my armpit. "Don't be sad, you'll soon be back on your feet. Good, your temperature is down. If we can keep it that way until tomorrow, then you can be moved into HDU. Oh dear, what did I say? I thought you'd be pleased."

She dabs a cloth on my eyes to collect the wet.

"IwantJack."

She leans down close to my mouth to hear me. "And who might Jack be?"

"Myboyfriend."

"I'm sure he'll come and see you soon."

"He'soutside."

"In that case, he can probably see you after you've rested."

"Nononohecan't. Dadwon'tlethim."

"Well, perhaps I can explain to that dad of yours how much you want to see him. He might come 'round if I tell him it's not good for you to get upset. Oh dear, you see your blood pressure's already too high. I'm giving you something to help you rest; too much excitement today, I think."

"Thankyouverymuch."

"That's a lovely smile."

I'm smiling all over. The nurse will get my Jack to me. She twists up a red button. A cold feeling runs along my arm. I put a home-with-Jack picture in my head. The nurse checks the water bag on the pole.

"Jackisoutsidethedoor. CanIseehimalittlebit? Please, thankyou."

The nurse wags her finger at me. "Five minutes, then you sleep."

I start to float across the room. My eyelids fall. I pull myself back. My head spins in a circle. Through my eye gaps someone stands over me. It's not the nurse. The green uniform has vanished. This is black... I think it's Janek.

He's found me.

I watch him. He bends right over me and kisses me. I fold my lips in. Helpmehelpme.

"Rosie, I know you can't hear me."

My heart slows down.

My Jack.

Not Janek. My best Jack is here. JackJackJack. My mouth can't talk. It's too weighted with sleep. The nurse gave me my Jack for five minutes.

I smell lemon and Lynx.

He picks up my hand and covers it up. I want to hold him tight. Tell him it's okay. But I can't talk.

"I couldn't find you when I got to the hospital. It was driving me nuts. Then a cleaning lady said you'd probably be here. I looked through the window and saw your red hair spread out over the pillow, with all these wires going into you. I felt sick 'cause I was going crazy not being able to be with you. Your dad doesn't want me here, so I'll get into more trouble, but the kind nurse told me I could see you for five minutes. My mum's coming to get me and I don't want to fucking go—sorry, I know you hate swearing. There's so much I want to ask you and so much I want to tell you. I sent you all these cards but I know you didn't get most of them. I've got some more for you; I kept doing them as it felt like I was talking to you. It was all I had. I...I thought you didn't love me anymore, but that's stupid 'cause you're Rosie, the best Rosie in the world who'd never stop loving me, no matter what a dick I am. You even came to get me. Where have you been, Rosie? You've been lost forever, and it's my fault; if I hadn't gone mad, we'd still be together. I'm so angry at me I want to smash—no, not that, not ever again... I don't want to smash anything up, Rosie. Seb said I had to get my shit together, that I couldn't keep messing up. He was right, I'm not a kid any more...but I'm scared stiff I'll let everyone down again."

Jack rests his head on the bed. His curls spill over my hand. I want to touch them. He sits up again.

"I told you about Seb in my cards, he's cool. I owe him big time."

"That's five minutes!" A green shape hovers by Jack.

I don't want Jack to go. I want him to sit here forever and keep talking. So I can deep-sleep. And not be scared of monsters coming. I try and squeeze his hand.

"Please, just a bit longer, nurse?" Jack sounds quivery.

"I'm sorry, you have to go because Rose's blood pressure is far too high and she needs to rest."

"I love you, Rosie Tremayne." Jack's lips touch mine. "I'll be back tomorrow."

"Maybe not tomorrow," the nurse says.

Yes tomorrow, I want to tell her.

"The police are hoping to talk to Rose if we agree she's well enough."

"Police? Why do the police want to talk to my Rosie?"

"I don't know exactly, but Rose has been through a lot it seems."

"What happened to her? If anyone's hurt my Rosie, I'll kill them."

"I don't think we'll have any of that sort of talk, thank you very much, young man. It's time you left, I'm sure you'll see her very soon. The best you can do for Rose is be patient and do as you're told."

The nurse puts her arm 'round Jack. I want it to be my arm. I struggle to stay awake. Nothing on my body will do as it's told. The picture of Jack gets smaller and smaller.

I tumble over into nothing.

thirty-four
december 18th

The pain in my head has gone quiet. I can breathe in and out better.

I remember Jack was here. I know he was real. He's nowhere now.

My nurse comes over with a jug of water. She's wearing blue pajamas today.

"Is Jack outside?"

"Oh no, love, I think he went home yesterday."

"Yesterday? He sat here," I pat the bed, "before I fell deep-asleep."

The nurse laughs. "You've been asleep for a long time. Your boyfriend was here yesterday, Wednesday afternoon, and it's now early Thursday morning."

I lost Wednesday. I'm making habits of losing days.

I hope Jack is still waiting for me. I can talk to him today. "Your parents sat with you for ages after that, but I sent them back to their hotel to get some sleep too. They'll be here soon, I'm sure. They've been beside themselves with worry, and I think you've put a few gray hairs onto your dad's head."

"I didn't do that. Dad grew them himself."

The nurse laughs and laughs. She's still laughing as she leaves me.

A man doctor in a white coat stands at the end of my bed. They all wear whiter than white coats. He doesn't say hello. He checks my medicine board and makes a mark on it.

"Hello, young lady. I'm your consultant. I just wanted to check that everything is going to plan as you've had us quite worried, you know." He tips his head on the side. "I think that enforced sleep has done you good. How are you feeling today?"

"Abitbetterthankyou. My chest hurts and my throat is burny still. The knife in my head has gone."

"Good, good, you're doing as the doctor ordered then." He laughs loudly. "Right, let's see how your chest sounds."

He puts his listening tubes in his ears and a cold bit on my front. He stands up and does a big smile to his ears. "Much better."

"Have you seen Jack?"

"Jack? I'm afraid not. Were you expecting him?"

"He's my boyfriend. We're going to get married."

The doctor clears his throat up. "Your temperature's normal and since your lungs sound clearer and less crackly, I think we can probably move you to the HDU. That means a high dependency unit, so you'll still have to be really looked after, as you've been very ill. Now, your antibiotics—that's your medicine to get better—"

"YeahIknow."

"My apologies, Miss Tremayne, your antibiotics for the pneumonia have kicked in and hopefully will continue to work their miracles. The infection in your burn is clearing up with the help of some different tablets. They are both very strong doses, so you might have a sore stomach on top of everything else for a bit. But I think we can try you with a tiny bit of lunch later and see how you manage with eating for yourself; something soft and easy to swallow."

He smiles at me over the top of his glasses. "Good." He writes something on my board and clips it back onto the end of my bed. "Don't do anything silly!"

"I'm never silly."

He clears his throat again and walks off.

I don't want food. I want Jack and only Jack. Why can't anyone understand?

I don't want to be in hospital. But if I go home, I won't see Jack.

I'm worn out being Rose.

Outside the window, the sky is full of cloud. The sun has gone away. When Mum comes, I'm going to ask for my Jack. He will make the sun come back to me.

A siren *howls* outside. I remember the police. Mum said they were coming. I don't want police. I can't tell them about Janek. I don't want my family to be dead.

I want to stop Janek. I want to help Lisette. Janek will hurt her. And Danka and Courtney. Idon'tknowwhattodo. I'm scaredscaredscared.

Jack would tell me to, "*Go, Rosie!*"

Grandma would put my chin up.

I can do it.

But I can't stop Janek hurting us.

A little blue butterfly flutters on the window ledge. I smile and smile. He makes me strong. Jack sent him, and he found me. My lucky blue butterfly.

I don't think it can stop badbad people.

My nurse comes back to me. "We're definitely going to move you as you don't need to be here now. You'll be right next to this ward as you're not out of the woods yet."

"I haven't been in the woods."

"Ha ha! It's what's called an expression, sweetie, and it means you need a lot of looking after still."

I nod my head. "I know those. Mum says them all the time. Hers can be silly too."

The nurse smiles and nods. "You're right... If you carry on improving like this, you'll be home before you know it. Wouldn't it be lovely to be home for Christmas?"

"Do hospitals have Christmas?"

"Oh yes, all the doctors and nurses wear tinsel on their heads, and we have Christmas dinner and families come in with presents. There, that's sorted your IV tube out. We'll keep it in to give you your medicines while your throat's still a bit raw. Now, it's about time we gave you a wash."

"I can wash me! I'm not a baby."

"Of course not, but you're still very wobbly and you have these tubes in you, so for now it's best that I help you."

The nurse pulls the blue curtain around me. She sings a Christmas song as she washes me. I like her singing. I feel lots better when she's finished. Last of all she brushes my hair and puts a clean nightdress on me.

"This is so pretty. Your mum brought it for you."

There's a bang and something rattles on the floor. It stops by my curtains. The nurse pulls the curtain open.

"Ah, here he is. Chati is going to help us wheel you through to the HDU."

A little man with a black ponies' tail grins at me. He holds my drip. He pretends to be a car as we leave the room. "Broom broom." He nods his head up and down as he walks.

I try and see Jack in the corridor. It's no good.

Mum and Dad are in my new room. There are fairy lights around a picture on the wall. Mum has put lots of cards on the shelf. Two gold balloons bob up and down over the radiator. A bed sits on the other side, but it's empty. Lots of machines sit on the wall.

"Darling, you look so much brighter. You've got some pink in your cheeks, hasn't she, Mike?"

"She has indeed." Dad kisses my nose.

Chati wheels my drip up next to me. "Good luck, *anak.*" His eyes twinkle.

"Byebye. Thankyou."

The nurse checks everything's in place. "I'll come back in a bit."

When they've gone, Mum and Dad sit on each side of me, holding my hands.

"Do you remember what I asked you yesterday? About the police coming to talk to you? Well, they're here now and want to know if they can have a little chat."

Dad scrapes his chair back. "You don't have to do anything if you don't feel up to it."

I take a deep breath and blow my scared out the window. To follow the blue butterfly to a safe place.

"I'lltalktothepoliceman." My words stumble over each other.

A knock on the door makes me jump. Dad opens it up. Two police people stand there. A police lady and a police man. The man is tree-tall and has one big, black eyebrow in a row. I don't look at him.

"Would it be all right to ask Rose some questions, Mr. and Mrs. Tremayne?"

"Why don't you ask Rose that?" Mum does her eyebrow lift at them.

The blonde police lady nods. She takes her cap off and tucks it under her arm. "Do you feel able to answer some questions, Rose?"

I'm frightened again now they are here. I check at the door for Janek. Mum squeezes my hand, and I squeeze hers back.

I can't do it. I want to, but I can't.

The police lady asks Dad to move. He doesn't look happy, but he sits on the end of my bed. She looks at me for a long time then leans forward to whisper to me. "It's okay, Rose. No one can hurt you or any of your family now; we will protect you and keep you all safe."

I don't know how she knows. Did I talk the words in my head out loud?

I make a picture of Jack holding my hand and start to talk. Before I can stop me talking. Sometimes the police lady asks me questions. Sometimes I have to cool my throat with water. I tell them about Lawrence helping me get the right color tube train. And how kind he was. And then how the snow made the trains go away. I talk about Paris and how horrible Leo was. Mum shakes her head and looks sad. I tell them about staying at the Youth Hostel. Mum smiles and looks pleased. 'Cause I was being in-de-pen-dent. Dad frowns. Mum frowns too when I say about Mia with the freckles. And how she took my stuff away. My mouth stumbles when I get to Janek. But I make myself brave. I have to tell them about him. I have to help Lisette. And Danka. And Courtney.

I start to tell but Dad keeps barging into my words with huffs and puffs and bad words.

The police lady frowns at him. "Tell me about this Janek if you can, don't be afraid, we're here to protect you."

"H...he wore sunglasses. That's silly in the winter. His blond hair was stuck down to his head. His coat was plasticky and Tesco mustard color. He was nice to me. He picked my clothes up. He stopped me crying. I blew my nose on his hanky. He said I could keep it. He promised to help me find Jack. He took me to his house. His promises weren't real. It was a badbad house."

Dad jumps up and shouts, "This is too much, let the poor girl rest—she's just got out of ICU, for Christ's sake."

"No, Dad. My mouth won't stop now."

Dad bites his lip. "This is too bloody much."

Mum is still and white. I squeeze her hand. I can hardly feel her squeeze mine back.

"Don't exhaust her." A cross looking doctor with big hair and a flappy white coat flies into my room. She didn't knock. "I need to check Rose is okay." She picks up my notes on the end of the bed. "She's only recently had her breathing tube out, so her throat will still be very sore, and we don't want any setbacks."

"I'mokaythankyou."

The doctor shakes her head.

"I promise we'll stop if it's getting too much for Rose," the police lady says.

"I'll be back soon." The doctor's coat flies back out of the room.

I don't want to stop. I want to let it all out of my head now.

"I met Janek in the park."

"Do you know where this park was, Rose?"

I take myself back to the place. "It had some swings. And a little statue of a sad lion. He'd lost his ears."

"That's great, Rose."

I shake my head. "No, it isn't. He wouldn't be able to hear. I remember! It was near the Youth Hostel. By the red post box."

"Can you remember the name of the hostel?"

"Green line. Four stops. Going west. From Victoria."

The police man checks his phone. "Green line—that's the District line. Four stops, that's Earl's Court. We had a report of a girl with Down syndrome staying at a hostel there."

"Yesitwas. Nearest to Victoria. I had a private room. All by myself. No extra cost."

Mum and Dad have their mouths open.

"You got a private room all to yourself?" Mum's words are all spluttery.

"I found Grandma's thinking cap."

"Thank you, Rose, that's a great help." The police lady writes something in her notebook. "Let's go back to Janek. He took you to his house after the park, in his car?"

"Yes. His house."

"Do you know where the house was?"

"No."

"Was it a long drive from the park?"

"No, not long. All the houses looked the same."

"What was Janek's car like?"

"It was like Dad's car. But gold."

"BMW coupé," Dad tells her. He's pacing up and down by my bed.

"Could you sit down, please, Mr. Tremayne?"

"My daughter was picked up by some sick bloody bastard, who I want to kill, so, no, I can't sit still!"

"Mike!"

"This won't help Rose, Mr. Tremayne. Please calm down, I promise you we will be doing everything we can to find this man and stop him. We're already tracking someone who fits his description. He's known to us from previous investigations. I can assure you, we will find him and he will be punished—for a long time."

"What, you knew about this man and yet he's still out there? What the hell is the matter with you people? Were you waiting for someone to get hurt?"

Dad flings his hand out, knocking my water all over the floor. I don't want his angry now.

"Sit down, Mike, right now. No, leave it, I'll clear it up."

The police lady stands up. "If it wasn't for the circumstances, Mr. Tremayne, I would ask you to leave."

That takes Dad's huff and puff away. I am all upset and confused now. I want to get my words back. Mum glares at Dad.

"Do you want to carry on, Rose, or would you rather stop for now?"

"Carryon."

"You are in Janek's car and he takes you to his house?"

"Yes. The houses were like the ones outside my college on Gravel Hill. But very dirty. There were two girls living there. Lisette and Courtney. And Janek's girlfriend, Danka. She had a brother like me. But he didn't live in the house. He didn't live in England."

"Do you know how old the girls were? Don't worry about what they looked like—we can get that later."

"Lisette was fifteen. She told me." Mum makes a funny noise in her throat. "I don't know about Courtney. They had to do bad sex with men. Janek wanted me to party with a man. The man had a sparkle in his tooth."

Mum starts to cry. Dad's face has gone sheet-white.

"I didn't party, Mum, Dad."

"Thank God, thank God." Mum holds my hand so tight it hurts me. Dad covers his eyes with his hand.

"Mr. and Mrs. Tremayne, would you rather we talk to Rose alone? This is clearly very distressing for all of you."

"No! Thank you, we're fine, just give us a moment. Rose needs us, don't you, darling?"

I nod.

Mum stands by the window. I can see her shoulders shaking up and down. I rest my eyes, and Dad and the police people talk quietly. I'm so tired I don't think I can tell anymore.

289

But I have to finish. Or it will never get out of me. Hurry up, Mum.

Mum returns with red, puffy eyes and sits on the bed next to me. "I'm ready." She smiles a see-saw smile at me.

The police lady flips a page of her notebook. "You told us that you didn't have to be with that man. Why was that?"

"Janek said pigs were looking for me at every house. In the street. I don't know what the pigs were, but Janek hid me under the stairs."

The police lady sighs. "It's a rude word for 'policeman,' Rose."

"Oh... But I like pigs."

The police lady pats my hand. "Now, you were under the stairs."

"Yes. Janek had to pull the wood out. I thought I was going to die. My back was pushed up on a hot bit."

Mum and Dad look at each other.

"I prayed to God, 'cept it came out muddled. Thinking of Jack made me de-ter-mined. In the black-dark I remembered what he said on Henley-on-Thames Bridge. He told me I could do anything I wanted to. He told me I was brave and strong. And that he loved me for always. I told me that over and over again. Then I didn't think about dying or spiders getting me. When Danka let me out, Lisette helped me. She gave me money that Janek gave her. And I gave her my special blue butterfly to look after her. I hope she's not hurt... I want her to be safe."

"We'll be doing everything we can to help those girls, Rose."

"Yes? You take them away from Janek?"

"Yes, we will make sure they never see him again. They will be looked after and safe... What happened next, after you were under the stairs?"

"Janek dumped me by the river. A mix-up dog called Bella rescued me from the snow. She was Tom's dog. He looked after me and helped me not be scared. Tom lives under a bridge. Not like Henley-on-Thames Bridge. He had sunset hair. And a big spot on his chin like Ben."

The police lady smiles.

"He kept me warm with a fire in a dustbin with holes. He gave me food. We found some clothes to make me different. Then Tom put me on the train to Jack. Bella gave me a blue teddy bear with one eye as a present. She got it from a bag outside a charity shop. It's in my coat pocket. I'm going to keep it always. Will you take me to see Tom, Mum? He saved my life and helped me get to Jack. He was more kind-good even than Lawrence."

Mum blows her nose. "I'd love to meet him, one day."

My voice gets more whispery and croaky as I talk. Everyone leans nearer to me, to hear what I'm saying. I'm coming to the last words my mouth can make. I take a big breath to help me say them. "I thought I'd got to Jack. A taxi was taking me to him. But the radio in the taxi gave me away and the driver said he had to give me to the police. I could see

Jack's house with sea-green shutters on the hill but I couldn't reach it. My heart was falling into pieces. Then the taxi got in a sandwich between a truck and a RV."

"Good grief, what knob would be stupid enough to go camping in this weather?" Dad bursts out.

"Shush, Mike, let Rose finish, she's exhausted. And don't be rude." Dad rolls his eyes up at Mum. "You were stuck in the taxi, Rose."

"ThankyouMum. The driver man got out the car to see what to do. I saw a gap in the hedge outside my window. I opened the door and ran into the field to go and hide behind a roll of hay that looked like a big Swiss roll. I waited and waited in the snow. I nearly turned into an ice statue. After a bit I started to walk toward Jack's house. I was so cold my feet wouldn't move properly."

The police lady takes my hand and squeezes it. "And then Jim Bowden picked you up in his tractor and drove you to Manor House Farm—and Jack." Her voice wobbles.

"Yes, he took me to my Jack."

Mum gets a tissue out her pocket and pats her eyes.

"I was going to ring you straight away, Mum, when I got to Jack's house. 'Cause I saw you crying on the television and it hurt my heart." I fall back on my pillow. "I'm sorry."

All my words are emptied out of me.

Mum hugs me so tight I can't breathe properly and Dad has to pull her off me. Dad's eyes are shiny wet, and he keeps clearing his throat.

"Go and get a cup of tea, Mr. and Mrs. Tremayne," the police lady tells them. "We've finished, I've made all the notes I need for now. Rose is an incredible young woman, you should be very proud of her."

The police man blows his nose very loudly. He follows Mum and Dad out of the room.

The doctor with the hair comes back. "Everyone out, please."

She shoos the police lady out of the way. As she leaves, the police lady turns to me. "Thank you, Rose."

The doctor fuss-pots around me. She pushes her glasses up her nose. "Sleep now, that's an order. You look exhausted. I don't want anymore talking for the rest of the day."

"Can I see...Jacknow?"

"Who's Jacknow?"

thirty-five
december 18th & 19th

I've sneaked out of my room to find Jack for myself.
I can't wait any longer. The floor is cold under my feet. I can't
walk very well so I'm holding onto the wall. It's hard 'cause
my drip is walking with me in my other hand. It squeaks
along the corridor. I tell it to shush or someone will hear us.
Everyone's in bed, but the nurses watch over you. I waited
until my nurse went out.

Mum said Jack was in the waiting room opposite the ICU.
She says his mum took him away. I have to check.

I can see the doctor who was looking after me on the ICU
ward. She's writing in a book. I hold my breath as I go past.
There are two doors opposite. They both have words on. I'm
too full of upset to work out what they say. I see the doctor fold
her book and stand up. I go into the nearest door. I stand in
the dark and make myself calm down. It smells of coffee air.
I don't like the dark. Shadows move toward me. I panic-grab
onto the wall by the door. I hit a bump. I press and press it.
The light comes on. It flickers on and off before it stays.

I think I've found where Jack is waiting. My tummy fills with bird wings. Then they die. He's not here.

In my head he was here.

There are paper cups on the floor. It's sticky under my feet. A chair lies on its side. Poking out from under the sofa is a scarf. It looks like Jack's. I pick it up and hold it to my nose. Jack smell. Sweat and Lynx. I sit in the sofa dent. I wonder if this was where he sat. I shut my eyes and picture him next to me. "*Come here, babe, and give me a kiss.*" That's what he'd say. And I'd fall into his arms and kiss and kiss him. And we'd want more than that. I hurt so much, it's a real pain-hurt. I try and stand up. Everything goes wavy.

I need to walk in Jack's footsteps. In this room. Where he sat for me.

I shuffle round. I think Jack made the chair fall over. The cups are all over the place. I pretend-see Jack kicking and kicking them. Kicking his angry round the room. Kicking his hurting around the room... I hope no one saw him.

I start to cry. It doesn't sound like me. It sounds like an animal. It fills me with frightened.

"What are you doing in here, my love? What's the matter, honey? Are you in pain?"

I didn't hear the doctor come in.

"You're too ill to be here on your own and you're frozen stiff. Hey, hey, don't cry any more. Come on, let's get you back to your room and you can tell me what the problem is."

It takes forever to get back to my room. After halfway, a night nurse runs along the corridor. She's upset-cross at me. 'Cause I left my bed. The doctor says she'll look after me. My sad has worn me out. I'm tired of everything.

When I'm back up in bed, I wind Jack's scarf round my hand. The doctor pulls my blanket up and tucks it under my arms. I tell her about Jack. That I'm not allowed to be with him. I tell her he won't hurt anything again. But no one believes him. 'Cept me.

"Whatcanwedo? WhatifIneverseeJackagain?"

The doctor takes her glasses off and rubs her eyes. She takes my face in her hands. "Both of you have to show your families that everything really is different with Jack... Then you just have to wait, be patient, and hope." She sits down on the visiting chair. Her skin is so dark against my white. Her eyes hold mine in hers and make me full of peaceful. "Do you understand that?"

"YesIdo. Patient is hard."

"Never is harder, honey... It's time to go to sleep now." She gets up to go. "Let me tell you, Rose, tomorrow is always a new day."

I hear her belly-laughing out my room. I like it.

I stay awake. My head is full of buzzing bees. I can't make them into pictures. The wind screams outside the window. Through the glass, hundreds of seagulls shriek and circle round the sky.

In my heart I have Jack. In my head is a big empty space. Me and Jack fit together. Without him I am only a bit of Rose. I must talk to Mum and Dad. I need to work it out.

I close my eyes and try and push words into my brain. Sleep grabs my words away. I open my eyes to stop it doing that.

I see Jack at the indoor window. I smile and smile with happy. He blows me a kiss. I hold my hand out and catch it. I hold it on my heart.

When I open my eyes, a nurse is in the room. She checks my drip and frowns at my blood pressure. The next time I wake up the room is filled with pink. The night has gone away. I watch the indoor window for Jack. I don't know if he was real Jack or dream Jack. I slip out of bed and stand at the outdoor window. The sun has painted the sky in red. It touches the rooftops and makes the snow blush. A church cross winks gold at me.

I call out to a seagull flying toward the blue-black sea. "It's a new day!"

My legs are stronger. The cold from the floor cools my feet. A breath of salty wind sneaks through the window gap. I'm glad it's not open. I climb back into bed and curl up in my blanket. I make a head plan.

A lady with hair like the Queen of England wheels my breakfast in. "Oh my goodness! You're famous!"

"Whois?"

"*You* are, you're all over the news on the radio. Didn't you hear it?"

"No, it's not loud enough. Why?" I can't understand the words the lady is saying.

"Everyone was so worried when you went missing and then you turned up safe in Brighton, so now they all want to know about it. It was like a wonderful Christmas present for everyone."

"I'm not a present. I'm Rose."

"Yes and a very special Rose too. What do you want for Christmas then this year?" She puts a bowl of porridge in front of me.

"I want Jack for Christmas."

"Oh—I'm glad you said that, I almost forgot." She pulls a piece of paper out of her pocket. "Here you go, I promised to give this to you as soon as I saw you. The night duty nurse gave it to me as she was leaving. It's from Jack; he made her promise she'd put it straight into your hands, but she didn't want to wake you up. Would you like me to read it for you?"

I grip the letter tight to me. "Nothankyou. I can read Jack myself."

"Don't let your breakfast go cold and try and eat as much as you can. Your night nurse says you've lost weight. Yes...? I can see you want me to leave you in peace. Nurse will come back in a bit to help you with your morning wash."

I wait until she's gone. I push the breakfast away and smooth Jack out over the bed cover. I read slowly, so I don't miss a single word.

My Rosie,

I hope you get this. Mum is writing it for me because we have to go home soon and it would take me ages to do it by myself. I don't want to leave you, but I have to be an adult.

Mum told me about the bad man who got you and I punched a coffee machine. Cups went everywhere ☹ I wanted to break every bone in that man's body, even after everything I promised. Mum said I shouldn't be hard on myself as it was a terrible thing to hear.

I ran away from Mum as I wanted to be alone. I didn't know where I was, so I got in a elevator and it went to the rooftop of the hospital. The wind up there was freezing cold and tried to knock me over, but I didn't care if it threw me over the wall because your dad was right when he said I'm not good enough for you.

The sea was black and angry like me and I swear it was calling to me, Rosie, which was crazy! I couldn't stop my feet walking toward it so I ended up on the top of the wall gulping in air, wishing I was anyone but Jack.

A weird, green moon glowed behind the clouds; everything felt freaky but I was part of it and part of the stormy water. The waves roared at me "Keep walking, Jack, don't stop," over and over to make me listen. I was scared, but I knew what I had to do; I held my arms high and opened my mouth and screamed.

Hundreds of seagulls took off from the roof, joining in with me. I screamed out all my anger and pain. I screamed for who I might have been. I screamed out the old Jack until I was nothing but a boy standing on a wall. I let it all go, Rosie.

I was done in, but in the distance I saw a bit of red where the line of the sea joins the sky.

Today was going, but another day would come after the night; and I was still here with you in the world. And I knew that losing you would be the stupidest thing I could ever do because I love you to the ends of the earth and back. I always will.

Sleep tight, my Rosie. I'm going to be strong for you and find a way for us to be together, for ever and ever.

Your Jack XXX

PS Hello Rose, this is Grace talking now.

I'll look after Jack for you. Get yourself better, be strong, and I will try and help sort everything out when you are home again.

I'm SO proud of you. Sending all my love and a big hug to you. Xxx

It takes me ages to read. When the nurse comes in to wash me, I have to ask her to do me later. 'Cause Jack's letter is more important. I don't get all the words. But I can feel the wind. And hear the waves. I can hear him. He threw away old Jack and found a new one.

I start to cry. The water falls onto the paper. I sad-cry for Jack's pain. Then I happy-cry for his strong. I smile for Jack and Rosie.

I have to talk to Mum and Dad. I made it up in my head. In the night. Then before the breakfast lady gave me my porridge, I went over and over it until I got it right. Jack's letter makes me brave. I can fight.

I'm waiting for them to get here, so I can say it. So I can see Jack. If it takes all my life to show them how much I love him, I will do it.

In the background I hear a song on the radio. It's very quiet. I realize it's our song. Mine and Jack's. I turn the sound up, and I hear the words happy-singing around the room.

The man sings about love. I can feel it. I feel it in my heart and in the air. And when I look in Jack's eyes. Just like the song on the radio.

I laugh and hug myself with happy. Love is everywhere. I can be strong. Mum and Dad will understand. This is our share song.

I fold my letter up. I tuck it in my nightdress pocket. I can do it.

There's a knock on the door. It opens before I can say "Come in."

"How are you, darling?" Mum walks into the room bringing her wide smile with her.

Dad holds a huge, gray furry elephant in his arms. It has a shiny purple ribbon round its neck. He bounces it up and down on the bed. "From everyone at college. They all send their love, especially Lou, who wants to see you as soon as she can."

"I feel sad about Lou. I didn't tell her the truth."

"Lou's mum told me there's been a lot of swearing from her iPad voicer." Mum grins. "They had to put her in her room to calm down. Don't look so glum, she's over-the-moon that you're safe now. Oh—and delighted that you'll be back to help her as she's had Danny Parker looking after her."

"Isn't that the boy with the bad stutter?" Dad asks.

"Yes and apparently he and Lou fell out because she kept finishing his sentences—on loud."

Mum and Dad laugh. I think of Lou all cross and upset.

In my head I promise to make it all up to her.

"Hey, little big sis!" a voice says from the doorway.

"BEN!"

Ben almost runs over to me. He knocks the doctor's notes off the end of the bed before giving me a bear hug.

"Careful, Ben! You'll pull her drip out."

Mum isn't really cross. And Dad has a smile going to his ears.

I take Ben's hand. He doesn't pull it away. "Imissedyou, Ben."

Ben goes all pinky. "Yeah, missed you too. It's cool you're back and Winniebago will poo herself when she sees you."

"Ben!" Mum says.

"What? I didn't say 'shit herself.'"

"Mum says you took my Tigger to your room."

Ben raises his eyebrows. "That's not cool, Mum, thanks a bunch. Did she tell you I put your picture up everywhere?"

"Yesthankyouverymuch. I thought of you lots."

"Yeah well, just don't go off on any gap years or anything without telling us."

We both can't stop laughing at the look on Mum and Dad's face at that.

"Come and sit down." I pat the bed and Mum and Dad sit down next to Ben.

I pick up the elephant and take the purple ribbon off him. I'll never like purple again. Not after the party dress.

Mum watches me. "That's a serious face."

"I have im-portant words to say."

Mum and Dad look at each other. Ben checks his phone quickly and then puts it in his pocket.

"I'm sorry I made you scared. I didn't mean to make you sad. I had to find Jack."

Dad snorts. Mum tuts and points her finger at him. Ben sighs. "She's only just started, Dad."

"Yes, Dad. Remember you told me, Mum, about when you

met Dad?" Mum nods. "You were sixteen. Like me. You said when you saw Dad you knew he was your husband."

"That's completely different!" Dad jumps up and goes over to the window.

"Why, Dad? Why is it different? Is it 'cause I have Down syndrome? Down syndrome isn't *me*. I am Rose."

Dad looks down. "You know I didn't mean that." Mum looks at him. "What did you mean then, Mike?"

"Don't start, Sarah, please—this is hard."

"It's more hard for me. I know you don't want Jack. Don't talk, Dad. Sit down, pleasethankyou... When I met Jack for the first time, he made my inside lonely go away. The sun came out in my head and my heart grew wings and took me up to the moon. I was *real* Rose. I was more Rose, Dad, than before I met Jack. Without him my sun is covered in cloud and everything inside me is rain. Jack makes me sky-tall and lion-brave...and I make Jack's angry fly away. No, don't talk yet, Mum, pleasethankyou. I can remember all the words I wrote in my head... Together we can be just Jack and Rose and not let the world make us different and stupid. Dad, I love Jack like you love Mum. We want what you want—and I want to get married like you and Mum and be together in our little house with two children and a mix-up dog. Without Jack I would curl up into a ball and shut my eyes in a for-ever sleep. Without him I am not Rose, I am gone away."

Dad looks at his hands then at me. "Oh, Rose." His eyes are full of pain.

Mum tries to talk but I put my finger on her lips.

Ben picks at a bit on his thumbnail and studies the floor. "Jack was hurt when he was born. His angry is bad. I know Jack messed up, but Jack is a new Jack. He WON'T hurt me... Jack hurts Jack more."

Dad sighs. "I'm scared that he might just lose control and... you'll...you'll be in the way." Dad's voice falls apart.

Mum stands behind him and wraps her arms around him. "Jack's doing well," she says. "I saw him before he left. He sat at the hospital and didn't make a fuss. He went home quietly with his mum."

"Great, you're both ganging up on me," Dad whispers.

"There aren't any gangs, Dad. I know you want to keep me safe. You have to let me be a grown-up. Grandma said that everyone deserves a second go. Remember? After you got cross? When Mum had been your girlfriend for six months? And Granddad said you were to keep away from Mum because you were trouble? And then you threw the cricket bat and hurt Muffin's leg? Mum still chose you. And Grandma gave you a second go."

Ben sits up tall. "Yeah, Dad. Grandma told us all about it, remember?"

Dad stares at the bed. "I can't deny I behaved badly in the past. I was hot-headed; but I didn't have a brain injury that means I *can't* control what I do."

"Doesn't that make what you did worse then, Dad?"

"Thanks, Ben. Look, I'm not trying to make excuses for myself but it terrifies me lately that Jack explodes and then thinks about it after the damage is done; because he has no control over the injured part of his brain. I know how dreadful it is that this happened to Jack, but it did, and I couldn't bear it if anything happened to you, Rose."

"Jack *can* control his broken bit of brain. That's what he's been learning. He's thrown the old Jack away. He's a new Jack—and he's always been a different Jack with me. Now he will be for everybody, 'cause he's learning. Dad, I want to choose for me. I choose Jack. Please give him a second go."

Mum sits back down next to me. She rolls up the edge of the sheet. "I won't make any promises, Rose, but I'm open to a second chance for Jack—I think you both deserve it."

I lean over and hug her. My heart is jumping up and down on clouds. "Dad?"

Dad gets up. He sweeps the hair back off his face. Then he picks up his coat. "I'm going for a walk." He shuts the door behind him.

I'm too lost for my words.

"He needs time to think, sweetie."

"He's a dick."

"BEN! That's not helping. It's difficult, he just wants to protect you, we both do, because it's hard letting go of your little girl."

"I'm not little any more, Mum."

"I know, you're my grown-up Rose. But you'll always be my little girl, the same as Ben will always be my little boy."

"No I won't," Ben grumps.

"WhencanIseeJack?"

"I don't know, darling, I just don't know."

I slide under the covers. I can't bear Mum not knowing.

My happy puddles on the floor.

thirty-six
december 20th

I stand by the window watching the clouds make dragon shapes in the sky.

Mum crashes through the door, making me jump. Her cheeks are red and rain damp.

"I'm so sorry I'm late, darling. What are you doing out of bed? You'll catch your death of cold!"

She's all out of Mum sorts. She makes me get back into bed. I hug her tight.

"I'mokaythankyou. Stop fuss-potting. Can I see Jack?"

She puts my little blue bear on the table by my bed. "He was in your coat pocket like you said. He nearly went off to the dry-cleaner." She sniffs him. "Mind you, he could do with a wash."

"WhencanIseeJack?"

"Your dad didn't get home, I mean back to the hotel, until really late last night, so I was in bed. He left again very early this morning, muttering about things to do, but he said he'd come to the hospital later, so you can talk to him then. I'm sorry, Rose, I wish I could give you a better answer than that, but I can't." Mum won't look at me.

"Put him down, Mum." I take the blue bear away from her and hold him tight. I don't want to lose my strong. "I walked and walked to Jack. I didn't give up. I won't ever give up."

Mum has gone all pink-flushed. "It was lovely to see Ben yesterday, wasn't it? Grandma's coming later, now you're getting stronger."

"Don't make the point go away!"

Mum smiles and takes the bear back. She dances him on the bed. I do my big frown at her. "I'm getting very crosspatch, Mum. You're not listening to me."

"Oh darling, I'm sorry, I'm just happy to see you looking so much better."

She tucks a bit of hair behind my ear and grins.

"Mum! When—"

My door opens and stops my mouth. Dad walks into the room. He's wearing the same shirt as yesterday, and his hair is standing up. He comes over to me and wraps me in a big hug. When he gets up, he won't look at me. Like Mum. I pull his face 'round. It's full of light and dark. His mouth does a wobble.

"Dad—"

"Rose." He swallows his words down. Then he shakes his head. He shadow smiles and takes a big breath. "Sarah, it's time for us to leave."

Mum picks up her bag. "You just came here!"

"I know but we'll be back soon, Rose, I promise." She holds me in her eyes.

"Then we have Jack talk."

Dad kisses Mum on her forehead. "Come on, Sarah."

Mum nods and blows a kiss to me. "Okay." She takes Dad's hand. They walk away leaving my head full of tangled words.

Dad turns back to me as I'm about to follow them. "I've brought someone to see you." He opens the door. "Go in, she's waiting for you."

Jack steps into the room. "Hey, you." He grins at me and the sun shines in my head. And my heart flutters blue butterfly wings.

All my hurt, all my sad, and all my ill go away.

Jack pushes his curls away from his eyes. "My Rosie." His voice breaks up.

I open my arms. "My Jack."

He runs into them.

"Rosie, Rosie, Rosie." Jack's eyes glow summer-sky blue. "I was scared I'd never see you again. I'm so sorry, Rosie, it's all my fault."

I lean over and kiss him to make his words stop. He holds my face in his hands and kisses me back. We look at each other and smile and smile. We don't need words to say what we feel. We can see it in our eyes.

Jack pulls something out of his back pocket. "These are the postcards I wrote to you when I found out you were missing. I wanted to feel close to you and I wanted you to know I loved you...even when I was being useless Jack who couldn't be with you to help you."

"Don't say that! You *were* with me. You did help. I found all your other cards that Dad stole away from me. I cried when I read them. I knew I had to find you. They kept me strong on the trains, strong in the bad house, and under the bridge. They kept me being Rosie."

I take the new cards from him and get his other ones I put under my hospital pillow. "I took these with me everywhere. When I was sad I looked at them. When I needed you I looked at them. I hid them in my bag pocket and kept you warm and safe. But I kept the real you in my heart."

"The real me is standing here in front of you. I'm your Jack, but a new one. Do you understand that, Rosie?"

"Yes, I do. You threw old Jack into the sea."

He takes the cards and puts them on the bed. He holds both my hands in his and puts his serious face on. "You made it through the worst time all by yourself. You'll never have to do that again. I love you, Rosie Tremayne."

He picks me up and is about to swing me round. He stops when he sees my drip. He touches where it goes in my arm. His eyes are full of unhappy.

Then a Jack grin lights up his face. "Rosie, look!" He picks up a postcard with our little blue butterfly painted on it. "He came back to me, our butterfly, and sat on my hand. I took him outside and blew on him to make him fly. I watched him disappear behind the clouds. How did he come out in the snow, Rosie? He should have been a caterpillar in a cocoon thingy."

"He's our magic butterfly. I saw him this morning, resting on my window. He was warming his wings in the sun."

"He brought you back to me like I told him to. My new friend Seb, at the unit, said I was bonkers and losing the plot. But we know better, don't we, Rosie?"

I smile. "Yes, we do."

Outside, winter-white clouds race across the sky. The sea churns green and flings foam up into the air. Jack and I lean against the glass and look out at the world. He slips his arm around my shoulders. Where our breath mists up the glass, I draw a heart with my finger. Inside it I write,

Rosie Loves Jack.

About the Author

Mel Darbon is a YA author who is passionate about giving a voice to those who might not otherwise be heard. Mel began telling stories to her autistic younger brother when they were children and never lost the skill. Her career has taken numerous turns. She has worked as a theater designer, a freelance artist, and a teacher for adults with learning disabilities, and run innovative workshops for teenage moms and young offenders. Mel is now focused on writing her second novel and developing her creative writing workshops that encourage students with mixed abilities to work together to help promote acceptance and inclusion. A graduate of Bath Spa's MA in Writing for Young People, she lives in England. Follow her on Twitter @DarbonMel.